The Perfect Family Man

M. M. DeLuca spent her childhood in Durham City, England. After studying Psychology at the University of London, Goldsmiths College, she moved to Winnipeg, Canada where she worked as a teacher then as a freelance writer. She studied Advanced Creative writing with Pulitzer prizewinning author, Carol Shields and has received several local arts council grants for her work. Her first novel, *The Pitman's Daughter* was shortlisted for the Chapters Robertson Davies first novel in Canada award in 2001. She went on to self-publish it on Amazon in 2013 where it reached the Amazon Top 20 in the literary bestseller chart. Her novel *The Savage Instinct* was shortlisted for the Launchpad Manuscript Contest (USA) in 2017 where it was picked up by independent publisher, Inkshares.

Also by M. M. DeLuca

The Secret Sister

M. M. DELUCA

THE
PERFECT
FAMILY
MAN

CANELO
US
San Diego, California

Canelo US
An imprint of Printers Row Publishing Group
9717 Pacific Heights Blvd, San Diego, CA 92121
www.canelobooksus.com

Printers Row Publishing Group is a division of Readerlink Distribution Services, LLC. Canelo US is a registered trademark of Readerlink Distribution Services, LLC.

This edition originally published in the United Kingdom in 2021 by Canelo.

Published in partnership with Canelo.

Correspondence regarding the content of this book should be sent to Canelo US, Editorial Department, at the above address. Author inquiries should be sent to Canelo, Unit 9, 5th Floor, Cargo Works, 1–2 Hatfields, London SE1 9PG, United Kingdom, www.canelo.co.

Publisher: Peter Norton • Associate Publisher: Ana Parker
Art Director: Charles McStravick
Senior Developmental Editor: April Graham
Editor: Angela Garcia
Production Team: Beno Chan, Julie Greene

Design: Brianna Lewis

Library of Congress Control Number: 2022946082

ISBN: 978-1-6672-0465-9

Printed in India

27 26 25 24 23   1 2 3 4 5

To all mothers, everywhere

I never expect to see a perfect work from an imperfect man.

Alexander Hamilton

Prologue

The lake is dreamlike under a shroud of ice fog.

Rime-covered trees ring the shoreline, rising like glittering sculptures out of the mist.

I crouch low and peer through frozen bulrushes at the thin crust of ice that glazes the lake. I'm panting – partly from fear, and partly from the adrenalin rush of my escape. Cold air rips into my throat like icy sandpaper, and a pungent scent of gasoline drifts through the air. My breath puffs out in pale clouds, crystallizing my eyelashes. I cover my mouth.

I can't let them see me here.

I'm supposed to be drowning.

Dying a slow, cold death.

I watch the tail end of the car. Black and shiny like a whale's tail. A sinking ship, its nose plunged downwards, the car slips inch by inch into the frigid water. Jagged fault lines zigzag across the ice. I turn my head away and dry-retch into the snow.

Sounds crowd into my head. First a low, tuneless creaking, then a groaning vibration that shakes the ground. Ice splinters and shatters as a network of cracks radiates across the surface, and the lake opens its yawning mouth to consume the car in a soft explosion of sound. The car slides gently under, leaving only the bubbling black water to mark its place.

My eyes sting with tears.

So many lies. So many lives ruined.

I sob into the crook of my arm, muffling the cries. My chest heaves in lungsful of icy air.

Then a plume of gray smoke wafts into the air beyond the trees. I taste ashes, feel the flakes settle, tickling my face like gray snow. Smell the sweet stink of gasoline on my fingertips.

I stumble to my feet, catching my knee on the edge of a fallen tree trunk. My nerves scream out, but one razor-sharp image cuts through the fuzz of pain.

Someone appears in the lake house window. The figure is silhouetted against the orange glow of fire, but it could be a trick of the light.

Clear thoughts now give way to confusion. Panic stirs my brain into a turmoil. I tear myself away from the bulrushes and will myself to start running before it's too late.

Sirens whine in the far distance. Louder with each passing second.

I have to get back to the lake house.

Now.

Before there's nothing left but a pile of burnt rubble and the person I truly love is buried beneath it.

1

ONE MONTH EARLIER

The lake house had stood empty for five years, but when a *Sold* sign appeared on its lawn, I moved my drawing board and easel from the upstairs office to the living room downstairs.

I'd convinced my husband, Nate, that the green light filtering through the deep bay window was better for sketching. Truth was, I felt stifled in my tiny office with its meager window. And worse, when I sat at my desk, I couldn't see anything but chimneys, rooflines, and the tops of trees.

Downstairs was different; I could look out onto the enchanted world of the luxury lakeside mansions from my smaller house on the opposite side of the street. Just like an awkward teen, forever craning my neck over a fence to spy on an endless party to which I was never invited.

Though my own home was large enough, with its tree-lined backyard and high stucco walls covered in Virginia creeper, it was modest in comparison to the massive lake properties, with their rambling gabled roofs and cultured stone frontages. Their polished teak or Brazilian wood doors, their manicured lawns leading to lush back gardens that looked out onto vivid sunsets from glassed-in verandas and sun-drenched balconies. Most of the lake houses had swimming pools, fancy rockeries, and hot tubs nestled in vine-covered arbors.

I could only see the front of the houses from my bay window. The back views were only visible in tantalizing glimpses from the top of the hill in the nearby park. A walkway led down from there to the lake shore, but a *Private: No Entry* sign slapped on a rickety wooden fence separated inquisitive onlookers from those luxury back gardens that led down to their own private piece of shoreline.

I'd often stand there and gaze down at those grand houses. On the opposite shore of the lake were other beautiful houses, all with their own fancy gardens, but only the one that faced mine held any interest for me. Sometimes I'd stand on tiptoe and strain to see the roofline of my smaller home from the top of the hill. Then satisfied that I did, in fact, live opposite the most beautiful properties on the block, I'd continue on my way. The walkway snaked towards a wooden bridge lined with ornate street-lamps that crossed a narrow channel linking the series of small lakes. At the other side of that bridge, a deep urban forest bordered the shoreline of the next lake.

It was my favorite walk. Repeated almost daily. I'd run or walk along that trail, my eyes drawn to the shimmering water visible in vivid glimpses through thick stands of trees.

-

The day I moved my drawing board, Nate was leaving for a three-week stint in Toronto. Nate, a pharmaceutical salesman, was always heading out on business trips, often two or three a month, twelve months of the year, including December.

I was just about to arrange my brushes and pencils on the ledge of my easel, when he lugged his large suitcase downstairs. He'd packed a bulging carry-on case and a garment bag stuffed with three suits.

I'd dropped one of the suits off at the cleaners the week before, and when the assistant reminded me to empty the pockets, I found something unexpected in the inside pocket. Something that made my heart race. I'd put it in my wallet. Couldn't deal with it until Nate was gone. Couldn't even think about it until he was out of my sight.

It was further proof that he was keeping secrets from me again.

The thought sickened me.

Now he stood under the arch by the front door, twisting his gloves.

"I hate to leave you like this, Olivia. I mean – are you gonna be okay here alone?"

I raised my head. He looked so clean-cut. Freshly trimmed black-brown hair immaculate against the pale skin of his stubble-dusted jawline. Ice-blue eyes fringed with dark lashes. The almost perfect symmetry of his face. During the early years of our marriage, I'd looked at him and marveled that I'd married such a beautiful man. Though sometimes it had felt like a weighty responsibility. At the time, I was furious with myself for being so superficial, but being with him had brought out some old insecurities, and I felt the need to try much harder to keep his attention. Meet a more exacting standard with my appearance. Especially at social occasions or dinner parties when he always managed to turn more than a few heads, while I was relegated to the role of the pale sidekick walking in his shadow.

I snapped back to reality, remembering he'd asked me a question and was waiting for my response. He adjusted his chunky silver watch and straightened his shirt cuffs.

"I'm good. Really," I said, distracted suddenly by the sight of a moving van sliding into view at the end of the winding driveway opposite. "I can make friends with the new neighbors."

He crossed the room and stood beside me, looking out. He made for an imposing figure in his well-cut navy overcoat and maroon scarf. On the surface, he was a kind and patient man. But glancing at those inscrutable blue eyes, I realized I never really knew what was truly going on behind them. And though for an instant, I was tempted to pull him towards me and kiss those finely shaped lips, I didn't make a move, sensing a chilliness and tension that made it difficult to cross the few inches that lay between us.

Truth was, Nate had checked out five years ago and in his place was a soulless clone going through the motions of day-to-day life.

"It's been empty for a long time. Wonder who bought it?" I said, conscious of a deep sadness creeping over me. Regret was a constant burden that wouldn't ease.

He shrugged and turned away. "Fill me in on their furniture. I like to know who I'm dealing with before we ask them over for drinks."

"Sure," I said, knowing a dinner date would never happen. We could barely talk to each other, let alone make polite supper conversation with strangers. And it was highly doubtful we'd ever set foot near that house again.

Not if I could help it.

Nate slung his garment bag onto his shoulder, then stooped to pick up his suitcase. "But you know what those

6

people are like. Only mix in their own privileged circles and damn the rest of us working stiffs."

It had always bugged Nate. The sporadic contact we'd had with any of the *lake people* as he called them. A cursory *hello* or a brief wave from the tinted window of a loaded Porsche SUV was the extent of our interaction.

Just then, a taxi pulled into the driveway and, feeling a last-minute pang of guilt, I climbed down from my stool. "You sure you don't want me to drive you to the airport?"

A furtive look darted across his face. He shook his head. "You need to rest, Olivia. Remember what the therapist said."

The blood rushed to my cheeks. *Damn him for reminding me.* I threw my pencil onto the worktable, wincing as the clatter echoed in the silence. "Don't patronize me. You know how I loathe it."

Nate put down the cases, an expression of blank restraint on his face. "It'll be good for us to be apart for a while." He spoke in a breathy, low voice, his hands clenching and unclenching into fists, which he promptly jammed into his pockets.

"Have a good trip then," I said, swallowing back the lump in my throat and turning back to look out at the street where the moving men were leaning against their truck. "I'll still be sitting right here in this exact spot when you get back."

It was a tired attempt at humor, but everything felt sluggish to me. The gray sky, the brooding clouds, the dull drone of the dishwasher and even the dry peck Nate placed dutifully on my cheek. I reached my arms out and held onto him for a moment longer, placed my face against his chest, seduced by the scent of his musky cologne. *He does have a heart.* I felt its soft vibration beneath

7

the fine wool coat. But he pulled away too quickly, causing me to stumble a little, and at that very moment I glimpsed a black SUV pulling up behind the moving truck outside.

A willowy young woman swung out of the driver's seat. She was dressed entirely in black with a mass of wavy blonde hair pulled into a thick braid. Animated, she moved with a sense of purpose that compelled me to watch her so closely that I barely registered Nate's parting *Bye, Olivia* as he slammed the front door shut. The blonde woman chatted to the movers, her arms moving in frantic accompaniment. The two men – bearish and burly – bent their heads to listen, then nodded and headed off to the back of the truck.

She pulled at her braid and made her way back to the SUV, only turning for a moment to watch Nate's progress to the taxi. He had that type of effect on most women, and I couldn't dispel the slight twinge of jealousy as he glanced in the blonde's general direction, paused, and then jammed on a large pair of sunglasses. Strangely, the woman stayed still, watching him as he stopped to smooth out his gloves before ducking down into the back seat of the taxi. My skin prickled with the chill of suspicion that was never far away.

As the taxi reversed down the driveway and turned onto the street, the new neighbor opened the back passenger door of her SUV and reached inside. I held my breath, aware of the pounding in my ears and a racing, dizzy feeling of inevitability as the woman pulled out a child. A tow-haired toddler dressed in yellow rubber boots, blue jeans and red quilted jacket. The woman plopped him on the ground and turned away, distracted by the sight of a dining table coming down the ramp.

I placed my hands flat against the window and watched the vulnerable child. *So small. So full of wonder. Oblivious to all the hurt and danger in the world.* Totally unaware that innocence can be crushed and destroyed in the time it takes a person to snap their fingers. And after that, it's too late to go back to the old life, because nothing can ever be the same again.

I had learned that cruel lesson.

Twice in my life.

I sighed, irritated that the mother was still nattering away, caught up with the moving of a large knotted-pine dining table, while the child stood unsupervised, gazing around at the street. Usually, the place was quiet on weekdays, though cars and contractors' trucks sometimes hurtled around the corner at top speed.

I willed the mother to pay attention to her son. Prayed she'd take his hand before he tottered out into the path of some speeding semi-truck that might come flying by.

The boy stuck his thumb in his mouth while his mother watched the movers guide the table to the bottom of the ramp. Then his little face lit up when he spotted a rabbit hopping over my lawn. Smiling, he pointed at the little creature, and looked as if he was about to take a step forward and cross the road. My heart crowded into my throat, stopping my breath.

Any minute now and he'll cross.

Hardly daring to take my eyes from him, I edged towards the archway that led out to the front hallway, figuring I'd lose sight of him for only a few seconds before I could dash out and rescue him from danger.

Time froze for a millisecond as I propelled myself forward, racing to the front door. I struggled with the lock and threw it open just as a semi-truck loaded with lawnmowers and landscaping equipment careened around the corner. The child was about to take one step forward when the semi-driver seemed to stand up out of his seat. The brakes screeched and wailed and the truck fishtailed sideways in a cloud of burning rubber. In a split second, the blonde woman grabbed the child's hand, yanking him to safety just as the truck slid sideways to a grinding halt.

I stood still for a few mind-splitting moments, trying to catch my breath as the truck driver leaned his head out of the window and screamed curses at the woman who picked up the child. The mother turned and hurried towards the front door of her new home, where she disappeared into the shadows.

I slammed the front door shut and fell back against it, chest heaving, mind buzzing.

A narrow escape.

Until the next time.

2

I woke up nursing a headache that pounded against the roof of my scalp. After the truck incident, I'd binged until two in the morning on some true-crime series about a missing kid. As always, after an exhaustive search, they never found him, so the ending was left wide open. I sat there, watching the closing credits roll, the words blurring into white fuzz. My mind was fixated on the short re-enactment clip of his disappearance. The images played over and over, flickering and nightmarish, like an old piece of film stuck in the shutter. The boy, throwing his plastic airplane into the air, watching as it sailed far ahead of him, then following it into the dark mouth of the woods.

He never reappeared.

All the bad things happened in the woods.

Everyone who's ever binged on thrillers knows the forest is a pathway to oblivion, a mystic place that preys on innocents, a sanctuary for the worst kind of predators. Animal and human.

The woods are a portal to some other world. A black hole that sucks in everything you love.

And once they're in there, they never come out.

That's how our son, Jack, had disappeared five years ago.

I'd spent five years since then living in a semi-comatose state. Though I'd finally managed to make some semblance of a life for myself, the memory of Jack stayed foremost in my mind, ready to emerge in all its horror and lay me prostrate with grief again.

It didn't matter that I'd packed up all his photos and clothes and toys and asked Nate to take them to the Goodwill Store. Any random event could trigger the memories of that day, reawaken the terror, and send me reeling into mental oblivion.

And seeing the neighbor's little boy in that moment of danger had brought it all rushing back.

I'd read somewhere that one of the reasons people cut or self-harm themselves is to get rid of emotional numbness and actually feel something. That's how it was with me. Remembering Jack reopened the wound and brought back the agony. It made me feel alive, but it was also a secret form of self-punishment for the guilt that surrounded his disappearance. Guilt that had never left me.

I pressed my sore eyelids into their aching sockets, then lay against my pillow, watching the morning light filter through the white and gray drapes. I willed myself to think about Jack.

He wasn't the kind of kid who fell asleep in his stroller while I browsed the racks at the mall. He was the kid who wriggled and squirmed until he escaped his seat belt, then crawled under clothes racks or – if I actually made it to the changing room with something to try on – he was the kid who lay on the floor peeking through the gap at the woman undressing herself in the next stall.

Another memory floated into my mind, as it always did when I dared to think about him. I'd been pushing him through the crowds on the first floor of a department store. As I approached the elevator to get to the second floor, Jack suddenly dove out of his stroller and flew towards the open elevator door. He slipped inside before I could maneuver the stroller in. The doors swished shut on his grinning face, and my heart just about left my body as the elevator traveled up to the next floor. Without wasting a second, I parked the stroller and tore towards the escalator, praying he hadn't arrived on the next floor yet. I sprinted up the moving stairs, shoving past the people that stood in my way. I ran past the mixers and the coffee makers and the toasters, until I arrived at the elevator just as the door opened. Jack stood there smiling and saying *ride, Mommy, ride.* I swept him up into my arms and kissed him all over, too relieved to even think of being angry at him.

I turned over and pressed my face against the pillow, trying to block out the morning light. A heavy pall of guilt engulfed me. I told myself for the thousandth time that I, and not just Nate, had to share the blame for Jack's disappearance. I'd known Jack was a hyper and inquisitive child. I should have kept my eyes on him the entire time we were at the party. Never let him out of my sight.

Never taken him to the party in the first place.

I should have hired a babysitter, and for a miserable forty bucks, my life might have taken a whole different direction.

3

FIVE YEARS BEFORE

It was hot, sunny Labor Day. We'd been invited to one of those swanky corporate parties Nate absolutely lived for.

He was a man who appreciated fine food and clothing, so he'd organized his side of the walk-in closet in carefully color-coordinated blocks of outfits wrapped in plastic garment bags. When we first met, I'd admired his sense of style and even found his attention to detail endearing. As a self-confessed slob who often used the floor as a dumping ground for cast-off clothing, I'd even hoped some of Nate's orderliness might rub off on me.

The day of the party he insisted on helping me pick something to wear, which removed one more headache from my day, because at that particular time, I viewed fashion as simply a chore. I selected clothes based on their comfort and washability, and with an active two-year-old, I barely had time to shop for new things. I tried on four dresses, parading like a model in front of him before settling on a pale green silk shift dress I'd never worn before. He planted a soft kiss on my lips and told me it matched my eyes. I remember looking in the mirror before we left and thinking that we really did look like a happy, attractive couple, and with our beautiful little boy we were the picture of the perfect family.

We walked across the street, towards the grand house with its polished teak doors, cedar siding and ornamental stone frontage. Polished brass lamps hung above the imposing front door and all three doors of the triple-car garage. Cultured stone planters displayed a riot of red and cream canna lilies studded with ivy and ferns. A stone statue of a deer and fawn stood at the center of a manicured flower bed.

The host was some hotshot lawyer with a Maserati and two gleaming Sea-Doos strapped to a monster truck in the driveway. It seemed an obvious display of ostentatiousness, left there for all the guests to envy and admire.

I'd torn my gaze away from all the grandeur to focus on Jack's head resting against Nate's shoulder. His downy auburn curls gleamed like burnished copper, his eyelids drooped, heavy with sleep.

Bring your kids, the host had urged. But Jack was tired. He should have been tucked up in bed for an afternoon nap, instead of going to a party. Nate persuaded me a bunch of other kids were going, and Jack would have a whole lot of fun because the host – some guy I'd never met, named Jude – had hired a clown to entertain them with magic tricks, face paint, and balloon sculptures.

Like a spineless coward I gave in.

Afterwards I'd tortured myself for my weakness.

The back of Jude's magnificent home consisted mainly of massive floor-to-ceiling windows that looked out onto the lake, bordered on its left shore by a wild forest, inhabited by deer, foxes and a multitude of squirrels and other tiny creatures. I sat on the tiled patio marveling at the intricately landscaped pool area, fenced-in and closed down for the fall. The terracotta stone terrace festooned with pots of blazing pink, red and white lilies, the trees draped with strings of white lights and the smartly dressed guests flitting between the bar and laden food tables.

Jack sat cross-legged on the lawn watching in rapt attention as a clown in a rainbow wig and red nose conjured rabbits out of hats, pulled endless strings of silk scarves from his ear, and made clever balloon sculptures. Afterwards, Jack had his face painted green like a frog. That was enough to send him running around in a wild frenzy, smacking everyone's knees with his balloon sword and saying *ribbit ribbit* until Nate and I were worn out chasing him and apologizing to the guests.

My second mistake.

I shouldn't have complained. I should have kept my mouth shut.

Nate suggested I take a break. He assured me he'd keep an eye on Jack while I went to get a drink.

My third, most grievous mistake.

I trusted him.

I was away from them less than five minutes, but every detail of those seconds was engraved into my brain. The barman in a snow-white shirt and skinny black jeans, the sweating bottle of Prosecco in his hands, the sharp pop of the wine cork, the fizz of bubbles in my nose, and the crisp, citrusy bite of chilled wine on my tongue. I took a few welcome slugs and wandered back along the terrace, marveling at the tiny white lights strung across the shrubbery. I felt relaxed and free for the first time in months. Free to study the bright summer hues of all the summer sundresses on display and how they merged with the riot of gorgeous flowers. Free to feel the warm breeze in my hair.

When I got back to Nate, he was deep in conversation with Jude, and Jack was nowhere to be seen. A rush of panic sucked all the feelings of elation away. The ground under my feet shuddered. My knees buckled.

"Where's Jack?" I demanded in a voice that was almost a scream.

Nate's nose wrinkled. "Take it easy, Olivia. He went to play with Jude's son, Abe."

Abe was an exuberant ten-year-old with nothing but food and practical jokes on his mind. Of course, Abe had no idea where Jack was. None of the other kids knew either. One girl said she'd seen him standing by the fence watching a deer move through the woods. Another girl, older, said she'd stopped him when he ran too close to the lake shore. Yet another said she'd seen him attempt to climb the willow tree that hung over the forest gate. Needless to say, by that time, I was a crazed animal, running around the gardens and walkways screaming Jack's name.

We never found him.

When the cops arrived, they scoured the woods and everywhere within a six-mile radius. They put up roadblocks on all the major routes and questioned every driver. Search parties of police and neighbors and well-meaning strangers did in-depth searches. Everywhere. The RCMP put out calls across the entire province, then went nationwide.

When they finally dragged the lake, they found nothing.

At least I found some small comfort in that.

In the weeks following Jack's disappearance, I turned to sleeping pills to cope. I gobbled up any prescription drug that numbed the pain, or knocked me out cold so I didn't have to relive those moments from the party over and over again, in minute detail.

After I finally woke from my drugged-up stupor, I screamed and raged at Nate. Cursed his neglect. Tore my hair out. Cried until my eyes were dry like sandpaper. And when my body was spent, I ran out into the street and collapsed in broad daylight, my body splayed out on the concrete.

My good friend and neighbor, Shanti, found me lying there, frozen like a corpse. She called her husband, Dev, and together they carried me back inside the house. Nate was out at the pharmacy, picking up more knock-out medication for me. I was so numb and disoriented; I didn't even ask if he needed some too.

I spent the next few months in bed, my face turned to the wall. I couldn't speak. My whole body just shut down. I lay there for days on end in a catatonic state. Protecting myself from the yawning loss that threatened to consume me entirely.

I remembered Nate coming into the room and leaving food, which I barely touched. Maybe I'd acted selfishly. Didn't even acknowledge his grief. But I was incapable of even communicating with another human being. The loss had killed something vital in me. I knew that I could never be the same woman, the loving wife and the mother of an amazing little boy. All that had been cruelly torn away.

The cops kept the investigation going strong for at least four years, following every crackpot lead and sighting. But at the end of the fifth year, they quietly put the case on the backburner. Didn't have the heart to tell me to my face. They just stopped coming to the phone when I made my daily call. Then the updates slipped to once a month, and finally twice a year.

I was left hanging – agonizing. Why did all the bad things happen in the woods? Which unseen person had watched my defenseless son cross from sunlight into darkness?

Right from childhood I'd had an overactive imagination. Always saw the clown doll's eyes blinking from the rocking chair in my room, or felt the unseen hand grasp my ankles as I ran up the basement stairs, or sensed the shower curtain parting behind my naked back to reveal the glint of sharp steel. That heightened sense of fantasy had made me a good artist and storyteller – or so my high school friends said when they clamored to see my weird and surreal comic strips.

But in reality, my imagination turned on me when my worst fantasies actually came true.

Twice in my life.

4

NOW

After a hot shower, my migraine had lifted a little. I'd swallowed three extra strength Tylenol and doused my face and eyes with cold water, so by the time I slathered myself with scented body lotion, I was ready to tackle the day.

With Nate away, the house was empty and quiet, but I welcomed the feeling of freedom. I could do whatever I wanted without him hovering in the background, scrutinizing my every move, worrying about me. Left to my own devices, I'd sit down and get lost in a book without thinking of meals and housework, or draw and paint until dark, or laze around on the living room couch and binge on Netflix. I didn't have to worry about Nate's suffocating expressions of concern.

At first, I started thinking about the thing I'd found in his suit pocket. It still gnawed away at me, needling my thoughts until I pushed it into the corner of my mind. Right now, I couldn't deal with it, but I knew sooner or later I would have to.

Usually, I tended to neglect food when Nate was away. There was no motivation for me to cook healthy, balanced meals. Instead, I existed on snack foods and takeout. Instead of a healthy breakfast of yogurt and fruit, I grabbed a chocolate-coated granola bar, took a slug of orange juice, and set out on a long walk. Exercise was the only thing that made me feel better. And when I was beginning a new project, it helped me think through new ideas.

The air outside was crisp and smoky. The scent of burning stubble drifted in from the farmers' fields. I loved the fall. Loved the bare, twisted trees against the overcast sky, the carpet of orange and gold leaves crunching under-foot, the gentle strangeness of the light. My imagination was always at its peak during this time, stoked by a steady diet of gothic horror novels during my teens. *Dracula, Frankenstein, The Turn of the Screw*, everything by Edgar Allan Poe. I lapped them all up. My mother always said I had morbid tastes for a young girl, and would get really flustered when she found her offerings of *The Baby-Sitters Club* and *Little Women* hidden under my bed under a pile of dark horror novels.

I took my usual path around the crescent, along the little track that led past the school then up the winding hill. The geese were there in force, crapping all over the footpath and the school playing field. I always wondered why the teachers let the kids roll around in all those goose droppings? Didn't they contain micro viruses? Couldn't that cause all kinds of nasty diseases? I gritted my teeth and carried on up the hill.

At the top, I stood under the sheltered seating area. Teens toked up and drank beer under the wooden canopy on Saturday nights, but during the week it was quiet. Only a couple of seniors doing t'ai chi and a man walking a large German Shepherd on a tight leash.

I glanced to the right, looking at the back of the lake houses that stood opposite my house. The blonde neighbor was nowhere to be seen, so I made my way down to the bottom of the hill and crossed the bridge over the channel linking the two lakes. At the other side, I took the winding track that snaked through the deep suburban forest.

I was just sidestepping a lanky teen on a skateboard when the new neighbor came into view, approaching me from the opposite direction. She was the picture of casual chic in her chunky designer sweater, her bright hair scraped up into a messy ponytail and eyes obscured by designer shades, even though the sun was nowhere to be seen. She yakked nonstop into a cell phone, barely taking a moment to breathe and seeming to argue with the person on the other end. One hand held the phone, the other sketched wild shapes into the air. I was about to say hello as she passed by, but the blonde looked oblivious and kept on talking.

Then the kid appeared. Way behind his mom. Perched on a tiny blue bike, his legs pumped like skinny little pistons. He flashed a panicked look at me, eyes wide and sea-blue, just as his bike swerved off the pathway. His skinny legs flailed in panic and he wiped out face first on the gravel. I turned to run to him. *The bitch was still talking on the phone.* She hadn't even looked back.

Sprawled out on the ground, the boy lifted his face high enough to let out a loud wail. Then he started bawling. Nonstop. His mother stopped dead, turned around and marched back, still talking on the damned phone. I stood silently cursing her, frozen to the spot as the blonde looked up and mouthed, *He's okay*, then picked up the bike, grabbed his hand and yanked him upright. She wiped a Kleenex across his face and marched off still yakking.

They disappeared across the bridge.

I bit my lip until I tasted blood.

All the wrong people have kids, I thought, annoyed that I'd even considered paying the woman a neighborly visit later. *But maybe she isn't really my kind of person*, I rationalized. For starters she was way too pompously *busy*.

I'd met her type before. People who measured their importance by their lack of personal time. Always complaining about how they just got off the phone and needed a few private moments to themselves, away from all the people craving just one more moment of their precious time.

The geese were squawking too loudly and a faint ache pulsed across my chest. I pushed on along the trail, putting off the inevitability of going home and starting the project I was supposed to have started three days ago. A debut author's picture book about a magic lunch bag.

I'd already done some research. Checked out the local stores for the perfect lunch bag. Marveled at the many variations: zip-around bags that opened out into intricate compartments, click-down plastic boxes, baggie-types with fold-down flaps, even vintage metal suitcases, or weathered-looking treasure chests. But one in particular stood out. It was a simple design. A brown and yellow plastic zip-along bag with a bright yellow spotted dinosaur on the front holding a chicken drumstick in its mouth. The words *feed me* were splashed across the top in bold, white letters. And the dinosaur gazed at me with such pleading eyes. I held onto the bag and let the words sink in. *Feed me. Feed me.* It reminded me of Jack. He would hold out his red and white plastic bowl for more Cheerios. *More rings, Mommy*, he'd beg, fixing those earnest, blue eyes on me.

I remembered standing in a busy bookstore, holding the dinosaur bag, tears streaming down my face. People were staring. Nudging each other. Probably wondering if they should step in and steer the crazy lady to the customer service department. But I pulled myself together and grabbed another lunch bag – a red one with a ladybug saying *yum yum* – then headed to the checkout and bought both.

I was so immersed in reflecting on that awkward moment, I realized I'd walked deeper into the forest trail, past a very young jogger pushing her baby in a blue-striped stroller. He was fair and chubby and his hands made windmills in the sunlight. My heart swelled as I visualized my fingers crushing the throat of an imaginary attacker. I checked myself at the violence of the image.

Was this maternal instinct? Unfulfilled urges still lingering in my brain cells?

On the lake, the geese bobbed like small boats, resting before taking off on their journey south. I stood motion-less, hearing nothing but my heart beating against the whisper of the geese and the trickling of water from the concrete fountain.

Had Jack wandered this far on his own? And if he had, where on earth had he gone? Which heartless monster had taken him by the hand and led him away?

Then time suddenly shifted, the recess buzzer sounded in the nearby school, and three kids hurtled down the hill screaming. A sharp pebble zinged past my ear sending the geese into a flapping, threshing panic, like wild bats at midnight. In the distance, the baby was crying so loudly his mother couldn't comfort him.

I clambered back to the pathway and took an alternate way home.

I stopped on the opposite side of the street from the house I grew up in. The same house that almost burned to the ground all those years ago.

Turning away, I swallowed a sob and walked away from the forest trail. I'd vowed to stay away from there. I'd spent fourteen years trying to put that event behind me. And when Jack went missing, abject grief over his disappearance buried the memory of that terrible fire.

Too bad something always drew me back.

Unfinished business, maybe?

Suspicion about how it really happened?

I shook my head. There was no way I could even think about that period in my life. I had no room left in my heart for anyone but Jack. So I hurried away, trying to distract myself by counting how many houses had basketball hoops in their front driveways.

Back home, my preliminary sketches were pinned out on the easel. The dinosaur saying *feed me* suddenly looked too sad. I thought maybe the ladybug would work. They were such cheery little insects.

Distracted for a moment, I glanced out at the lake house.

No sign of a husband yet and somehow the idea of going over there seemed way more titillating than three hours of detailed planning and sketching. I'd gotten so used to the lake house being empty. The windows shaded like blind eyes, the driveway deserted, the once manicured flower beds growing wild. The silence.

Now someone had moved in and disturbed that sleeping house.

I could feel my nerve ends buzzing. My anxiety level ramping up.

It was only nineteen days till Nate came back and I still hadn't figured out what to do about the thing I'd found in his jacket pocket.

I couldn't ignore it anymore.

Because this time I was done with secrets.

5

Baking always calmed me. Watching the flour float from the sifter down into the bowl, then cutting sticks of butter into it, was a mindless form of relaxation. Luckily, I had little desire to eat anything I'd baked. Body weight was just about the only thing under my control.

I'd decided to take muffins over as a welcome gift for the new neighbor. I'd forgiven her for the slip-up on moving day. I thought maybe she was so harried from the move she'd been more distracted than usual, and accidentally let her attention wander. As for the bicycle incident, maybe she was trying to make arrangements with contractors to do all the repairs needed to get that neglected house back into shape. I would give her the benefit of the doubt; it could be the beginning of a new friendship. Perhaps we could have coffee together. Compare notes about our absentee husbands. Maybe I could even offer to babysit.

Besides, nobody else on the street would do the welcome-to-the-neighborhood thing. Sam, my neighbor to the right, had just lost his tech job and was training to be a real estate agent, while his wife waited tables at a fancy steak house. On the other side was Vera, a widow whose abusive, alcoholic husband had died a year previously, leaving her free to live the rest of her life as she wanted to. Now her days of conflict and self-sacrifice were over, she was always out at the casino or playing bingo, so it was unlikely she'd be dropping over for a friendly visit unless it involved a game of poker and a couple of cold gin and tonics.

An hour later, I had arranged six golden blueberry muffins into a cloth-lined basket and was wondering how this still-nameless neighbor would receive me. Whether she'd simply dismiss me as the pushy neighborhood busy-body, vying to be the first to get an invite into the house to get the lowdown on her taste in home décor.

I stood by the bay window in an agony of indecision, wondering if I should actually sling the basket over my arm and walk like an overgrown Red Riding Hood across the street. My phone vibrated, shocking me out of my inertia. It was Min, my editor, probably wanting an update on how the illustrations were going. I ignored the insistent buzzing, vowing to call back in the morning after cramming in at least four hours of work that night. Then a text arrived from Nate.

> How are you feeling today?

Impersonal. A chore. As if he'd checked off another item on the list of things he had to do today. Now he could cross out *call the wife*. I texted back.

> Okay.

> What are you up to?

> Not much. Work.

> Gotta go. Talk later.

I clicked the phone off. What a complete waste of thirty seconds.

In a fit of guilt, I snapped a picture of the muffins and texted it to Nate with a message.

> New neighbor's welcome basket. LOL.

His reply came back quickly.

> Are you sure you should intrude?

Nate had always encouraged me to reach out to our neighbors. I stared at his text for a moment, unsettled. I thought I was just being sociable. I thought for a moment longer, then texted back.

> Gotta break the ice somehow.

I waited, but he didn't respond to that one so, duty done, I headed out onto my front steps just as the blonde neighbor's garage door opened and her SUV pulled out. The driver's side window was down and, though the woman turned away before spotting the basket, I caught a glimpse of her tear-stained face as she zoomed by. The kid was fastened into his car seat in the back, howling and crying. He'd been crying ever since he'd arrived on the street. My heart went out to him. So vulnerable and probably missing his old, familiar home.

Just before the overhead door closed, I noticed the garage was empty. Obviously she was still alone, dealing with all the demands of a toddler and a move to a big, new house that probably needed a whole lot of work. Feeling a stab of sympathy, I thought about leaving the basket at the front door, but the fat tabby that crept around the top of all the fences would probably get into them. Deciding against it, I turned to go back to the solitude of my house, only to stop after taking a couple of steps. If no one was at the lake house, what was the harm in taking a look around the back? Seeing how it looked now?

Why not? I've done it many times before.

Forced myself to take that same walk over the street that Nate and I had taken five years before. Only then we were three – a family. Afterwards, only two of us walked away from that place, our hearts torn apart.

I'd slipped through the side gate many, many times after the owners moved out. I'd combed every square inch of that place for a fragment or fiber of Jack's clothing, a footprint, a clue – anything – then I'd sat and wept by the empty pool, broken by the futility of a ritual that produced nothing.

All I had left was hope. And that's why I stayed, living opposite the house that killed me inside every time I looked over at it. I'd convinced myself that if Jack came back from wherever he was, I had to be here, waiting for him.

The street was eerily quiet for a weekday, the silence interrupted only by the occasional raucous screech of the crows that inhabited the towering chokecherry trees. No cars driving by, or people out walking. Scanning my neighbors' houses, I saw only empty windows. The coast was as clear as it would ever be.

I hooked the basket of muffins over my arm and hugged it close to me so I could move more easily into the cover of the cedars that lined the broad pathway to the back of the lake house. The gate latch was a single fraying rope. I pulled it gently until I heard the familiar click, then let myself into the massive garden where elm and linden trees rose like giants surrounding the wide lawn.

Beyond the trees was the lake. Sunlight reflected from the surface of the water, gilding the skeletal branches of the weeping willows. Weeds grew out of cracks in the rough stone patio and the long cedar deck appeared tilted, needing to be leveled. The graying planks had warped and dried. The rockeries and shrubs were choked with a profusion of twisting, twining weeds. The entire effect was desolate and gothic. A dark memorial to a glamorous past.

I gazed hard at it. Pictured that same place on a warm, sunny day. Saw people in bright summer clothes mingling among the rock gardens and around the pool. Imagined the sound of muffled voices coming from the nearby balcony, the sudden pop of a cork and the gurgling of wine into glasses. Now the garden was wild and unkempt, filled with dried autumn shrubbery and damp piles of leaves. At its center was the drained pool.

I walked towards it and leaned over the cracked concrete edge. The pool was empty except for a shallow slurry of dirty water and slimy autumn leaves. A clock chimed somewhere as the sun broke through a cloud. My reflection shifted in the muddy puddle.

31

I heard a rustling sound and looked up. A little boy appeared between the trees, his back to me. He walked towards the broken fence that led to the forest. I blinked my eyes again and he was gone.

I ran towards the place I'd spotted him.

Find him. Find him. That boy.

Was it the neighbor's boy?

Or my boy?

But he was nowhere in sight. I felt the heat of tears on my face. The same hollow clawing of emptiness in my gut. I turned to look back at the house.

That too was deserted.

Dust furred its smudged windows. A storm door flapped on rusted hinges. Or maybe it was the sound of the garage door opening. Maybe *she'd* come back. Maybe she'd forgotten something.

I realized then how I would look to her. A disoriented, neurotic busybody carrying a basket of muffins, and snooping around in her backyard. Just then a light went on in the back window by the screened-in veranda. I retreated into the cover of the trees. There was no way out except over the broken fence and into the forest.

The same way Jack had wandered.

I turned and fought my way through the clotted branches and twisted vines, scratching my hands in the process.

The small gate was padlocked. Had the lock been there on that day five years ago when Jack slipped through? Or had Jude, the owner, been so overwhelmed by guilt, he'd installed it afterwards to protect *his* kids?

I heard the swish of a patio door and my heart began to race. I had no other option but to balance the basket on the top of the fence, step up onto the bottom rung, then hitch my leg over the broken part. The basket tipped over, sending the muffins tumbling onto the grass. I got my other leg over just as I heard the sound of voices in the garden behind me. Jumping down onto the other side, I heard a rip as my jacket caught on a jagged piece of wood. I crouched under the cover of a spruce tree and watched as the blonde walked out into the garden accompanied by three men with pruning machines and chainsaws.

They'd come to start work on restoring the beauty and order back to that glorious garden. To rebuild it back to its former splendor.

Only then did it dawn on me that the house and its gardens were probably closed to me for good.

Worse still, I'd lost access to something precious I'd clung to for five years.

The last link to my son, Jack.

6

I sipped my tea, enjoying the spicy scent of cardamom and ginger. From my seat on my front porch, I could see the school kids running by, happy to finally be out in the fresh air. Usually I tried not to think about what it might have been like walking Jack home, but I couldn't help myself imagining his little hand in mine, asking him about his day at school. I'd have a plate of sliced fruit, cheese strings and animal crackers waiting on the kitchen counter for him. Then we'd cuddle up and watch cartoons or do some drawing or read a book together.

I shook the painful thoughts away and glanced at my phone. It was three twenty-eight.

The branches on the weeping willow outside my house drooped in a sad arch and when the breeze blew, the remaining leaves shivered and floated to the ground. The front yard needed to be cleared. I thought maybe I'd hire a lawn service this year because Nate hadn't bothered to rake the dead leaves. It was just like him to shirk the practical stuff or complain that a lawn and snow-clearing service was too expensive. Even though he had a closet full of expensive custom-tailored suits, he refused to spring for a decent mower or even a usable snow shovel.

I slipped my hand into my hoodie pocket. My fingers tightened on the bank slip I'd found in his suit. From an unfamiliar bank. The account balance said $850,675. I'd thought my eyes were deceiving me when I saw that huge number, so I held it up to the light. The black, printed numbers stood out in stark relief against the white paper.

Last time I'd looked, our accounts had only $4600 in the checking and just over $6000 in the savings. Everything else was tied up in the house, and Nate was always nagging at me for being too extravagant with the groceries. I couldn't fathom the idea of possessing this amount of money. Where had such a staggering figure come from? Was this actually his account or had he just picked up someone else's bank slip? But what was he doing at that particular bank? And why had he taken the time to fold the slip so neatly and stash it in his pocket?

I remembered that old cliché – still waters run deep. The quiet ones always had something to hide, and ever since I'd first met him, Nate had been a private, unobtrusive guy who rarely made waves. Who held his emotions tightly to himself. I was the needy, paranoid mess. On a roller coaster ride that never seemed to end. Maybe that's why we'd lasted this long.

A burst of chattering and a familiar voice brought me back to the present.

"How's it going, Liv?"

I looked up to see Shanti, my old friend from the moms and twos group. She stood at the edge of the front lawn holding seven-year-old Rocky's hand. Shanti's husband, Dev, was a big Sly Stallone fan. Every weekend morning, he went out jogging in his gray wool hat, black sweats and muffler, crunching his hands into fists as he ran.

I held up my teacup in a mock toast. "Pretty good. You?" Shanti always looked so put-together, from her sleek black ponytail to the stylish charcoal zip-up sweater and the skin-tight yoga pants that emphasized her long, slim legs.

"Haven't seen you in a while. Come over for tea some time."

A chill breeze tickled my neck. "Sorry – I've been so busy with new projects and all."

Shanti sighed, her face clouding over. "At least come to the block party on Saturday. It'll be fun. There'll be pumpkin pies, sweet potato casseroles and probably some highly alcoholic punch for the adults."

"I'll try," I said, marveling at the way Rocky leaned against his mother's side, his arm circling her waist.

"Think he needs a snack," said Shanti, glancing from me to her son. "See you Saturday?"

"Sure," I said, my mind suddenly crowded with the image of two small heads – one with glossy, black-hair and the other auburn and curly – bent over a blue wooden table, sifting sand through stubby fingers. I turned away before Shanti could see my eyes tear up. I bent over the table to brush off imaginary crumbs. When I looked up again, she was gone. I fell back against the chair, a sudden rush of sadness choking the breath from me. It subsided at the sight of a massive pickup truck with glittering wheel rims and red flames painted across its shiny black sides.

With one last blast of exhaust from the chrome tailpipes, the truck stopped in front of the lake house. The door swung open and two boot-clad feet emerged, revealing a tall, husky man who resembled a caricature I might have drawn for one of my middle-grade books. A cross between a biker and a wrestler, he sported a gray ponytail, a luxuriant black beard and was decked out in a black Ozzy Osbourne T-shirt, faded denim vest and a Hulk Hogan-type bandana that peeked out from under a black baseball cap. His bulging biceps were covered with vivid tattoos of green and blue snakes coiling around scarlet flowers.

I leaned back into the shelter of the cedars to watch as the garage door opened and the blonde neighbor strode down the driveway. The little boy padded along behind. The man held his arms out towards the child who sucked his thumb and clung to his mother's leg.

They were too far away for me to hear anything, but the man became agitated as the woman shrugged and folded her arms, facing him with an air of blank defiance. He turned and took a large blue gift bag from inside the truck and held it out to the boy who peeked around his mother's legs to look. Like a magician pulling a rabbit from a hat, the man lifted out a plush Mickey Mouse almost as big as the kid, who skirted around his mother's legs, grabbed it and retreated to shelter again.

She looked angry. One hand on her hip, she waved the other in his face, spitting out a barrage of words I couldn't decipher. The man tensed up. A pit bull poised to strike. The woman backed off, almost treading on the child's feet. Then the man turned and glanced towards me just as the sun beamed into my eyes. I shifted sideways to dodge the rays, then picked up my notebook and pretended to flip through the pages, trying to keep my eyes lowered.

By then he'd started yelling as the woman swept the boy into her arms. The kid screeched as he dropped the giant furry toy on the street, then carried on screaming and waving his arms as she retreated up the driveway and into the garage. The door slammed shut, leaving the man staring down at the Mickey Mouse toy that lay face down in the roadside gravel. His face was livid red as he kicked the toy further along the road, then climbed back into his

37

truck. He revved up the engine, spewing noxious exhaust into the air, then reversed over the toy, back and forth at least three times, crushing it under the weight of the heavy tires before he screeched off, leaving the stench of burning rubber hanging in the air.

My heart jumped when I saw the woman standing in her front bay window, staring right at me. Oblivious to the little boy at her feet who screamed and cried as he pointed to the crushed Mickey Mouse lying in the dirt.

7

Nate's mystery bank was situated in the heart of the downtown business district, occupying the expansive ground floor of a charcoal glass skyscraper. A long, gleaming security desk greeted me as I walked into the airy reception area the following morning.

I'd put off this visit for too long, imagining all kinds of wild explanations for Nate hiding the existence of such a large sum of money. Now I had to know if it was his money or if it was just a simple mistake and he'd picked up a client's bank slip by accident. A small part of me felt I should wait until Nate was home, talk to him first. But things had been so strained between us following Jack's disappearance that talking to the bank actually felt easier, less complicated. If there was a simple explanation, then there was no need to start an awkward conversation, and I didn't have the energy for the inevitable confrontation when he found out I was snooping around in his business life.

Beyond the uniformed guard in the foyer, rows of offices were stacked in dizzying floors around a cavernous central banking hall with glistening marble floors. Water trickled down a slate wall-fountain and subtle artwork was dotted around the walls. It looked like an international investment headquarters, not your average neighborhood branch.

The teller, a doll-faced girl with shiny black hair and thick eyelash extensions, would neither confirm nor deny the existence of Nate's account. She tapped on her computer keys with talon-like nails, then stopped and scanned the screen.

"If it's not a joint account we can't give out any information."

I leaned closer. "Even if I'm the spouse? I can prove it. I have my marriage certificate."

I held out the document but the girl stared at it, unfazed. "That proves nothing. Separations and divorces can get nasty when one partner's trying to access the other's private assets and empty the accounts. You wouldn't believe what I've seen in my time here. I'm afraid those kinds of cases have to be left to the lawyers to sort out."

"But I'm not getting divorced."

The girl sucked at her teeth. "You're not listed as a customer of this bank."

"Is my husband?"

"I can't tell you that either."

I felt a smirk coming on. "You already did when you told me it wasn't a joint account."

"What if I did? It's not a crime," said the girl, looking beyond me at the growing line of customers. "So, if you're done, I'd appreciate it if you moved aside and let me look after another client."

I stepped aside, irked at her sassy attitude. Then I stood, looking around that glittering place, wondering if Nate really did have access to almost a million dollars. Or maybe the slip belonged to one of his clients. That was the simplest explanation. How could he possibly have that kind of money at his disposal when we'd just argued over changing the kitchen counter tops to granite, because it would cost upwards of ten grand to do the whole thing?

But then I'd sensed for some time that he was holding something in. Something big. Ever since I'd kicked up a fuss about going to see the therapist, he'd drifted away from me, his every move seeming cagey and furtive as if he was a B-list actor playing a supporting role in a movie. As if he'd forgotten his lines and kept looking to some unseen director to coach him for his next scene.

-

My nerves were so on edge by the time I got home, I couldn't work. The latest half-finished illustration was just a sharp reminder of my inability to keep to a deadline, and there was no chance of me getting my focus back with all the worry about the bank slip. The other thing bothering me was that Nate hadn't called or texted since the day after he'd left on his trip. Two days and I'd heard nothing from him. I tried his number again, but it kept going to voicemail.

Finally, I threw on my quilted jacket and runners, grabbed my sketchbook and headed out for a walk, vainly hoping the creative juices would start to flow again.

The lake was a gathering place for all the birds who were late to migrate. The dawdlers who had lingered too long, enjoying the unusually balmy weather for late October. Now the cold was coming in, the stragglers were marshaling themselves into ragged teams before they headed south. The water was the color of summer leaves. Geese swam between small islands of ice and a jogger held his collar up against the stiff north wind. A squadron of ducks swam beak to tail across the water. I made a mental note to use that perfect image somewhere in the book. Maybe the lunch box kid brought all his extra muffin crumbs to a park and fed the ducks.

A squawking gull flapped by, breaking the silence and marring the serenity of the moment. I felt a faint flicker of annoyance as I walked away, so absorbed in worrying about the book and Nate and the money, I didn't hear the cyclist swishing up behind me, alerting me to the fact that I'd strayed into the middle of the path. I quickly jumped away onto the grass, cursing at the way those speed demons monopolized the walkways.

Heading away from the lake shore, I waded through the crackling carpet of leaves until I reached the bridge with its row of ornamental black lamps. If I leaned far enough forward, I could almost see beyond the pine and linden trees into the blonde neighbor's yard. Second house from the end, a black wrought iron fence separated it from the houses next door. I spied the large garden shed and the fire pit. Piles of chopped-up wood and brush were stacked by the fence. The landscapers had been hard at work cleaning the place up. I felt a sudden urge to run over there and sift through the debris like I'd done so many times before. To look for any shred of child's clothing torn off by the jagged branches. A sock. A shoe. Anything.

Hard, cold logic always told me that after five years any evidence would be long gone. But maybe…

A lone red canoe lay on its side on the shingle beach beyond the open gate. I shivered suddenly as if I'd walked through a sheet of freezing rain. What if the neighbor's little boy opened the door and slipped unseen into the garden? It would take nothing for him to run down to the lake shore and get into the boat or try to wade into the freezing water. I gripped the metal rail. If he did, I'd dive in among the weeds and swim to him. Drag him to safety.

A rangy middle-aged woman jogged past, calling out a cheery *hello.* I snapped out of my stupid fantasy and hurried away, the muscles in my legs screaming as I drove myself up the hill. At the top I looked down at the school. Classes were in full swing. The soccer field was empty. Determined to take another stab at the lunch box project, I clutched my sketchbook and headed down towards some benches near the school. All day my head had been flooded with thoughts about the money in Nate's mystery account. And the only image I could conjure up was the ladybug lunch box bursting with hundred-dollar bills.

What was Nate doing with all that money in the mystery bank account, and where exactly had it come from?

Just then, the blonde neighbor's child burst from around the corner of the school and ran, arms waving and feet skittering through the gravel towards the nearby play structure. His mother and the biker husband – or maybe boyfriend, clad from head to toe in black leather – followed, deep in conversation.

I hadn't noticed the monster truck on the street that morning or, for that matter, before I'd set out on my walk. After yesterday's row, they must have kissed and made up, considering the animated way the blonde chatted to biker boy. Maybe they were the kind of people who screamed and slapped at each other one minute, then pawed each other's bodies like mating tigers moments later. The type for whom rage was a kind of aphrodisiac because anger and love were both expressions of passion – interchangeable, regardless of whether they were destructive or gentle.

Things were different for me and Nate. Our relationship was as lifeless as a dead battery, our interactions polite but devoid of real feeling, our daily lives filled with empty rituals like stacking the dishwasher or reading the newspapers or mowing the lawn. We lived a half-life – simply going through the motions with blank expressions and deadened senses.

I looked up at the play structure. The little boy was trying to launch himself onto a climbing frame intended for school-age kids. His skinny arms barely reached the first rungs. He ran around the perimeter of the structure trying to find a way in, a way up. After a few minutes of reaching and failing, he plopped down onto the gravel, head bowed and began to sift the grit through his fingers. How many dogs had peed all over that spot? And now he'd probably start sucking on his fingers. My nerves bristled. I was on edge. I glanced over at his mother, now completely absorbed in showing biker boy something on her phone. Both were oblivious to the kid who was licking the pieces of gravel one by one.

I tried hard to concentrate on my drawing, turning to a fresh page and carefully sketching the little boy in front of me, thinking he might make a good character for the book I was working on. Now he threw down the gravel, spat out a mouthful of sand and ran like a little comet towards the slide. His tongue licked the snot from his upper lip as he gauged the ladder carefully, then began to climb it. My stomach flipped as he went higher and higher until he finally stood poised at the top, surveying the playground from a dizzying height. By now I was poised for action, half standing on the balls of my feet, ready to spring to his rescue.

The boy called to his mother, but she was still yakking as biker boy leaned in so close, he could have licked her face. The kid called again. When they didn't respond, his thin shoulders slumped. I fought the urge to run over and wait at the base of the slide ready to open my arms and sweep him up with hugs and kisses.

At that second, the kid launched himself downwards at a crooked angle and came hurtling down the slide sideways, his head bumping against the metal sides. He landed in a crumpled heap on the gravel. I sprang to my feet, and lunged towards him, but biker boy beat me and grabbed the kid up with two meaty hands. The mother came close behind, her hand plastered across her mouth. I froze in place, chest heaving. Before the child could even gather himself up to howl, the man swept him up onto his shoulders and lurched around making the kid's head loll from side to side. The mother reached to get him, but biker boy sidestepped her, laughing as he trotted away. The blonde neighbor's head turned deliberately towards me.

"Want a picture or something?" she snapped, before hurrying away after the man and boy.

All the wrong people have kids, I thought to myself once again, as I gathered up my drawing things and headed home.

8

Nate hadn't called by five the next evening, neither had he answered the many texts I'd sent asking him to tell me where he was staying or simply to give me a call. Worse still, it looked like he hadn't even read them.

The neighbor across the street hadn't shown her face all day and Shanti didn't walk by with Rocky after school. I figured she was probably busy chauffeuring a van full of kids to swimming classes, kung fu or soccer practice. So, as early twilight settled in, I felt the weight of loneliness as the walls closed in on me.

The silence was messing with my head. Deprived of the sounds, sights and scent of human contact for an entire day, I knew it was only a matter of time before the mosaic of shadows on the living room wall would become creeping, shifting creatures and the quiet a dull thrumming in my ears.

I gathered up my coat, packed my sketchbook into the new maroon leather valise Nate had brought back from Chicago last spring, and drove to the local bookstore just to be around people. Even the company of strangers was preferable to another night spent alone.

The nearest bookstore was one of those airy two-story places with overpriced knick-knacks on the lower floor next to the bargain books. Scented candles, vegan purses, printed silk scarves and whisky sets no one ever used took up a whole lot of space that, in my opinion, should have been used for books. Upstairs, a white baby grand piano stood next to the escalator and a busy coffee bar lay beyond the long rows of books.

I settled at a balcony table that looked down on the sales floor below. The steady bustle and flow of customers felt comforting after a week of solitary confinement. But after one sip of the cinnamon confection masquerading as coffee, I cursed that I hadn't asked the barista to hold the syrup. A slice of yellow cake topped with thick white icing lay untouched on the plate in front of me. Gnawing anxiety had robbed me of any desire to eat. Lunch had been coffee and a piece of bagel, supper a bite of leftover pizza.

It wasn't like Nate to ignore texts or calls for this long. He always replied with some kind of acknowledgement. Usually something brief and polite, but each time I'd tried his number, it had gone straight to voicemail.

And then the bank slip was an ominous specter looming in the background. Such a shocking sum at his fingertips. Was it actually his? If so, what was he doing with that amount of money? How did he get it? I thought about trying the number of his hotel. Asking him point blank about the money, but I couldn't because I had no idea where he was staying, and that was out of character. Usually, he'd either text the name of the place or an itinerary of his trip, but this time I'd been so preoccupied with the arrival of the new neighbors, I hadn't noticed his vagueness about where he was going. I'd let him slip away free and clear. Now, even if I could get him on the phone, I doubted I'd have asked him about the money anyway. Honesty and candor were not part of our repertoire. We thrived on banal niceties and blank chit-chat.

47

Sighing, I flipped my sketchbook open to a drawing of a tousle-haired child holding a partially sketched ladybug lunch box. The young hero appeared genderless. A deliberate choice I'd made since learning the child was called Parker. Now I just needed a bit more detail on the lunch box.

I'd forced my attention to the task of etching a cheeky grin on the ladybug when I found myself staring at the woman sitting at the table next to me. A slim, olive-skinned beauty with gleaming black hair tied back into a ponytail that rested at the back of her swanlike neck. She sat with the poise of a ballerina. Her long, tapered fingers circled a cup of herbal tea in one hand, while the other clutched a phone to her ear. She chatted with nervous agitation, tapping her knee on the underside of the table, eyes blinking double time. Intrigued, I opened a blank page and began to sketch her, thinking she'd be a good fit for Parker's mom, a breezy yoga enthusiast.

After five minutes of nonstop chatting on the phone, the woman turned and stretched her elegant neck as if searching for someone among the far bookshelves. I followed her gaze to a tall man in a well-cut navy overcoat who leaned against the magazine racks and beckoned the ballerina over with an incline of his head. He looked eerily familiar and then it dawned on me. It was the blonde neighbor's boyfriend. He'd lost the biker denim, smoothed his hair back into a ponytail and slipped into something tailored and stylish. With the groomed black beard and craggy face, the hipster-chic look was a surprising contrast to yesterday's hulky wrestler vibe.

Scrambling from her seat like an eager kid, the olive-skinned woman nearly tipped her tea over in her haste to get to him. I glanced around at the other customers, who were glued to their laptops, oblivious to the unfolding scene, then bent my head over my sketch pad, making sure to keep the couple in my sights.

The woman's loose burgundy coat had slipped from her shoulders by the time she reached the magazine rack, where the man reached out to her, snaked an arm round her waist and drew her in close. She tipped back her head, allowing him to plant a lingering kiss on her lips. They stood for what seemed like an eternity, caught up in a tight embrace like two high school kids skipping class to make out in the library. Then he pulled her around to the other side of the racks, so that they were concealed from my view.

Was this hot and heavy little affair the source of all the friction between him and the blonde neighbor? Or maybe the guy was leading a double life. Brash biker dude by day and artsy hipster eccentric by night.

I flipped my sketch book shut. Now I was way off course. At this rate I'd be far off my deadline and this assignment had been a favor from Min, who'd been a huge support during my tough stretch after Jack's disappearance.

"I feel for your loss," Min had said, "so I went out on a limb to vouch for you."

"I'll be okay. I'm in regular therapy. It's really helping," I'd lied without blinking. I hadn't set foot inside the therapist's cinnamon-walled office for at least a year. And I hated Mila, the therapist with her gelled nails and her Botoxed face. All through our sessions my attention would drift to the woman's rigid cheeks and the two little grooves that appeared each side of her mouth every time she pasted on the fake empathetic smile meant to win my confidence. She reminded me of a ventriloquist's doll whose mouth was the only feature that actually moved in that porcelain face. Nate hadn't a clue that each time I set out for a therapy appointment, all I did was go to the park and sit by the pond in the sculpture garden to read or sketch.

But I'd found some solace in work. Min had been delighted with the early sketches. Now all I had to do was come up with a few more pages of finished pieces to keep her believing in me. There was nothing for it but to go home to the darkness and quiet again. It was my only chance of getting anything done.

Poised at the top of the escalator, I glanced down and saw biker guy and ballerina already heading towards the front door. They must have sneaked through the warren of bookshelves and slipped out without me seeing. They held hands in a way that suggested raw passion, tangling their fingers together and rubbing at each other's fingertips as if the touch of skin on skin was an addiction – a craving. My own skin ached with the absence of touch.

Nate hadn't touched me that way in months – even years, if I was honest with myself. The few times we'd come together since Jack had gone, sex had been preceded by half a bottle of rye that Nate poured liberally into a can of coke as if he was trying to hide the fact of his drinking from me. Reeking of stale booze, he'd reach for me wordlessly in the darkness and then roll over on top of me, his half-shut eyes gazing at some undefined point on the wall.

When it was over, he'd slump over to his side of the bed, his back a brick wall. Afterwards, I'd lie rigid, the sheets pulled up to my chin, wondering when I'd become such a pushover. Someone who'd lost all sense of herself and her emotional needs.

Outside, the air was like a slap to my face, bringing me sharply back to the present. The bright moon glowed from a star-studded navy sky and bathed the lovers in a cone of blue-white light as they leaned against the man's monster truck and embraced, oblivious to passersby.

I stood, transfixed by the magic of the scene until a loud tapping broke the spell. The man pulled away, turning his head towards the rear window of the truck. He opened the door and the interior light went on illuminating the little curly-haired boy strapped into his car seat. Alone and unprotected, he'd waited there while the man I assumed was his father, had gone to meet his lover. He strained to talk to the child, hampered by the ballerina woman who draped her arms across his chest and leaned her head on his shoulder as if she couldn't bear to be torn away from him.

The man seemed irritated, his head darting from his son to his lover, who pushed him abruptly away and went to open the passenger door. The man moved to block her but she was too quick for him, ducking under his arm and planting herself in the passenger seat. The child's cries echoed across the parking lot as the man slammed the passenger door shut then stomped around to the driver's side. The screech of tires on concrete sent up a cloud of dust into the air as they zoomed away down the street.

I leaned against my car, chest pounding. That child was an innocent, caught up in a troubled adult world that left him a vulnerable target. Collateral damage. All the people around him were so immersed in their own angst, they barely paid him attention. It was only a matter of time before the unthinkable happened. Tragedy struck. I'd seen it before. Lived it. Breathed it. Was almost destroyed by it.

Breathless, I clambered into my car. I had to speak to someone. Anyone. The black thoughts were coming back. I took off and used the voice prompt to call Nate's number – pictured him lying on the bed of some anonymous hotel room, sipping on a beer and watching a movie or hockey game. The call went through and somewhere in some far-off city, the comforting ring was abruptly followed by a sharp click and then an automated message that said, *I'm sorry this number is no longer in service.*

I blinked at the sudden rush of oncoming headlights and swerved just in time to avoid an oncoming SUV.

9

I woke to a dull throbbing behind my left eye, and my stomach twisted and clenched. Mornings were always the worst time of day for me. Every anxiety seemed amplified. Every worry heightened. My nerves quivered like steel wires.

I lay there thinking over the events of last night. The bookstore. The biker guy and his ballerina lover. The little boy that no one seemed to be thinking about. My husband who'd suddenly disappeared.

When I'd got back home around nine, the neighbor's house had been lit up like a Christmas tree – windows blazing and the driveway crowded with an expensive array of import cars. Everything but the monster truck. I couldn't imagine that they'd had time to get there, drop the child off and leave before I'd reached home. But then I convinced myself that maybe it was better the kid was out of the house when a huge party was going on. Maybe biker guy actually did have some vestige of paternal instinct.

I'd stood at the bay window trying Nate's number over and over, and each time the mechanical voice delivered the same message. *No service, no service.* I tried to think rationally. Maybe he'd lost his phone and had to terminate his service. Maybe he was in the process of setting up another phone but had just been too busy to let me know about it. After downing a couple of glasses of wine, that theory had seemed reasonable, but in the cold light of morning I knew he would have called to let me know from the hotel phone. He was too polite not to. Something bad was up. I could feel it.

After ignoring a couple of Min's calls, I finally dragged myself out of bed. Min was tenacious, and the ringing sound seemed to escalate in intensity the longer it went on. A sure sign of her desperation. There was nothing else for it but to make a concerted effort to put all the worry aside, take a long shower, try to force some food down and do an eight-hour stint to catch up to my deadline. There was also the promise of the block party Shanti had mentioned. Something to kill the long, lonely hours. Another night spent alone was unthinkable.

I toweled off my hair and decided to forgo the tedious blow-drying ritual. My auburn curls had once been a source of insecurity, but eventually I came to see them as something to be proud of – something that marked me out from the other girls with their silky flatironed hair. At one time I'd cultivated a romantic Pre-Raphaelite image after reading about Elizabeth Siddal and the thread of tragedy woven through her life. So I pulled on a loose green sweater and fluffed the curls around my shoulders. Nate preferred my hair swept up in a bun or tamed with the flatiron. But now I didn't have to please him.

The aftereffects of the sleeping pills and wine made me feel light and disembodied as I padded down the stairs, the curls swaying like a soft veil. I went straight to the window. Three or four cars from the previous night were still parked opposite but still no monster truck. And all the blinds were drawn. No sign of life there. I put on a massive pot of coffee, did a few warm-up exercises for my arms and moved my easel away from the bay window. I was determined not to look outside at all today.

–

That night when I set out for the block party clutching a plate of spiced pumpkin bars, I felt better than I had in weeks. Dogged persistence had yielded three pages of finished drawings that were bound to pacify Min for at least the next month. And it was so mild outside for late October, the air soft with moisture that dripped from the bare branches. Thin ribs of cloud stretched across the moon creating a perfect pre-Halloween backdrop for witches on gnarled broomsticks to swoop across the sky. Bats hung from black, twisted tree branches. The glow of illuminated pumpkins burnished concrete doorsteps and massive blow-up ghosts and spiders billowed out on lawns and driveways.

It had been liberating in a way not to worry about talking to Nate, and as the day had worn on, I'd felt an unfamiliar thrill of freedom, found my mind drifting back to my single days in my tiny bachelor pad in Toronto. That place had been a refuge from the empty husk that was my family, its heart gouged out after my brother Alex's death. Leaving all that sadness behind, I'd felt truly carefree for the first time in years, and able to flit between concerts and openings and crowded house parties, without feeling a nagging sense of guilt.

Immersed in those giddy memories, I walked straight into a wispy sheet draped like a ghost over someone's tree. The more I tried to unravel it, the more it became tangled in my hair, and as I swatted and cursed to free myself, I heard a voice that sent a tingle of recognition across my skin.

"Need help there?" the voice said in a light but rich tone. Then someone flipped one side of the sheet up and loosened it from my neck. In the soft beam of the streetlight, I made out a tall man with a pale, heart-shaped face, catlike eyes with thick lashes, light stubble above full lips and a tiny tattoo above his left temple in the shape of a sun. His dark eyes gleamed.

"Livvy. Livvy Carroll?"

"Stefan. Stefan Tang."

My mind flew back to high school. The first time I met him when he joined my English class. Miss Glow, our teacher, had turned to the class and announced, "So everybody – I want you to meet Stefan Tang. He's just moved here from Toronto, and I have to say, it's pretty tough coming into a new school in twelfth grade. I hope you'll all welcome him into your community. Show him around. Give him a good Stoney Oaks welcome."

A young guy walked in, eyes downcast. He wore a short black leather jacket, a plain black T-shirt with a most unusual bead and chain necklace hanging down his front. His short, black hair was cropped at the sides with a thick burgundy crest on top. Black bone earrings stuck out of his earlobes. His hands were stuffed in his jean pockets. The final touch was a pair of gold runners. It was hard to see his face, but his lowered eyes had a sleepy look. Like a young Keanu Reeves, who'd just stepped off the set of *The Matrix*.

"So how d'you get a name like Stefan Tang?" said Cory, the class clown, as Stefan took the seat next to him and just in front of me. I was wondering the same thing.

"My dad's from Hong Kong and my mom's Polish," he whispered, without averting his eyes from the teacher.

I had hardly been able to take my eyes off him back then, and it was even harder to do so now.

"God, you've changed," I said, looking up at the well-groomed man now standing in front of me.

"Lost the burgundy hair and crazy earrings you mean?" He smiled with that familiar twitch at the corner of his lips. "You look the same – the hair and all."

"Sure, only I'm fourteen years older." I took in his slim black puffer jacket and dark jeans. "And you grew up too – toned down the style."

He swatted away the muslin sheet that fluttered against his hair. "Steel chains and gold shoes don't exactly work in my particular field."

"You still have those shoes?"

He grinned. "Actually, yes. Shoved somewhere in the back of my closet. You never know when they might come in handy. Never know when I might get an invite to a dress-up Halloween party."

"You still have the tattoo," I said, searching the familiar lines of his face.

He touched the tiny sun. "Haven't summoned up the courage to get it removed. I use a lot of concealer."

"Good. I always liked it."

A sudden whoosh of air inflated a massive *Beetlejuice* figure on the lawn beside us. I stumbled sideways. Stefan reached out and steadied me, his touch sending an unfamiliar thrill down my arm.

A sudden heat warmed the back of my neck. "That's Halloween for you. Strange apparitions in the night."

"You headed to the block party?"

I nodded. "You too?"

57

"Yeah, I just moved into a bungalow on the other side of the crescent. Short-term rental until I find something more permanent."

"That's incredible," I said, falling into step beside him, and for a few dizzy moments time seemed to shift gear and we were two teenage loners walking home together from school, shoulders aching from the pull of heavy backpacks. "I live just four doors back. Opposite the lake houses."

He shrugged. "Living among the elites, eh? My place is opposite the people on the park. Not quite so salubrious."

We rounded the corner of the cul-de-sac where a crowd of darkened figures thronged the grassy boulevard at the center. Silhouetted against the orange glow of pumpkin lights, they swarmed around three long picnic tables, loaded with food, pop cans, beer bottles and stacked paper cups. A gruesome skeleton was perched atop a massive beer keg, and someone in a Jason mask was dispensing punch from a huge plastic barrel. The loud buzz of adult conversation vibrated in my ears just as a tiny vampire pursued by a larger werewolf slammed into my legs.

I glanced over at Stefan who stood open-mouthed at the mass of babbling parents chugging back beers, oblivious to their screaming kids. He chewed his lower lip, hands dug deep into his jacket pockets.

"Wanna go for a walk?" he whispered, already turning to go.

"Preferably a long, quiet one," I said, handing my plate of pumpkin bars to the nearest kid over the age of ten.

"C'mon before they see us." He placed his hand on my elbow and steered me back into the moonlit darkness. We power walked away along the street, keeping silent until we were well away from the party.

Stefan had been in my creative writing group. I remembered the first time we shared our work.

Miss Glow, our teacher, arranged us into small groups and asked us to share our pieces. I'd squirmed in my chair, my face flushed as it always did when I was feeling self-conscious. The curse of being a redhead. "I'll pass."

The other kids urged Stefan to share next. I studied his face, fascinated, noticing his eyes were hazel with amber flecks.

"It's nothing," he'd said, shrugging, though his eyes scanned the crowded page in front of him. When everyone encouraged him, he took a deep breath and grasped the edges of his book so tightly the whites of his knuckles stood out.

"I have this dream where I can fly. Like a phoenix, I swoop across molten red skies, leave burning rocket trails as I blaze through the cosmos, fingertips piercing the clouds until I reach the blistering face of the sun."

Everyone was silent. Stefan shrank back into a slouch. Cory's brow knit into a frown. My ex-best friend Sasha watched me with wide eyes and I could barely breathe.

I knew what they were thinking. *After what she's been through, I can't believe this guy is writing all about the f-word. Fire.*

For a moment, I couldn't speak.

"It doesn't make sense," said Cory, the class clown, wrinkling his nose.

"Yes, it does," I said. "It's incredible." My mind was alive with dazzling gold and scarlet shards of light that weren't scary, only beautiful.

And now, fourteen years later, gold and scarlet light danced before us from lanterns hung outside an elaborately decorated yard. We'd fallen into a silence filled with memories, questions – what had our lives been like in the time we'd spent apart, and what had we become?

"Weird we should run into each other like this," Stefan said, nudging me back to the present. The light from the streetlamp cut across his face, and I still couldn't believe I'd run into him again after so long.

"I was just remembering our first writing class. When we shared our free-writes."

He scratched his head and hunched his shoulders. "I believe I wrote something lame about a burning phoenix."

"It was beautiful."

"I wish I'd known about your brother at the time," he said, turning to study my expression.

I pushed on ahead, past the house where a witch hung on a noose from the upstairs balcony. "It was okay. Believe me. The things you wrote about and the beauty of your words, helped me see what happened to him in a different way."

"I'm glad," he said, his voice softening. "Your mom and dad still around?"

"Dad passed away five years after I graduated high school. Complications with the skin grafts. And Mom went a couple of years later. Guess she couldn't manage without him."

"I know you had a tough time at home, Liv. I should've stuck around longer."

I touched his shoulder. "Don't feel bad. You had to be with your dad. And you had that offer from Carleton on the horizon."

"Yeah, and it didn't do me much good."

"You mean you didn't go into journalism?"

He shook his head. "Had a change of plan," he said as we turned the corner into the field. The elementary school was situated at the bottom of the hill. At the top was the shelter where we'd sat on spring and summer nights drinking beer and contemplating the state of society, the world and the universe.

"Shall we?" he said, his eyes glinting in the moonlight.

"What are we waiting for? Race you to the top."

Cool night air rushed through my hair and whistled in my ears as I ran, chest heaving, up the steep hill. At the top I slumped onto the bench under the wooden canopy.

"God, I thought I was in better shape," I wheezed, the breath rasping from my throat. "Guess I'd better start jogging instead of walking."

"I'm not much better," he said, flopping down beside me.

"Too bad we didn't bring a couple of beers with us."

"Major slip-up," he said.

I turned to watch him. Moonlight illuminated tiny pearls of sweat on his temples. "I always wondered what happened to you. Where you ended up."

His brow wrinkled. "Last time I saw you I had to go back to Hong Kong – to see my dad. I hadn't realized how sick he was. I stayed there until he passed."

"I had no idea. I'm so sorry."

"I should have stayed in contact. Should have called you, but I didn't know if I was ever coming back. Guess I hadn't realized how much his death would affect me. Mom decided to stay in Hong Kong. She convinced me to take the scholarship to Carleton, but I guess I just couldn't fit in. I tried for two years. Then I missed my granny so much I came back here to live with her. It really helped her get over Dad's death to have me around. Gave her some closure, because she hadn't been well enough to take the journey back to Hong Kong when he was sick."

"She still alive?"

He grinned. "She'll be ninety-six this year and she's the unofficial leader of the bridge club at her seniors' home."

I felt the comforting dig of the bench into the back of my neck as I gazed up at the stars. My heart ached. *If only I could go back fourteen years* – before Jack. I swallowed and tried to remember the vigorous old lady. The memory of her made me smile. "I remember your gran so well. A tiny, energetic woman but she was always larger than life."

"And sometimes a real pain in the ass. She was real old-school Chinese. Suspicious of strangers. Especially females. She used to tell me all the girls were sluts, out to cast love spells on me."

"And did they?"

"None that lasted any length of time. How about you? Are you married?"

I nodded. "It's been eight years. He's away on business."

"Kids?"

The lightness slipped away, and a cold, dead weight settled on me. I shook my head and picked at my thumb-nail.

His eyebrows rose. "Sorry, I'm being too personal."

"It's a long story." I blinked back the pressure of tears behind my eyes. "Maybe some other time?"

The dull vibration of a phone broke the silence. He reached into his pocket, checked the screen, then held up a finger. I watched him, marveling at how much he'd changed. When I'd first met him, he was a kid whose mind never stood still, whose imagination had no bounds, who could conjure up blazing images in a few glorious words that I faithfully tried to capture in sketches. We'd started our comic strip only weeks after we met.

He ended the call and stood up abruptly. "So sorry, Liv. Gotta run. Work calling."

I felt a new awkwardness between us as we walked back down the hill. Of course, the mention of Nate had put up a barrier. How could I expect it not to? And yet I'd chatted more with Stefan in thirty minutes than I had in days with Nate.

"How did you end up using all your talents?" he said as we stood outside his small, slate-trimmed bungalow.

"I went to art school in Toronto. Thought I'd write graphic novels and get a major deal. Too bad reality hit. Now I illustrate children's books."

"That's incredible," he said, his face lighting up.

"Really not as glamorous as it sounds. And you?"

His eyes dropped as he kicked at the gravel with the toe of his shoe. "I'm a cop. Plain clothes detective." He glanced up at me, eyebrows raised. "Not exactly what you expected, huh?"

"Definitely not. You were so… so…"

"Nerdy? Weird? Say it, Liv. Don't hold back."

"We both were, Stefan." I touched his arm. "We were loners. Oddballs. And you helped me get through a tough time. I owe you big time."

He smiled. I'd forgotten how bright his smile was. "Don't be a stranger, Olivia. Now we've found each other again. Come over for a drink. Bring your hubby."

He held my arms and leaned forward to drop a friendly kiss on my cheek.

"Coffee's on most mornings. Drop by any time."

He turned and waved when he reached the front door, and I walked on past the giant inflated witches and pumpkin heads, feeling an unfamiliar tingle spread to my fingertips. This was the second time I'd been going through a troubled time in my life, and he'd showed up like a guardian angel.

Turning the corner, I stood under the streetlight and checked my phone. Nothing. No messages, emails or phone calls. No word from Nate. What the hell was he up to? I decided I'd take the last resort and call his boss on Monday. I didn't want to cause trouble or embarrass him at his workplace.

The roar of a powerful engine drew my attention over to the neighbor's driveway, which was packed with cars again. The front windows were dark, but if I looked down at the side of the house, I could see the glow of lights from the back of the house reflected on the lake. That woman had a crazy busy social life. How did she manage it all with a small child around? And where was the poor kid? Locked away in his room with no one looking in on him? That nagging sting of anxiety prickled at my nerves again.

I sidled up my driveway keeping an eye on the big house opposite, watching to see if anyone of interest came out, to give at least some clue about what was going on in there. Then from the corner of my eye I noticed a black Dodge Viper crawling along the street, its dark tinted windows obscuring whoever was inside. It stopped, idling at the foot of my drive, the red brake lights bleeding onto the weeping willow tree. The dull whirr of the driver's side window opening made me step into the shelter of my front porch. Hiding in the shadows, I watched the two dark shapes inside. The glint of glasses told me someone was watching me, scoping out my house. Heads were moving as if they were talking. Then they made an abrupt turn and pulled into the lake house driveway.

I breathed easy again.

Maybe it was good to have a friendly cop living nearby.

I decided not to return to the block party. A good thing because the cop assigned to keep Jack's case alive called me just as I poured my first glass of wine for the evening. It was a brief conversation intended to deliver just another gut-wrenching assurance that they were still keeping the case open but had no new leads.

I took my drink and sat in the big easy chair by the bay window. I needed to collect myself. Stop my mind careening down an endless tunnel of hopelessness and futility. Think instead of the one bright spot of the day. Seeing Stefan again.

I always wondered if and when he'd come back into my life. On the one hand, my pulse raced at the thought of seeing him again, but there was also a dark side to our reunion.

He'd awakened a whole raft of memories from high school. Memories I'd put aside long before losing Jack. After all, losing Jack was only the latest tragedy in my life. The first tragedy had been a loss that marked my teen years with heartbreak.

My older brother, Alex, died in a fire in my eleventh-grade year.

10

BEFORE

One year older than me, Alex was a guy who loved to talk. And I never got tired of listening to him. When other girls at school got all pissed off about their jerky, asshole brothers, I could truthfully say that my brother was one of my best friends. He was what people would call a sunny guy. Always positive. Forever joking around. If Dad was in an off mood, all it took was one wisecrack from Alex to have Dad in stitches.

"This boy could sell hair color to a bald man," Dad would say, holding his palms up to the ceiling.

Here's what else I remember most about him. Long discussions about how the universe began, the origins of human life, environmental catastrophe. Deep, important issues that siblings don't always talk about, especially in their teen years.

We'd talk for hours about our future ambitions, lounging on the Adirondack chairs in our sun porch and staring at the night sky. He planned to go on to university and study philosophy or astronomy or quantum physics. I loved listening to him, and loved that he made me feel confident about myself.

"You might be quiet on the outside, Liv," he'd say, tipping his chair back and turning the peak of his baseball cap around, "but you've got a powerful inner dialogue going on."

Alex was really a walking contradiction; a handsome jock with the mind of a philosopher and scientist. It wasn't surprising that a whole lot of girls at school had crushes on him.

Life was great. Going into eleventh grade I found an outlet for my imagination in the drama club – backstage, of course – and Alex sailed into senior year as first-string quarterback on the football team. It was shaping up to be a glorious grad year for him and a tantalizing preview of what my senior year might be. Everything seemed rosy until Chad Hayes and Renny Beaumont got onto the football team and muscled their way into Alex's tight-knit friend group.

The change happened in the space of a week.

One moment Alex was the cheery, optimistic brother and son – an open book, always there to talk and listen. Days later he was like a ghost in the house. Slipping out first thing in the morning, returning late in the day from school, his jaw set in a strange, tight expression, his conversation reduced to brief three-word sentences. At weekends his bedroom door was locked and no amount of knocking on my part could get it open.

Dad cornered me in the hallway. "Is he on drugs, Liv? You'd tell me if he was, wouldn't you?"

I nodded, a cold, sickly feeling in my stomach. "I'll ask around," I said, unsure exactly how I'd broach that task.

"Maybe it's just a natural phase, Ted," Mom reasoned to my dad, but her face was tight with worry as she looked up the stairs towards Alex's bedroom. "Sometimes the prospect of big change ahead can stress young people out."

I wasn't convinced. Neither was Dad. "This change has been too quick – and besides, he'd talk to us if he was worried about graduation. It has to be something else."

At school, the word was that Chad and Renny were trouble.

Turned out Dad was right.

That spring I learned a terrible lesson. The world I'd believed was simple and perfect, was actually a cruel, dark place.

I came back late one night from drama club, wondering why a thick blanket of smoke was hanging in the air. I felt the acrid bite of it in my throat as I turned the corner and saw my house surrounded by fire trucks. Red and blue lights swirled in the darkness, lighting up the blackened frontage of my house. I ran screaming towards it, dropping my backpack on the ground, straight into the burly arms of a paramedic who caught me as I fell forward, screaming my lungs out.

Strong arms held me back and pulled me away when a stretcher emerged from the house, carrying my dad who was moaning and bellowing in a way I couldn't comprehend, his face and arms charred and blackened. Mom was nowhere to be seen. I thought the body bag that came out next was her, and I started up my howling again as my legs gave out from under me. But when I spotted her, lying propped up on another stretcher, tranquilized and semi-comatose, I knew the awful truth.

After the fire, we moved to live with Gran. Mom couldn't stay another night in the burned house. Said every space, every corner, every doorway and window reminded her of Alex. For months after, she was drugged up with heavy knock-out stuff – slept all day as if she'd checked out from being Mom because the pain was too much to bear.

When Dad finally came home from the hospital, he'd changed both mentally and physically. Shiny scales and raised wheals of scar tissue crept up from under his collar to the soft places in front of his ears. The skin on his arms had transformed, too, knotted, twisted skin stretching from the backs of his hands to his elbows.

But he always tried to keep them covered, even though, to me, they were badges of bravery. The indelible marks of his ultimate sacrifice for his beloved son.

He'd got those burns when he tried to rescue Alex from the fire that started in the basement. He'd reached his bare hands into the flames and pulled Alex out, but it was too late.

He never forgave himself for surviving.

I never forgave myself for being out when it happened.

After the fire there was an investigation. The fire commissioner's findings reported evidence of drugs among the basement rubble. Shreds of tin foil and traces of crystal meth among the scorched pieces of glass from the bowl of a glass pipe.

When Dad found out about the drugs, it was like he'd lost Alex all over again. Only this time it was not just a death, but a betrayal of everything he'd treasured about his beloved son.

I knew deep in my heart that Alex wouldn't try that poison. I refused to believe it possible. Someone else had brought those drugs to our house. And that someone started the fire and was too cowardly to take the blame.

I carried that doubt with me for years, vowing to find out who was responsible.

Until Jack disappeared and a new, fiercer kind of pain consumed me.

11

NOW

A light snow was falling Monday morning. The first snowfall of the year. Transforming all the drab muddiness of fall into a pristine wonderland. Trees sparkled with frost and a thin white blanket was spread over everything. I bundled up in a parka, wool hat and scarf and went for a long walk. I'd always loved the milky, muted light that came with the snow. The ornamental lamps were still lit on the bridge and the creamy-pink sky created a melancholy magic that sparked my imagination. As I walked through the frozen landscape, the watery scent of fresh snow brought my brain to life and I planned a bunch of eye-catching winter pictures for the lunch box project.

By the time I got back home, I was so focused on thinking about the pictures I was going to draw, I only gave a sideways glance at the lake house, but stopped in my tracks when I saw the driveway was empty for the first time in a week. I hadn't seen the blonde neighbor since the day at the playground and wondered how her little son was surviving the endless parties and the constant coming and going all night.

The air was so fresh I felt reluctant to go inside. I opened the garage to get the shovel out and do some clearing before the snow got too thick, but as soon as the overhead door whirred open, the sight of Nate's empty car set my nerves on edge. A sharp reminder of his absence, it swept away all my newfound serenity. I tried the passenger door – locked. But I thought maybe he'd left a spare set of keys in the house. I'd look for them later. Maybe something in his glove compartment might hint at where he'd gone.

While I scraped away at the driveway, pushing the snow onto the lawn, I decided I'd waited long enough to act. It was time to call Nate's work. I just had to come up with a good excuse that wouldn't get them wondering what the hell was going on.

I was about to go back into the garage to hang up the shovel when a loud screeching noise cut into the silence. Biker boy's monster truck rounded the corner with a thunderous roar, its rear wheels fishtailing on the slick road surface. The truck skidded to a halt, the driver's door flew open, and the guy slid out, just taking a second to pull up the fleece collar of his denim jacket before he stomped up the driveway. I moved into the shadowy corner of the garage so I could watch events unfold.

He stood at the massive front door ringing the doorbell nonstop. Then he waited for a while. No answer. After about a minute of constant ringing, he began to pound the door with his fist. I moved closer to the entrance of my garage.

"I know you're in there, Heidi – you'd damn well better open up."

So, she was called Heidi. The name seemed to suit her cool, blonde looks.

By now he was pounding like a maniac and nobody had answered. The thought of that innocent little kid listening to the sudden deafening noise tugged at my heart. In troubled relationships it was inevitably the kids who suffered, the vulnerable ones. And Jack was always somewhere in the depths of my consciousness – a faint little figure urging me to watch out, take care, *don't forget me.*

Never. I'll never forget.

The guy bent down and scooped up a handful of snow. He fashioned it into a snowball and hurled it at the side window, then turned to go, yelling, "I'll be back, bitch, and this time with the cops."

I thought I saw a faint smudge of a face at the window. Maybe, maybe not. Could've been a trick of the light, but I was so intent on figuring it out, I hadn't noticed the biker was standing at the foot of the lake house driveway watching me, hands planted on his hips. I pulled back into the shadows, but it was too late. He was already stomping up my drive. Reaching my hand up towards the pin pad, I was about to close the garage door, when he waved and called out to me.

"Wait. Don't close it."

His desperate tone told me he wasn't coming to ream me out, so I paused, aware of the steady thud of my heart. But then I remembered Stefan lived just around the corner and that was enough to give me a comforting sense of security.

"How can I help you?" I said, stepping out into the daylight and blinking in the sudden glare.

He reached out a hand towards me. "Rick – Rick Dubeau." He crushed my hand inside his huge one.

"Olivia Barnett," I said, trying not to wince at the pressure on my fingers.

"Pleased to meet you, Olivia. Guess we didn't exactly get off on the best foot."

73

I pulled my hand away. "Not sure what you mean."

He grinned. "The other day at the playground and then now." He tilted his head in the direction of Heidi's house. "I probably look like a first-class nutcase and the world's worst dad."

"You have an adorable son," I said.

Up close his features were large but well formed – smooth, fair skin, prominent brow bone above pale gray eyes, and a well-shaped mouth hidden partly behind the full, dark hipster beard. One ear was pierced with three gold rings and a colorful riot of tattooed hearts and flowers was visible at the neckline of his faded black T-shirt.

"You mean Toby? Yeah – he's cute but he can be a bossy little tyke if you cut him too much slack."

"I've seen him in the park with your... with your..."

"Ex-wife. Heidi."

I nodded. "He fell off his bike the other day. I went to help him but..."

"She probably told you to take a hike," he said, putting a hand to his forehead. "Typical Heidi. She was probably on the phone."

When I nodded again, he kicked at the snow with the toe of his boot. "Dammit, he's gonna get hurt some day and she'll be responsible."

Panic stabbed at my heart. "It just takes a second and then you live with the consequences your whole life."

His brows knit above narrowed eyes. "Say what?"

"Sorry. I get carried away sometimes."

He touched my arm. "No... hey... if you know something, you have to tell me. I love that kid."

Blood pounded in my ears and rushed to my head. "You left him alone in your truck. At the bookstore."

74

He backed away, hands held up, palms forward in supplication. "Just for a few minutes." He shook his head. "I never meant to be long."

"That's all it takes. I took my eyes off my son for a few moments and then… and then…" I fought back tears. Bit the inside of my lip. Not again. I couldn't cry in front of this stranger.

"I'm so sorry, Olivia." His voice softened. "Wanna tell me what happened?"

I shook my head. "I can't… not right now."

"Okay. I respect that, but let me just say, you're absolutely right to give me shit. I'm a fool for leaving Toby alone even for a few minutes. I swear, I'll never do it again."

"He's your kid. Why make the promise to me?"

He sighed. "I don't want you to think I'm a bad guy, because I need to ask a really important favor."

I took a deep breath and folded my arms. My toes were tingling with the cold. I wanted to get inside. "Okay, what?"

He smiled sheepishly. He had even, white teeth that looked like veneers. I thought about the beautiful ballerina he'd been with the other night, and Heidi who could be a model. This guy was heavily into appearances. "You seem like a really caring person – and trustworthy. And you've probably noticed what's going on over there. All the parties and the cars at all hours of the night? Am I right?" he said, moving closer and reaching into his pocket.

My cheeks flushed. "Yes. It's pretty busy over there."

He held out a small card. "Here's my contact info. If you see anything out of line, or if you think Toby is in any danger, you call me. Truth is, I don't want him living with Heidi. I want him with me. All the time. But I need evidence. Hard facts. Understand?"

I scanned the card, which read, *Rick Dubeau, Custom bike designs.* "Okay. I'll keep an eye on him."

He backed away, down the driveway. "Thanks, Olivia. And you can call me any time." He took a few more steps, then stopped and seemed to think for a few moments before turning back to me. I was about to close the garage door. "But you should stay away from that house. Heidi hangs out with some pretty sketchy people."

I nodded, feeling a slight tingle of fear. Had I imagined someone watching me from the Dodge Viper the other day?

I waited until Rick swung the truck door open and leapt inside. With a blast of loud acceleration, he was gone in a few seconds, leaving only a faint trail of exhaust fumes hanging in the air. Before the garage door closed, I thought I saw a pale figure watching me from the lake house window, but in a split second it was swallowed up in darkness.

Back inside the house, I cradled a hot cup of tea and thought about Rick. Maybe I'd misjudged him. Jumped to conclusions because of his appearance. Maybe he really was a good dad with his son's best interests at heart. And maybe Heidi, in her big, fancy house, was up to something illegal. Something that might put a vulnerable kid like Toby in danger. I took another look at the card Rick had given me. I couldn't save my own kid, but I could play a part in rescuing someone else's.

Determined to get my mind back to my work, I wandered into the living room. My latest painting showed a small, curly haired boy standing under an ornamental streetlamp, its light spilling out onto the snow-laden fir trees. His eyes were wide-open in surprise as a tidal wave of peanut butter and jam sandwiches erupted from his red lunch box. Just up the hill behind him, two glittering sets of eyes watched intently from the cover of a low-lying bush.

Jack had always loved peanut butter and jelly sandwiches, cut into long strips and arranged like the petals of a flower on his plate. He'd loved waffles with lots of syrup and a soft-boiled egg in a frog egg cup. I'd stroke his blond curls. Blond? *They were blond, weren't they? Or was I thinking of Toby?*

I looked back at the painting. I'd given Parker fair hair but Jack had auburn curls. *That's what made him stand out among all the other little kids. His flame-colored curls.*

I was forgetting him and I could never do that.

I took the tube of titian red and repainted Parker's hair. I knew once that was done, I would finally have to make the call that I had been dreading.

12

By lunchtime, I'd seen no movement from the lake house so I had nothing new to report to Rick. I hadn't heard anything from Nate either. My self-imposed deadline had arrived. It was time to call his work. Pacing back and forth, I rehearsed what I would say. How to seem nonchalant. Unconcerned. But everything sounded lame or fake. I decided spontaneity was the best course, so I scrolled through my contacts and found Alec's number. Alec was the area sales manager and had been Nate's boss for more than ten years.

His secretary put me straight through to him. Alec was loud. The life and soul of every office party I'd been to, with his quips and one-liners. I turned down the volume on my phone to save my ears.

"Livvy. Long time no hear. How are you?"

"Good. And you?"

"You know what they say, if you can count your money, you don't have a billion dollars, so I'm still here plodding away."

"And Jenny?"

"She's on so many boards I have to make an appointment for an audience with her these days."

"You should've been a stand-up comedian, Alec."

"They wouldn't be able to afford my hourly rate, Livvy. So what can I help you with?"

I swallowed. "It's about Nate…"

"Oh, you want to pick up his things? He said he'd do it, but he didn't show."

"Which things?"

"Last year when he left us, he forgot to empty his desk. So, we put it all together in a box."

My mouth felt dry and woolly. I tried not to stutter – to give away my surprise. "Oh… okay. I'll come tomorrow and get it."

"Sounds good, Livvy."

"Just leave it at the reception desk."

"Will do. By the way, how's Nate doing? We were sorry to lose him, but he couldn't turn down the opportunity of a lifetime. Even I said he'd be a fool to do that."

I plunked myself down on the sofa, trembling. *How many more lies was I going to uncover?* "Yeah, you know Nate. He seems to do well in whatever situation he finds himself in."

"Well, you tell him to give me a shout. I'd love to catch up with him."

"Sure," I said, my mind racing ahead. "By the way, he wanted me to ask you about his HR file. Could you send him a copy? Seems he's in need of it right now."

There was a slight pause before he answered. "We don't usually do that, but I'll make an exception for Nate. I'll get my assistant to send him the file."

"Just email it to my address and I'll get it to him."

I texted him my email address and then closed the call. So, Nate hadn't worked for them in almost a year. What was this *big opportunity* he'd left the company for? And where had he gone when he'd claimed to be on all those business trips? Who was he working for? Worse still, why was he lying to me?

I cradled my aching head in my hands and waited for the HR file to come through.

A sharp *ting* alerted me to an incoming email. I clicked on the message and saw the attachment. The little icon that held some of the answers I was looking for. *Nate Barnett: HR file.*

I opened the folder and scrolled through the contents, scanning reports and spreadsheets, performance reports and sales numbers. It seemed he'd been an exemplary employee. Always met or exceeded the sales targets. Performance reports were glowing, commenting on his *professional approach with clients*, his *superior communication skills*, his *drive and initiative*, his value as a *team player*.

His *integrity and honesty*.

I almost choked on that one.

But I stopped when I came to the record of his business trips. For the past three years, Nate had taken at least two or three business trips a month. At least, that was the story he'd given me. But as I scanned his personnel file, the list of business trips for the two years before he'd left the company was way shorter than I expected. Only four out-of-town trips for each year. I looked at the next page in disbelief. It seemed that at the beginning of that three-year period, Nate had apparently switched to part-time remote working from home, and all those dates spent supposedly *working from his home office*, roughly corresponded with the dates he told me he'd been on trips out of town.

I felt the fluttering of panic in my stomach again, and a sour, sick feeling when I glanced over at Nate's photograph on the side table.

I couldn't even confront him with this new information. Couldn't ask him why he'd been lying to me for over a year now, because he'd chosen this time to disappear and leave me searching for even more answers about the man I thought I'd known for the past fourteen years.

The man I'd been married to for at least eight of those.

13

THEN

It hadn't always been like this with Nate. Not at the beginning.

I'd first heard of him at high school. He was on the football team of our rival school and was friends with some of Alex's football buddies. But he was always a background character, a shadowy figure on the outside of my brother's social circle, showing up at some of the football parties, sitting with people I didn't know at the local coffee hangout. I paid little to no attention to him.

He was a year older than me and the kind of guy who would never even glance at an artsy nerd like I was. My best friend at the time, Sasha, had a temporary crush on him, but moved on to someone else when Nate faded from our lives after Alex's death. The whole tragedy had shaken up the football party scene, and all Alex's buddies seemed to drift away. Sasha figured Nate had just disappeared back to his own school again.

I never thought about him or saw him again until I was an art student in Toronto. We met in a perfect way. The way you see in movies and Hollywood musicals. It was on a Friday night get-together with my two college friends, Grace and Mimi. We'd stocked up on munchies: tacos and guacamole, lime and black pepper chips, buffalo chicken pieces, hot pickled eggplant, olives and a selection of sinful cheeses. On top of that, we'd each brought a bottle of wine. We sat back, sipping wine, nibbling on our favorite snacks, and watching old movies. Mimi chose *All About Eve*, while Grace had raided her DVD cupboard and come back with the original *Superman* movie.

After a couple of hours of Bette Davis and her rosebud lips, we were ready for some escapism, so we plugged in *Superman* and drooled over Christopher Reeves's tight pecs and sky-blue eyes. We were almost bawling when we got to the part where Superman lands on Lois's balcony then whisks her into the air in a cosmic piggyback for an intimate flight above the towers of Metropolis.

"I swear I could claw Margot Kidder's eyes out," said Mimi, mopping at her eyes. "I mean, why doesn't anything like that ever happen to me?"

"You're afraid of heights for one thing," said Grace.

"Maybe you could do a helicopter ride," I suggested.

"Hey, I'd take a frigging elevator ride to the stars if Superman was pushing the right buttons," said Grace, finishing off the guacamole.

After Superman had flown off into the sunset and all the salsa was gone, we drained our glasses and decided it was a good time to head to an art exhibition our professor had recommended.

The exhibit was at a dingy downtown gallery – a warehouse-type place with a real urban-industrial vibe. Stained brick walls, concrete floors and wide metal pipes spanning the ceiling. The whole thing consisted of grotesque twisted metal sculptures that looked like tortured lizard bodies.

The after-party was set up in an adjoining room, where an eighties-style disco had been set up. It was magic. A spinning disco ball scattered white flakes of light across the floor, dappling the walls with stars; lovers snuggled together in plush blue velvet booths, and I floated into the room feeling like a fairy-tale princess, flying high on almost an entire bottle of cheap Pinot Grigio.

Mimi grabbed us a booth right near the dance floor and we ordered more drinks. Together we raised our glasses to toast the approaching summer holidays. At that moment, I almost chewed off the end of my cocktail stick when I glanced across the dance floor and saw a man gazing right at me.

"I'm hallucinating," I said, rubbing my eyes before fixing them yet again on the six-foot-plus vision with black-brown hair, chiseled face and ultra-white smile, who was not only staring but walking towards me with purpose.

"What the hell?" said Grace. "It's… it's Superman."

"No… it's… it's Nate Barnett. From my high school days."

"My God… I think he's coming this way," said Mimi, nudging me. "He's actually looking at you, Liv."

"It's your lucky night," said Grace's voice from somewhere far above the stratosphere. And before I could blink, those blue-violet eyes were looking down at me, melting my insides with their cool intensity.

"Would you like to dance, Liv?" said the vision and the next minute I was walking on air towards the dance floor holding Nate's hand. We were Maria and Tony in *West Side Story*, our eyes locked in an electric gaze. All the other dancers faded into a blur when I heard him say, "I knew it was you as soon as I walked in."

That night he took me for coffee at a chic French pastry café. We shared so many memories about home and mutual friends, it almost seemed as if we were two old friends reminiscing about our school days. At first, I was so flattered he remembered me, but he seemed like a changed person – humbler and more accessible than he had ever been at high school.

At the time I thought it a little strange, considering we'd barely said two words to each other during those years, and now he was acting like we'd been best buddies. But I put his easy, intimate manner down to the idea that maybe he was just relieved to see a familiar face in a big, anonymous city.

After that night, whenever he was in Toronto, he'd call me up and take me out to the ritziest restaurants, buy the best wine and shower me with small but expensive gifts: a sleek Scandinavian watch, a pricy watercolor set, a leather portfolio and many other trinkets.

He was so attractive and so persuasive; I couldn't help myself from drifting into a physical relationship with him. He was a gentle lover and our sex life was incredible, but before long, I discovered I was pregnant. I got the news just around the time my father passed away.

Nate proved to be a lifesaver. So understanding and supportive. And with all the inevitable emotional turmoil, it seemed like a natural transition to get married and return to Winnipeg with him. We became Mr. and Mrs. Barnett at a small but intimate civil ceremony in Toronto, attended only by a few of my art school friends and one or two of his work colleagues.

As soon as the plane landed on the tarmac, I knew I'd made a mistake coming back home. The familiar pall of gloom descended on me when I scanned the vast, flat expanse of the prairies, and I had the strongest feeling that

I'd be sucked back into the dark spiral of memories I'd escaped when I left for art school.

Nate had already told me he had no family – that his parents died a couple of years previously in a car accident while holidaying in Greece. I totally empathised because I was in the same situation. Mom had totally withdrawn into herself after Dad's death and barely knew me anymore, so I was more or less an orphan too. We decided that all we needed was each other, and then Jack came along, bringing a level of joy and contentment I hadn't felt since before Alex died.

We bought a house across from the lake – the lake I'd always lived nearby. Nate wasn't keen at first, saying it might remind me too much of Alex, but I wouldn't take no for an answer.

Too bad he'd given in to me.

I never forgave myself for that. We might still have had Jack if we'd bought the townhouse on the south side of town near the perimeter highway.

But something always drew me back to the houses near the lake. Some unfinished business related to Alex.

Maybe a mystery still waiting to be solved.

And now Nate was my new mystery. The perfect man I thought I knew.

14

NOW

I sat in my car under the shadow of the looming office tower where Nate used to work, his neatly taped box of belongings on the passenger seat next to me. I hesitated before opening it, wondering if I should wait until I got home, but my curiosity overcame me, and I ran my car key across the tape, wondering if anything in the box might throw some light on the big opportunity that caused Nate to leave his job. But I doubted I'd find any clues, considering how secretive Nate had been lately. He'd probably made sure to clean up any incriminating evidence when he left.

Folding back the flaps, I peered inside. The box was only half full. On top was a framed picture of me and Nate, taken a few weeks after our marriage. He looked so handsome in his black tux and bow tie. My eyes shone as we smiled and held our glasses towards some unknown waiter. I clutched my virgin Caesar, while Nate nursed a dry martini, his other arm wrapped around my shoulders.

I remembered I was at that irritable stage of pregnancy, when I could barely stomach my bowl of asparagus soup, while Nate chomped down on a rare steak with all the trimmings. I'd glanced briefly at the blood pooling at the side of his plate, staining his garlic-mashed potato a dull crimson. My stomach turned and I grabbed my glass of sparkling water, gulping it down until the nausea passed.

He'd started talking about baby names. We agreed that if it was a girl, we'd name her Robin – such a cheery, pretty name. When it came to boy's names Nate cleared his throat and said, "How about naming him Alex?"

I felt like my head was on fire. I almost choked on my drink. "How can you even suggest that? Why would we saddle our child with bad luck before he even starts out in life?"

Nate's face flushed. He swallowed loudly. "I... I just thought it would be a way to commemorate your brother. A mark of respect."

The burning in my head subsided, but I could still feel my scalp prickling, as if the anger was trying to force itself out through my skull. "You don't know what it was like to live with tragedy hanging over my family day in and day out. I just want our baby to mark a fresh start for us. I don't want any bad memories associated with his birth."

Nate clammed up after that and for the rest of the meal we ate in silence. I relented afterwards, apologized for being so snappy and persuaded him to come up with another boy's name, since I'd picked the girl's name. He came up with plain, simple Jack. The quaint, old-fashioned name surprised me, but I smiled and said it sounded perfect. A happy, unaffected name that couldn't be shortened to a silly nickname. I never asked the significance of it. Never understood until much later.

I pushed the photo aside to find a small paperweight from Niagara Falls. I turned the smooth glass cube around in my palm, studying the white lines of the falls burnished inside.

We'd gone there two years after Jack's disappearance.

Nate had thought a change of scenery might help lift my spirits – get me away from the family room couch that I curled up on every day, sleeping on and off for hours.

I'd read somewhere that over 600,000 gallons of water falls every second over The Horseshoe Falls on the Canadian side. Close to 85,000 per second over the Bridal Veils Falls on the American side. Those dizzying facts and all the crazy stories about daredevils tumbling over the falls in barrels, were bizarre enough to distract me from my depression.

But the actual trip turned out to be a disaster.

The Falls were dazzling. All that foaming, greenish water blasting down the steep gorge and below, the sight-seeing boats bobbed like tiny toys. At first, I just stood by the railings, marveling at the crashing torrent of water and the mist of fine spray that cloaked the surrounding area.

Nate stood dutifully watching for a while, then became restless, wanting to drag me up into the main tourist area. To Clifton Hill with its wax museums and haunted houses, its tacky chain restaurants and sports bars. Over foot-long margaritas he persuaded me to go with him to the nearby Fallsview Casino. When we pulled up to the brightly lit hotel with its cascading fountains at the entrance, Nate acted like a kid about to enter a video arcade. He strode off ahead of me at a brisk pace, barely looking back to see if I was keeping up with him.

Inside the glitzy casino, the noise was deafening: ringing bells, wild electronic music, spinning wheels and crazy sound effects provided background noise for the chatter and laughter of row upon row of gamblers hunched over slot machines. He handed me a wad of twenties, told me to have fun and then disappeared. At first it was a blast, all the mechanical button pressing and flashing lights and the occasional win. But soon the machines swallowed up every penny I had, so I set off to find Nate. When I caught up to him, he barely acknowledged me. Perched on the high stool, he appeared hypnotized by the slot machine. His blank, expressionless eyes reflected the bright electronic lights and whirring columns of shapes and symbols and pictures. His hand kept darting out towards the button, pressing it mindlessly as if he were a monkey in a lab experiment.

Distracted, he handed me another hundred and told me to keep playing. After an hour and a half nursing a couple of mojitos at the bar, I set off to look for him again. I felt a chill inside when I found him at the cash machine withdrawing more money from our checking account. Five hundred dollars to be exact.

"I lost everything," he said, a wild look of panic in his eyes.

I took his arm. "Let's just walk away. Cut our losses. Go get something to eat."

His eyes blazed and he shook my hand away, then clutched at my arm so hard his fingers dug into my flesh. "You don't understand. I have to win it back."

I couldn't say anything to convince him otherwise. Three hours later, after I'd sipped the dregs of my fourth cocktail, he appeared with a huge grin on his face, and waved a bunch of money at me. "I'm up four hundred. Had a lucky break."

I spent the rest of the weekend trying to persuade him not to go back to the casino. Instead, he grudgingly went on a visit to a winery. But on our final night, I woke to find his side of the bed empty. He came back at four in the morning, his face pale and drawn. Turned out he'd lost everything he'd won the previous day, and another six hundred he'd withdrawn in the hopes of chasing a win.

We never spoke about that night again. Ever. Though it showed a side of Nate I hadn't seen before. An uncharacteristic loss of control. For a long time afterwards, I thought he'd learned a valuable lesson that night, and he never went back. But as I rustled through his belongings, under the small stack of papers at the bottom of the box, I pulled out a club card from a local casino. One of those plastic cards you insert into the slot machines to accumulate reward points. I tried to reason that maybe he'd gone once or twice with some guys from work. But there was always the chance he'd started going regularly, and allowed it to become part of a bigger problem. One he'd kept secret.

A crazy thought flashed through my mind. Was the large sum of money somehow tied up with his gambling? Surely, he couldn't have won such a staggering amount at a casino? A further search revealed some business cards and more bank slips, all showing different six-figure amounts of money.

Outside, the snow was falling more steadily. It was time to head home before the roads got too bad. I thought maybe I could take another look through the box back at my place, but the corner of a bright photograph caught my eye. I pulled it out and my heart sank.

It was a photo of Jack.

He stood in the middle of our back lawn. It must have been summertime because the trees were in full leaf. He held both arms up in the air, and his face was a picture of pure joy, frozen in a precious moment of time. His blue eyes gleamed at the cloud of bubbles floating above his head.

The pain of seeing him was like a knife stabbing into my gut. I doubled forward. Rested my forehead on the steering wheel and howled. Great, body-wracking sobs that shook the car. I cried until there were no tears left.

Nate must have kept a picture at work because I had banned all pictures of our son at home. I'd packed up all of Jack's clothes, furniture, and toys into boxes that Nate took to the Goodwill Store. I couldn't bear to see his things. Unlike those people in the true crime shows that keep their missing kids' rooms all intact and untouched like shrines to their grief, I wanted no reminder of my terrible loss. I couldn't bear it.

Except I remembered that in the top shelf of Jack's old bedroom closet, I'd kept two things that he'd loved.

I started the car up and raced out of the parking lot. I couldn't wait to get straight home and find them.

15

On the drive home, I remembered how, when Alex died, I'd secretly kept a few of his treasures. I was kind of a magpie like that.

My mother did the same. When we moved out of the burned house, Mom stuffed tablecloths and teapots on top of some of Alex's football sweaters and water bottles. She couldn't bear to let go of objects he'd touched. But after Jack disappeared, I didn't want to be reminded of him. The grief was too much to bear. Too visceral.

I always had this feeling that certain objects, especially treasured ones, capture the essence of that person, far more than photographs. They have substance that you can hold onto, feel their weight in your hand and sense the energy from the person who loved them. Maybe they retain miniscule particles of that person's skin. Their life force. Their soul.

That's why I couldn't bear to let go of absolutely everything that belonged to Jack, and also why I stashed a whole box of Alex's treasures under my bed all those years ago. Sometimes I'd take them out and look at them so I could remember what he'd treasured in life, and how he acted when he used them.

In the box was Alex's Sam Roberts T-shirt, his under-15 soccer trophy and a framed picture of him and me taken outside the monkey house at the zoo. I'd given it to him on his sixteenth birthday. He loved those monkeys. Said they were smarter than some people he knew. But of all the people in his life, he always said I was the smartest. That's a pretty crazy thing for a sixteen-year-old to hear from her brother. And it was that kind of respect that drew us closer – made us seek out each other's company.

Back home, I carried Nate's box into the house and set it down in the back coat closet. I wanted nothing to do with the old memories those objects had stirred up. Even the photo of Jack would set me back four years. I'd be incapable of going on with my everyday life if I took another look at it. So, slamming the door shut, I took a deep breath and headed upstairs to the second bedroom. Jack's old room.

I'd convinced Nate to hire someone to repaint the walls. Neutral cream replaced mint green. We'd donated Jack's bed to the Goodwill Store. In its place a queen-sized guest bed with a gray-striped cover stood, dominating the room. Pictures of anonymous wooded landscapes replaced the hand-drawn pastels I'd created during my pregnancy, and the alphabet curtains had been stripped off, leaving plain white blinds in their place.

My heart slowed as I opened the closet, empty except for one white box on the upper shelf. Inside were two of his favorite toys. I hadn't been able to bring myself to part with them. I remembered one was a red and yellow Hatchimal. I pictured its furry body, blue beak and green glass eyes. Jack thought it was a penguin. He'd laughed and said *no feet, no feet*. Nate and I had both cracked up over the weird little footless creature with its tiny flippers, and to Jack's delight, we'd christened him Nofi. The other was a brown, furry puppy with a pink tongue and big lolling head. Jack had wanted to call him Rory and we'd written that on the star medallion that hung around his neck.

I pulled the box down, thinking how light it felt. How little was left of my only son. Placing it on the bed, I pulled off the lid, moved the tissue paper aside and took a deep breath. Tiny pinpricks of light sparked in front of my eyes. Only the red and yellow penguin toy was there.

The puppy was gone.

I looked back into the empty closet, my head reeling with uncertainty. I hadn't taken the box down since I'd put it there four years ago. Had I sleepwalked and taken it out without knowing? I stood there for a moment trying to search for some memory of taking the box down and removing the puppy.

Nothing.

I raced back into our bedroom and searched my closet, pulling down boxes and rooting through them. I reached into the far back corner to see if I'd stuffed it away somewhere, but came up empty-handed. Nate's closet was on the other side of the floor-length mirror. I pulled open the door to reveal a neat row of suits and shirts in dry-cleaning bags on one side and shelving that contained perfectly folded sweaters and T-shirts on the other. His closet was spartan compared to mine. While the floor of my closet was cluttered with boxes that overflowed with scarves, purses and shoes, Nate's closet floor was clear, with only a long shoe rack holding a selection of well-polished shoes. But the number of empty hangers and spaces on the shoe rack took me aback. It was as if he'd known he wasn't coming back and had actually planned to disappear for a good, long time.

The closet was a perfect reflection of Nate – ordered, anonymous and impersonal.

In the last few years since Jack had gone, I'd searched my mind wondering where the charming, empathetic man I'd married had disappeared to. The romantic who'd won me over in Toronto with all the dinners and excursions and declarations of love. But the more I remembered it all, the more I began to see everything in a different light. As if our relationship had been a carefully rehearsed string of scenes performed by a man who was a polished, professional actor, changing his approach to suit his purposes.

The more I tried to conjure up my husband, the less I discovered I really knew about him. Standing in that dark closet I felt my reality shift with the realization that I'd existed in such a stupor these last few years, I hadn't recognized the emptiness of my marriage.

As my eyes adjusted to the dark, my gaze fixed on a small box at the back of Nate's closet, hidden behind a pair of brown ankle boots. For some strange reason, I looked behind me before reaching down for it. Maybe it was the cold, prickly sense of being watched, or the idea that Nate could just walk in on me and catch me prying into his private stuff, but the house was empty and quiet. Only the low whirr of the furnace fan echoed in the vents.

I held the dented old cardboard box, its lid decorated with stickers of NFL teams. The most authentic and genuine thing I'd known about Nate was that he'd been a football player, though nowadays he never watched football. I wondered what had turned him off the game.

I placed the box on the bed. It was the kind of object that didn't seem to belong to Nate and all he represented. Dog-eared, messy and old – a relic of the boy he used to be. Inside were a couple of yearbooks from his old school, some ribbons from a cross-country meet, a couple of banners from his high-school football team, a grimy pair of football gloves and a small box holding a gold and onyx team ring. The box was lined with a sheaf of photos: His team picture in which a seventeen-year-old Nate knelt in the front row grinning, eyes sparkling, expression animated. I felt a certain sadness. I'd never really known that guy.

Another portrait showed him in action, jumping for a catch, his body taut. The next picture was at a beer party around a campfire in a forest near the high school. I recognized Alex's buddies from his team, arms linked, all holding open beer bottles. Alex was at the far end of the row, his broad grin and open face beaming in the light of someone's phone flash. Nate stood behind his shoulder. But something jarred me about the way he was positioned. Maybe it was his proximity to Alex. The intimacy of the gesture as Nate clinked his beer bottle against Alex's. I'd never regarded the two of them as close buddies. Only football acquaintances.

Maybe it was the glare of the camera flash in Nate's face, but for a split second I imagined his eyes weren't focused on the photographer, but onto Alex. I blinked again and saw it was just a trick of the light. My over-active imagination at work again. I shivered and placed the picture back into the box.

Too many strange things happening in succession always made my imagination run wild and that's when it went to bad, scary places. At times like those, I wondered how I ever represented myself as a children's book illustrator, considering the dark thoughts that dominated my mind.

Drained emotionally and physically, I trudged downstairs picturing the sweating bottle of Pinot Grigio chilling in the fridge. My right hand trembled so much as I poured a generous glass, I had to steady the bottle with my left, and it still sloshed onto the counter. I sipped until I felt the slow buzz of the alcohol warm my body, then wandered into the living room hoping to distract myself with my work. But I took one look at the easel and the unfinished drawing and plunked myself down in the chair by the bay window. After another large gulp of wine, I closed my eyes and tried to steady my nerves. A few deep breaths and I could face the world again.

Outside, the evening was drawing in. It had been a damp day, snow turning to slush and frost coating the trees. Now ice fog hung in the air, blurring the edges of the houses and smudging the streetlight's glare into a yellow cloud.

The more I drank, the more I obsessed about the missing toy. I clearly remembered wrapping it with careful, loving tenderness, as if I was handling my own child. I remembered whispering goodbye before I placed the lid on the box, my tears blotting the tissue paper.

I never opened it again. Why would I?

The most logical explanation was that Nate had taken it. He'd kept a photo of Jack, so maybe he wanted his own memento. Maybe I'd been so immersed in my own pain, I hadn't considered his feelings. Maybe I'd acted like a selfish, cold-hearted bitch. But Nate and I didn't talk about difficult subjects like emotions. Hadn't since we married. Had I driven him away with all my misery? Should we have found comfort in each other's company instead of pulling away from each other to live our own separate lives?

And now I couldn't even ask Nate about the toy. I hadn't heard from him in over a week. Nine days to be exact. Perhaps it was time to report his disappearance and yet – I wasn't missing him. I was actually enjoying the experience of being here alone, living my life without him. Could I simply carry on as if nothing was wrong? He'd go his way with his secret stash of money and I'd go mine – with what? I had no idea if he was being paid. I didn't even know where the money we'd been living on for the past year had come from, and now he'd disappeared, I wondered if it would keep on coming in.

I realized right then and there how little I knew about the man I'd been married to for eight years. It had been at least thirteen years since I'd seen Stefan, and yet I'd felt more comfortable in his company than I ever had with Nate.

Resting my head against the back of the chair, I stared into the starry sky and wondered what would have happened if Stefan had stayed instead of going back to Hong Kong to see his father. Had he tried to get in touch with me when he dropped out of Carleton? Or simply given up on me when he found out I'd left the city and gone off to art school? Now it seemed really odd that he'd shown up again in my life, just when Nate disappeared.

Was it all just a weird coincidence?

He'd showed up at a time I needed help. Advice. And it wouldn't be the first time. He'd helped me once before when I was in need. Now he lived just around the corner.

Why had I been surprised that he'd become a cop? When I'd first got to know him, he'd vowed to do his own secret investigation of my brother Alex's death. I never got to ask him what he'd found out.

Well, now Nate was my new mystery. The perfect man I thought I knew.

I had a new mystery for Stefan to solve.

16

BEFORE

The first day Stefan came to our class, I stopped by our old house on the way home. The stucco was still singed black from the tongues of flame that had rocketed up the basement stairs. Alex's only escape route. His friends said something about a candle falling over while Alex was experimenting with meth – trying to smoke it in some kind of glass pipe that cracked and burned his hand. They said he panicked and threw it away. It knocked over a candle that sent sparks over to Mom's Christmas craft supplies. All the glue and flammable materials flared up in a second.

But I knew it was a lie. He was no druggie. He was an amazing, honest guy. The best brother a girl could ever have.

I'd walked on towards the forest trail, dragging my feet through the mushy leaves left from the previous fall, then suddenly I couldn't hold myself together. I flopped down onto the metal bench and let all my sorrow out in big howling gulps.

"You okay?" someone asked.

I looked up and Stefan hovered over me, hands stuffed into his pockets, shuffling from one foot to another.

"Oh… yeah. It's nothing." I wiped my sleeve across my face.

"Looked like you were crying."

"Must be getting a cold."

"Whatever," he said, pulling his backpack up onto his shoulder and adjusting the strap. He kept clearing his throat and glancing down at me then away, like he was afraid to rest his eyes on my face.

"What's up?"

He bit his lip as if he was trying not to say something stupid, then reached into his backpack and pulled out a book. "I'm not a weirdo or anything, but you look just like Brigid."

"Who the hell is Brigid?"

"I'll show you," he said, opening a brightly colored book with a glowing sun on its cover. "Check out this picture of Brigid, Celtic goddess of poetry, art and fire."

My stomach lurched when I heard the *f* word but I was intrigued. I leaned forward to see a beautiful red-haired woman with pale skin and green eyes like mine. She was holding a harp with a cluster of pale roses at its tip.

"She's gorgeous."

"*Yeah*," he said. "Why are you so shocked?"

"Most people think red-haired people are ugly. Or at least weird looking."

"That's because they're jealous."

"Tell me about her."

He took a deep breath and started to talk fast, his words tumbling over each other. "Well, first important thing – she was born with flames shooting out of her head and that united her with the cosmos. Her original ancient Gaelic name means 'fiery power' or 'fiery arrow' and her parents were…"

He was just about to tell me more when I heard someone calling my name. I looked behind at Sasha, my best friend, heading towards us on her bicycle. Stefan slammed the book shut.

"Guess I'd better go then."

"No, stay. Hang out with us," I said, wanting to hear more about the fire goddess.

"Maybe tomorrow." He slung the book into his backpack and hunched his shoulders again as he stomped off down the path.

Before I could stop him, he was halfway towards the bridge, his burgundy hair like a patch of autumn smoke.

Not long after that, we were inseparable. Feeding off each other's creativity and love of strange, quirky stories, we created a comic book strip inspired by my late brother, about a guy named Alex Apollo; a shy, straight-ahead guy by day, and a blazing, fiery superhero by night. Alex Apollo possessed the power to use fire to fight the forces of evil.

Those comic strips made me think a lot about my brother, but in a good and positive way. Like he was a giant firebird somewhere up in the cosmos. I'd always loved the idea of the vast expanses of space. Even as a little kid, I'd imagine infinite universes, collapsing stars, swirling galaxies, black holes, cloudy nebulas. The comic strip made me wonder if Alex had found a place in those great sweeping heavens. Maybe he was out there swooping around the endless universe, lighting it up with all his beauty.

I still remember those little comics, at first produced on the library copy machine, then distributed in the student cafeteria, lounge and gym. We gained quite a following until the librarian complained about the amount of paper we were using and we had to go online.

Then, towards the end of the year Stefan got bad news. His dad, a successful businessman in Hong Kong, had fallen seriously ill with cancer and wanted to spend his last days with the son he'd neglected for so long. When the airline ticket arrived, Stefan had to leave with only a day's notice.

I remember the night before he left, we were both so stunned we could barely speak to each other. For ten months we'd spent the better part of every day in each other's company. He was ingrained in my daily routine – we'd walk to school together, take English together, eat lunch at the same table, walk home side by side, hang out at each other's home, message and Skype when we were apart. I'd often fall asleep talking to him at one or two in the morning. I didn't need any sleeping pills.

That final night we stood on the front veranda of my house. It was a warm summer evening. Moist air, rich with the scent of leaves and flowers, a chorus of chirping crickets in the background and the occasional mournful cry of a loon on the lake.

"I guess that's it for the comic strip," I said, feeling a cold fist pressing at my heart.

"We can still keep it up even if I'm in Hong Kong," he said, placing his hands on my shoulders. I remember marveling at the shadow of his thick eyelashes on his cheek. The bluish shadow of stubble above his upper lip that I hadn't noticed before. The aching realization that we were both growing up and moving on.

"Not the same," I said, my lower lip trembling.

"Why not?" he said, dipping his face close to mine. So close I felt the prickle of static electricity.

"If we're apart we can't shoot the shit – you know, confer on ideas."

"We can if we make the effort," he said, holding my chin with a steady hand.

But I was so pissed at him. So stubborn I could barely form a word. Couldn't offer a glimmer of hope for us. How I cursed myself afterwards.

He twisted one of my curls on his finger. "I'll send you new stories for the comic strip. I promise, Livvy."

I shook my head. "Once you get there, you'll forget about me."

"Never," he said, his expression so earnest it shook me to the core.

And now he was back. As if he'd sensed I needed him.

Coincidence or fate?

I didn't care.

17

NOW

After finishing half the bottle of wine, I was so restless I couldn't sit still. I had to go and see Stefan – take a chance that he'd be in. Too many unanswered questions had rendered me totally unable to work and I was damned if I'd sit there and just wait for something to happen.

Outside, the fog was thick, the air damp and dewy. I pulled my collar up and jammed my hat over my ears. After closing the garage door, I glanced across at the lake house. Workers had been buzzing around the back and front of the house all week, trimming the trees, pruning the bushes and clearing snow-covered piles of leaves away from the lawns. The tangle of dead summer flowers had been ripped out of the flower beds and Christmas lawn decorations had been put in their place.

I was about to set off down the street when in an instant, the blurred outline of the house was transformed by a massive array of white lights that outlined the walls and gables and doorways. Glowing blue lights illuminated the trees and a row of red and white candy canes lined the driveway. Sparkling deer grazed on the snow, and potted cedars loaded with white lights stood either side of the front door. The garish colors seemed out of place in the misty air, but I hoped the light display would give little Toby some much-needed pleasure.

Higher temperatures had turned the snow into slushy ice, so I picked my way slowly down the driveway, not wanting to slip and land hard on my ass. Once I made it safely to the road, I thought again how weird it was that Stefan and I had run into each other again after all this time.

I was so immersed in thinking about him, I momentarily lost all sense of my surroundings, but I became gradually aware of the low purr of a car engine. Turning my head, I made out the headlights of a car crawling behind me. I moved onto the side of the road thinking it would pass by, but it just kept edging along, its yellow headlights fuzzy in the fog. I walked faster, glancing behind me every now and again. Stefan's house was just at the end of the block. But the car accelerated, nosing ever closer.

Someone was toying with me.

I immediately sidestepped onto the nearest lawn and stood waiting, daring the car to pass. To go on its way. I even considered giving the driver the finger, but remembered Rick Dubeau's words of warning about the sketchy people visiting my neighbor and clenched my hand into a fist. The car slowed momentarily, then with a sudden roar of the engine, sped off, its exhaust trail blooming into the fog, blurring the unmistakable outline of the black Dodge Viper. The same car that had idled at the foot of my driveway a couple of days ago.

Breathless, I hurried on to Stefan's house before the car had a chance to round the crescent and come back again.

Though the front windows of his house were dark, I prayed he was in the back somewhere. I rang the doorbell – once, twice, three times – checking behind me now and again to see that the car hadn't returned. Finally, a light went on in the hallway and the front door opened a crack to reveal a sleepy looking Stefan wearing gray sweats and a baggy, black T-shirt.

"Sorry, were you sleeping?" I said, noticing his startled expression.

He shook his head and beckoned me inside, ruffling his hair so it stood up in little spikes along his forehead. "I probably look like shit. Passed out watching the hockey game. I thought I was dreaming about the doorbell ringing."

He helped me off with my coat and hung it on the bannister, then I followed him through into a large family room decorated with spartan furnishings – black leather couch and chair, glass dining table, massive TV, bare walls. It had the feel of a temporary resting place with no pillows, ornaments, photos or knick-knacks to personalize the place.

Scanning the room, he shrugged. "Sorry, it's a bit of a blank canvas. I just never have the time to do anything with it. In fact, you're lucky to find me here. I just got off a string of fourteen-hour days."

"Don't worry about it. It's clean, which is more than you can usually say about most bachelor pads."

He stood by the fridge. "Want coffee – or maybe a glass of wine?"

I couldn't stop smiling at him. "Wine sounds great. Whatever you have open. We have to celebrate our meeting up again."

He took a half bottle of white wine from the fridge. "I've been thinking about you a lot since we met the other day," he said, opening the cupboard to find a glass.

I noticed only one shelf was full. The others were bare. This guy was traveling light.

I leaned against the counter, scanning the bare necessities of a coffeemaker, a stainless-steel toaster and an open bag of bread scattered across it. "Me too. I was thinking about our little comic strip."

He laughed and handed me a glass. "You know, I kept some of the originals, if you ever want to take a look at them. I still think they're pretty good. Probably good enough to adapt into a graphic novel if you ever feel the urge to strike out on your own."

"Maybe. You never know when I might get inspired." I sipped at the wine, relaxing as it burned its way down my throat. "Don't think I'm paranoid, but I believe some asshole tailed me all the way here in his fancy car."

His face clouded over. "You okay, Liv? Is he still out there?"

I shook my head and tried to smile. "You know me. It might be just my crazy imagination. But I could swear I saw the same car idling at the bottom of my driveway the other day."

"Maybe he was looking for a particular address."

"You're probably right," I said, gulping the wine down.

"Is something wrong, Liv? Is that why you're here?"

"Guess I'm that transparent," I said, settling down onto the sofa and placing the empty glass on the coffee table. He refilled it.

"You were always pretty easy to read. Didn't hide your feelings."

"I've changed since then, Stefan," I said, hanging my head.

He sat next to me and touched my arm, pausing for a moment before he spoke. "Look, Liv, I know about your son."

The stinging at the back of my eyes started up again. "How did you find out?"

"I saw a note about it back at the office. A buddy of mine was reassigned to keep the case open."

"I don't think they're doing anything, Stefan. They've given up."

"I gotta be honest with you, Liv, it gets tougher after five years, but we do still follow up on leads, and I've seen cases where new information comes up even years after the disappearance."

"I've learned to live with it, Stefan. After a whole lot of stupidly expensive therapy, I've managed to make some kind of life for myself."

"You're a strong woman, Liv. With all the grief you've gone through in your life you still manage to hold things together. I'm in awe of you. Always have been. Remember I was your greatest fan fourteen years ago."

I play-punched his shoulder. "You always knew how to boost me up."

"I'm just an all-round nice guy," he said, clinking his glass against mine. "So, tell me how I can help you, Liv?"

I settled back onto the sofa. "This may sound crazy, but I think my husband has gone missing."

His brows knit. "What exactly do you mean – missing? I thought you said he goes off on regular business trips."

"He does, but… well… we haven't been getting along for a few years now… not since…"

"It's only natural, Liv. Many marriages can't survive a tragedy like you went through."

"But this time I haven't heard from him in well over a week. No texts, no calls, no emails. And I don't know where he's staying. He's usually religious about keeping in contact when he's away."

"Have you called his boss?"

I nodded. "I'm embarrassed to admit it, but he's been lying to me. He left his job last year. Didn't even think to tell me about it."

"Weird. Maybe he was afraid to tell you. Maybe he didn't want to get you stressed out and worried again."

"He wasn't fired. He left voluntarily. To pursue a *big new opportunity* according to his boss."

He reached for a small green notebook on the side table. "Sounds odd. I could do a little digging around if you know what city he was going to. Maybe check with some hotels."

"That'd be great. He said he was going to Toronto, but I was so distracted by the new neighbors moving in across the street, I forgot to ask him the name of the hotel. Guess I thought he'd text the details to me, but he never did."

"That doesn't narrow things down a whole lot."

"Sorry. It's all I can give you."

"What's his name?" he said, his hand hovering above the page.

"Nate – Nate Barnett."

The moment his hand froze, I knew something was up. But then he suddenly snapped into gear and wrote down the name.

"What's wrong, Stefan?"

He sighed and looked straight at me. "The name just took me by surprise."

"You knew him?"

"I knew *of* him, Liv. Saw him around the school a few times. So did you."

"He knew Alex, too."

"He was on the rival football team, so of course they'd run into each other."

The image of that photograph I'd found in the closet flickered across my brain. "As far as I knew they weren't close. Do you know anything else about him?"

"I don't want to say too much, Liv. That was a long time ago."

"You know you can't hide anything from me."

He pursed his lips together and sighed, his expression intense, almost worried. "Remember fourteen years ago I did a little detective work around your brother's friends?"

"And what did you find out?"

"Sorry, but not too much. You probably also remember how I had to leave on a day's notice to go back to Hong Kong."

"I was just thinking about that before I came here. But you have to be honest with me, Stefan. If you know something, tell me."

"I had a tough time finding out anything about Nate. His friends were tight. The moment drugs were mentioned they all clammed up. But there were a few rumors."

"Like what?"

"He was into gambling. Basement poker tournaments and all that. He was friends with Renny and Chad. Word was, he blew through a whole lot of money. Won a lot but spent it just as quickly."

"Lots of guys were doing that, Stefan. You'd see them playing poker in the stairwells as well as in everyone's basements."

"I also heard a rumor that his parents were deadbeats. That he didn't want anything to do with them."

I sensed that prickly, cold feeling across my skin. "Parents? When we married, he told me they were dead."

"Remember, that was a long time ago. A lot could've happened in that time. And if he was estranged from them then, it's unlikely he'd have wanted them as wedding guests, even if they were alive."

I took a deep breath. Steadied my heartbeat. "Could you do me a favor, Stefan? Look them up? See if they're dead or alive. I don't care who they are. I want to know all Nate's secrets."

"Sure. I'll check it out for you."

I closed my eyes and pressed my hand against my forehead. "Sometimes I curse the day I ever ran into that guy. My life could've been a whole lot different if I'd stayed here."

Stefan's eyes softened. "But you wouldn't have had your son."

"Yeah, and I wouldn't have lost him," I said, covering my face with my hands and trying to hold back the tears. I stood up abruptly. "I have to go, Stefan. Before I say something I shouldn't."

Immediately he was up and following me as I stomped into the hallway and grabbed my coat. "I promise I'll do a search on Nate's parents, Liv. See what I can find out. I'll come by your place if anything turns up."

I nodded. I couldn't speak. If I'd opened my mouth, I would have broken down like a blubbering child. I held onto the front doorknob realizing that my life was a mess of my own making and there was nothing I could do about it.

He caught my shoulder. "Liv... I hate to let you go like this. At least let me walk you home."

I threw the door open. "The fresh air will be good for me. I'll be okay. Call me." I strode out into the night without a backward glance. I knew he was standing in the doorway watching because the door hadn't slammed. I walked away, cursing myself. Fate had delivered me some hefty blows, but then I'd made some stupid choices in my life. Now the thoughts ran over and over in my head. What if Stefan hadn't gone away? What if I'd waited for him to come back instead of running away to Toronto? What if I hadn't fallen for all Nate's sweet talk? Why had I been such a pushover? Falling for the first guy to shower me with gifts and attention and flattery, as if I couldn't believe that someone thought me worth all the effort.

I'd betrayed Stefan. Taken up with Nate and his polished act. Nate, the shadow with no substance. The chameleon who could be anyone you wanted him to be.

And now he'd been lying to me for so long, I didn't even know who he was.

18

I was glued to my phone the next day, waiting for a message from Stefan, sure it wouldn't take him long to find some information regarding Nate's whereabouts. In the meantime, I drank four cups of strong coffee and finished three more pictures for the book. I was on a roll, flying on blind energy. Driven by an urge to finish the damn project so I could concentrate on everything else that was going on in my life.

A few hours later, my work was looking great and I'd opened a bottle of Nate's best Pinot Noir. I was coasting on an alcohol-fueled high, and figured since my own husband didn't even give a damn about me now, why should I care?

At around four o'clock the action in the lake house began.

I hadn't seen Heidi for a few days, but I put down my wine glass when the front door swung wide open and she strode outside in a skimpy, hip-hugging black sheath dress. It was well below zero outside, so she must have been freezing.

Three black SUVs were parked in the driveway. A Lincoln, a Lexus and a Mercedes. By now I'd realized Heidi loved the big spenders. The guys with the luxury rides. The hotshots and high riders. It was too bad Nate was away. They'd probably have found a whole lot in common.

She sashayed down the driveway waving her arms in the air. Then some guy with a shaved head and a studded leather jacket came running out after her and grabbed her around the waist from behind. Swaying her hips against him, she pulled his head onto her shoulder, her eyes vacant, her mouth fixed in a slack grin. Either they were drunk or high because they didn't seem fazed by the cold. Then another long-haired guy in a Metallica T-shirt came jogging out of the house with Toby perched on his shoulders. The little boy was clinging to the man's shirt, wobbling precipitously as the guy loped around like a clown.

Leather jacket pulled himself away from Heidi and started grabbing handfuls of snow and flinging it at her. She quickly retaliated by scooping up even bigger armfuls and throwing it up in the air in a cascading shower. The long-haired guy caught a whole wack of it in his face and stopped dead, letting go of Toby's feet and allowing him to fall off his shoulders and tumble sideways into a big mound of snow. I stood up, almost knocking my easel down in my haste to see if the boy was hurt.

It took Heidi a few seconds to register what had happened, but then she raced over to the mound where Toby lay. I held my breath, but within seconds the welcome sound of a child's piercing wail burst out into the silence. Heidi scooped him up in one arm, shoved bald head and long hair away with the other and stalked off back into the house. Toby's little legs were scissor-kicking with fury.

I realized then I'd never seen that kid smiling or happy for longer than a few seconds.

I watched as the other two guys filed inside and shut the door, then sat back on my chair at the corner of the window. My heart was still racing, so I slugged back the rest of my wine to try and settle myself. Within seconds, as the night closed in and the streetlamps flicked on, the colored lights on the lake house flooded their brilliance into the darkness. I strained to see into the bay window opposite and hoped the ghostly shape was Heidi holding Toby up to see the display.

Instinctively I drew back into the shadows. I felt pathetic. The lonely, crazy woman at the window, living vicariously through the neighbors. But that poor kid over there was at the mercy of his party-animal mother and a whole string of dubious-looking guys who didn't really give a damn about him. Not to mention the alcohol and drugs that were probably lying around the place.

What would happen if they were all too drunk or high to hear him if he was in distress or something? What if he fell down the stairs or got into the cleaning cupboard or found laundry detergent pods and tried to eat them? My brain was alive with all the terrible possibilities.

It seemed clear then that I had only one option. I'd failed Jack, but I wouldn't fail this innocent kid. He wouldn't be a victim. *Not on my watch.*

I sprang up from my chair, almost knocking the wine bottle over. Strange that there wasn't much left in it. I could've sworn I'd only had one glass. I tottered to the kitchen feeling wobbly, and found Rick's card propped up against the coffee machine. Then it was only a matter of dialing and waiting to tell him exactly what I'd seen.

After I finished, there was a long silence on the other end. Someone else was there with him. I heard muffled whispering in the background, as if his hand was covering the phone. It was probably his ballerina girlfriend.

"Are those other cars still there, Olivia?" he asked.

I glanced outside. "I see at least three of them."

A pause. "Okay. Thanks for the tip off, Olivia. I really appreciate you looking out for Toby. You're his guardian angel."

"I don't want to be too nosey, but can you do anything about the situation?" I said, the wine emboldening me.

"I'm gonna come around tomorrow morning. I hope those guys will be gone."

"Can you tell me what's going on in that house, Rick? I mean it's right opposite me. Is there anything I need to be concerned about?"

Another pause. I heard his quick intake of breath. "I can't really say anything about that, Olivia. Just don't get friendly with Heidi. Like I said, it's probably best if you stay away from her."

I felt a sudden chill. Prickles over my skin. "Why Rick? What's going…?"

The phone went dead. He'd cut me off. When I tried to call back, his voicemail came on.

I looked over at the lake house again as the colored lights suddenly switched off and the whole place was plunged into darkness, except for a dim light that seeped from the basement windows.

What on earth were they up to? I felt a sudden, deep and primitive loathing for that house. Nothing good happened there, and how long could that innocent kid survive in such a place?

19

I'd just flipped over my breakfast omelet when the deafening roar of an engine shattered my quiet morning routine. The piercing screech of tires on slick snow was soon followed by the slam of a car door thrown shut.

I ran into the living room in time to witness Rick stomping up Heidi's driveway like a man on a combat mission. He pressed the doorbell once, twice, three times, and when no answer came, he pounded on the door with a closed fist. For a few milliseconds I felt panicked. Maybe it had been an overreaction to call him. After all, what did I really know about him as a man and a father? Maybe it had just been a harmless accident when Toby fell off the long-haired guy's shoulders. He'd fallen into a big snowdrift, so he probably wasn't hurt.

And what if Heidi found out it was me who called? Unless she suspected Vera next door, who was probably just the right candidate to be watching out for some scandal.

I chewed the inside of my lip. Convinced myself I'd done the right thing looking out for that innocent kid. If someone had found Jack and acted in the same way, maybe he would've still been here. Instead, the whole world had turned its head away. *I saw nothing. I'm not involved.* That was the safe way to act. Keep your nose clean and nobody will bother you. Well, I was damn well not going to do that anymore.

Rick had started thumping at the door again, only this time it swung open revealing the shaved-head guy, dressed in a black sweater and jeans. He was shorter than Rick, but solid, with the shoulders of a linebacker. They began talking at each other heatedly, but I couldn't hear anything through the window. Then, when Rick started swinging his arms, bald guy pulled both arms back and shoved him so hard in the chest, Rick went staggering backwards and landed on his ass in the snow. Bald guy cracked his knuckles, gave Rick the finger and slammed the door shut.

I backed away from the window as Rick stumbled to his feet, brushing the snow from his jeans. I wasn't in any mood to talk to him. He stood for a moment, shouting at Heidi's closed door, then turned and walked away, head bowed. He glanced over at my house before swinging himself up into his truck and gunning the engine so hard, the spinning tires sent a shower of snow into the air.

All that effort and nothing to show for it except for a snow-covered rear.

My omelet was tough as leather by the time I got back to it, so I tipped it into the garbage and toasted a bagel instead. So much for the high-protein breakfast.

I sat at my kitchen counter sipping coffee and gazing out at the trees that lined my backyard. The grinding in my stomach had subsided a bit after the Rick and Heidi incident, but I decided to keep a low profile today. Didn't want to run into Heidi and risk her grilling me about Rick. In his fit of anger, he may have let it out that someone called and snitched on her. Hopefully, he kept his mouth shut, since I was the person who had to live steps away from that house and all its crazy goings-on.

The dull ache began to spread across my forehead again. I didn't need all this new worry. I just wanted to live a quiet life with my drawing and my stories and my family. That's all I'd ever wanted. Now that seemed so far away. So out of reach.

A rustle in the trees out back distracted me. Those huge fifty-foot trees were havens for an army of squirrels, and I watched in awe as a cheeky red squirrel sat on a mid-level branch and shook a shower of snow onto an unsuspecting rabbit below. The rabbit's nose was twitching like crazy trying to figure out where that pesky snow was coming from. For once, I started to laugh. Surely, I could capture this perfect moment for the lunch box story? Suddenly the day seemed brighter. Strange that the dark cloud over my life had gradually been lifting since Nate was out of the picture and Stefan reappeared.

Did that make me a cold-hearted bitch? That I wasn't worried for his safety? Maybe he was ill or injured, lying on some remote country road? Hell, I hadn't even called around any hospitals. But I wouldn't have known where to start.

I was just considering the next layout for the lunch box project when the doorbell went, not once but several times as if someone was pressing it continuously. Surely, Stefan would have called first? Hurrying over to the front door, I made out a tall, willowy shape through the frosted glass. Blonde hair, one hand on her hip. Heidi.

I swung the door open just as she was about to pound on it with a clenched fist. Up close her face was flawless – ivory skin, full pouty lips and a slim, sculpted nose. Bold, well-groomed eyebrows knit into a twisted frown and ice-blue eyes blazed at me. She opened her mouth to speak, but I cut her off, reaching my hand out to her.

"Hi, I'm Olivia. Great to finally meet you."

Her lovely mouth drooped and the wide eyes narrowed as she seemed to calculate me carefully. She gave a slight laugh. "You can cut the girl-next-door happy neighbor act, and you can also keep your damned nose out of my business."

I glanced to my left, hearing Vera's garage door slide upwards. I looked back at Heidi. "I'm not sure what you're talking about. Maybe you'd care to explain."

"You're always watching me. Showing up everywhere. Smirking. Judging. Getting in my face. Nosing around. Don't you have a life of your own?" She glanced beyond me at the empty hallway. "Guess you don't have kids. That figures."

The sudden swell of anger was bitter in my throat. I stepped towards her, in an attempt to assert myself. "First of all, I'm an artist. My studio is in my living room. My easel is placed in the bay window to get the best light, so it might seem like I'm always watching but I'm really just working."

"Sure," she smirked. "You think I believe all that BS? You called my ex. Told him something happened to my kid."

I tried hard not to look away, a sure sign of a lie. "Who told you that?"

"Bullshit. I saw him talking to you the other day. He probably asked you to spy on me. He's always hounding me. Won't leave me alone. And you... you probably can't keep your eyes off other people's kids. Creep. You're pathetic."

I clenched my fists. Her comment was a sucker punch to my gut.

I was about to snap back at her when my neighbor, Vera, stepped out onto her driveway. She was snappily dressed in a black wool coat, fur hat and tan leather boots. She waved at me and walked towards us over the grass. Heidi took a few steps back.

"What's this? The neighborhood watch meeting? Everything okay here, girls?" she said, smoothing her gloves out.

I glared at Heidi. "It's okay, Vera. Just a misunderstanding. Our new neighbor was just about to leave."

But Vera persisted, standing at my side. "No, she can wait. I need to tell her something. It's shameful what that little boy of yours has to put up with. Whoever called your husband or boyfriend – or whoever the hell he is – was doing that innocent child a favor. I saw those hoodlums throwing him around yesterday. That's not a fit way to treat a child. And do you really think a house that hosts endless all-night parties is the best environment for a child? You're lucky I didn't call the police or the child protection services."

Heidi was looking from me to Vera, her mouth gaping open. "I'll get a restraining order on both of you if you ever think of interfering in my life again. I happen to know a lot of well-connected people, so I'd advise you to keep your fucking noses out of what I do and when I do it."

With that, she turned and stomped away, her long braid swinging from side to side like a heavy pendulum.

Vera made a *tutting* sound. "She's a real piece of work. Thinks she's a cut above the rest of us. I liked it better when the house was empty."

I sighed. It had been such a good start to the day and now the cloud of conflict was hovering, threatening to quash my new enthusiasm. "Me too. And she doesn't seem to give a damn about her little boy."

Vera touched my arm. She had a calm face etched with deep lines. The result, no doubt of a lifetime of stress. But her smile was warm and genuine. Silver curls peeped out from beneath the dark fur hat.

"If you called her husband, you did a good deed, Olivia. I know it must be hard for you to watch her take that precious child for granted. But those empty threats won't bother us any. We'll keep an eye out for the boy. Someone has to. Besides, I doubt she'll call the police."

"What makes you so certain?"

She laughed. "That woman wants to stay under the radar. Have you ever wondered what's going on over there in her fancy house?"

I nodded. "I've seen some pretty odd characters coming in and out of the place. And those big parties. At all hours of the night too."

"Exactly. It has to be something illegal or under-the-table. That's my hunch," she said, checking her watch.

"You going somewhere?" I said, just as a taxi rounded the corner.

"Meeting my friend at the airport. We're off to Niagara Falls. Staying at the Fallsview for a few days. Have a little fun – do some gambling, have a few drinks and probably a whole lot of laughs. I've always wanted to see the Falls in winter."

"Sounds chilly, but fun."

She shrugged. "Gotta enjoy my golden years somehow. Try to make up for lost time. You should get that husband of yours to take you. He seems like a fun-loving guy."

I felt my face flush and hoped she didn't notice. "He's away on business right now."

"Must be a guy who knows how to balance business with pleasure then."

"What do you mean?"

"I've seen him at the Fallsview Casino a few times over the last year. He probably popped over there from one of his business trips to Toronto. Hell, one night, maybe three or four months ago, I was there with Carol. We played the slots until almost midnight, then called it a night. I passed the poker tables and your husband was there on the high-stakes table."

I was starting to get that breathless feeling again. I swallowed and tried to look politely interested. "He does like to gamble. I know that."

She leaned in closer. "The thing is, when Carol and I got up next morning to go to the breakfast buffet, he was still there at the same table. Had a few stacks of chips in front of him. And he was still drinking. Didn't look in any shape to go to work."

And I'd been at home, imagining him sitting in board-rooms or conference rooms for tedious meetings, or traveling to meet clients. He'd been lying all the time. Playing games with me.

"Why didn't you tell me about this before, Vera?"

She backed away. "I thought about it, dear. I've been around the casinos enough to know that some people just can't control themselves when it comes to the slot machines or the roulette table. Maybe your husband has that problem, but I usually draw the line at getting involved in other people's marital troubles. I've had enough of my own. Your husband seems like a nice man. I'm sure you two can work things out. If I thought he was abusing you, it would be different. Don't forget. I know the signs." She glanced around at the taxi. "Well, I must dash. I have to get to the airport. I hope I haven't upset you, dear."

I shook my head. "We'll deal with it, Vera. Don't worry. I'll talk to him when he gets back."

"You do that. In the meantime, keep an eye on our little prince over there." She winked, then walked back over to her driveway to retrieve a leopard-print weekend case before clunking it along behind her.

"I will," I called, wondering if this further evidence of Nate's gambling was connected to the *big opportunity* that caused him to leave his job. And whether it had anything to do with his disappearance.

Now maybe it was time to do some digging of my own. To peel away the layers of lies before he came back.

If he came back.

20

Later that evening I picked at an instant microwave curry, only to abandon it halfway through and open a fresh bottle of Chardonnay instead. Vera's information about Nate had thrown me into confusion.

So he was gambling again. In a big way.

But all those sums of money on the bank slips I'd found in his pocket and in the box from his office were way too much for winnings from a slot machine, and even a poker table. He had to be into something bigger.

I sat by the window nursing my glass and waiting for the bright lights to switch on across the street. Maybe I'd catch a glimpse of Toby again. See him happy for once.

Right at six o'clock the colored lights blazed into the darkness. The front door flew open and Toby careened outside. Heidi followed, the red tip of her cigarette glowing like a pinhead in the night. She stood listlessly watching him, one hand cupping her elbow as she drew hard on her cigarette. He tumbled like a puppy in the snow, then stood up and ran along the line of candy canes, touching the tip of each one as if trying to count them.

The glow of yellow headlights lit the street as a long lean car crawled around the corner. The Dodge Viper. It slowed down and nosed its way into Heidi's driveway. Toby stopped his antics and ran back to his mother, where he cowered behind her legs. Barely registering him, she dropped her cigarette and ground it into the snow with her shoe as she went to greet them, her face glowing with the kind of smile she'd never directed at Toby. The kid clung on for dear life as she headed down the driveway.

Three people got out of the car. Two men in dark parkas and a tall woman wearing fur. Heidi embraced the woman and bumped fists with the two men. They chatted for a moment, huddled close, the women's heads nodding in agreement to something the tallest guy had said. But then they all suddenly turned and looked in my direction. Staring as if they could see into my window. I slid down in my chair to make myself invisible.

Heidi reached behind her and scooped Toby up into her arms. Holding him tight, she stepped away from the others, took his little arm and shook it hard as if to make him wave at me. The others began to laugh and wave as well. Toby squirmed and nuzzled his face against her neck.

Bitch. She's taunting me. I squirmed, my face burning with embarrassment. *She's painted me as the meddling neighborhood busybody. The sad, childless woman spying on other people's children.*

I ran into the kitchen and refilled my glass, gulping the cold liquid down until I felt the warm buzz spread through my body. What had happened to me? In my teens, my future had been filled with promise. I'd dealt with the tragedy of Alex's death. Forged ahead, with Stefan's help, and used the grief to create something – to give myself a purpose in life. As the wine slipped down and blurred the edge of my frustration, I tried to redirect myself towards something positive. Perhaps I'd take Stefan up on his offer and look over those Alex Apollo comic strips. Maybe I could create a graphic novel and maybe Alex could have a little sidekick with flaming red curls, who possessed the special power of being able to appear and disappear at will. They'd fly hand in hand through space, swooping through galaxies of stars, leaving a burning trail of fire behind them.

I felt something warm drop onto the back of my hand and realized I was crying again. Not necessarily from grief, but from the kind of joy that comes when you think of someone you love unconditionally whether they're with you or not. Tears trickled down my cheeks and a fierce sense of purpose gripped me. This would be my best work ever. And it would be fueled by raw passion.

The ringing phone ripped me back to the present. I put it on speaker.

"Liv? Are you there?"

It took me a moment to register Stefan's voice. "Oh... sorry. I was working," I said, my voice catching.

"I called you earlier. Guess you were busy."

I checked and saw one unanswered call earlier today. Probably when Heidi was reaming me out at the front door.

"You okay, Liv?"

"I'm fine. In fact, I was just thinking about the graphic novel you suggested. I'm going to go ahead with it. You inspired me *again*."

"Then I'll drop by tomorrow night and bring the old comics. Also, I have some other news for you."

I sat up straight, my throat strangely dry. "About Nate?"

"Yes. Tell me, have you heard anything from him yet?"

"Nothing. Did you track down his parents?"

"I did."

"Dead or alive?"

"Very much alive."

A rolling, sickly feeling made me double over. *Liar. Liar. My husband is a liar.*

I slammed my glass down onto the counter. "You need to give me their address. I'm going there. I have a whole lot of questions to ask them about their son."

There was a long silence before he answered. "I can open up a missing person's file on Nate if you want, Liv, but then I'll have to hand it over to another colleague. That's not my field."

"Just give me the address, Stefan. I'll check it out myself."

Another silence, then I heard him sigh.

"Let me swing by the address tomorrow to give it a look over. See if there's any danger, then I promise I'll take you there."

"You're not just stringing me along?"

"Trust me, Liv. I *will* take you there."

"Then you come right over as soon as you know anything, Stefan. I'll be waiting."

"You got it, Liv. Gotta go now. I'm still at work."

"Which unit do you work on, Stefan?"

But the line was dead. He'd gone. Back to his world of murder, robberies, assaults, break-ins – or whatever he was involved with.

Nate had lied about his parents. Why? Why would he want to keep them away from me?

That meant he'd been lying the whole time I'd known him.

I felt dizzy. Disoriented. Maybe it was the wine. Too much in such a short space of time. But maybe something dark was closing in on me. Past and present had begun to collide. Images and incidents revealing themselves like pieces of a scattered jigsaw. Separate, but somehow connected.

And I was afraid to start fitting them together.

Afraid of what that might reveal.

21

Around four o'clock the next day, I watched from my window as all the kids filed home from school. My heart ached when they stopped for impromptu snow fights or rolled in the snow to make snow angels. Laughing and screeching, limbs flailing, they seemed oblivious to their raw, red faces or their runny noses, and probably glad to get out of the classroom with its musty stink of damp coats and boots. I remembered that smell from the moms and twos group. Shanti and I had gone there twice a week at the nearby school.

The kids played outside for the first fifteen minutes, circling the field in endless games of tag or hiding in snow forts the older kids had made. They'd try to make snowmen, and we'd step in to help them to roll the snowballs and make the facial features out of pebbles they'd gathered from around the play structures. Back inside, we filed past the row of coat hooks assigned to the gradeschool kids. They held a rainbow array of parkas hanging above rows of fur-lined boots. Radiators blasted out heat and the musty stink of damp coats was everywhere. I remembered unrolling Jack's frosty scarf away from his scarlet cheeks, then taking out a Kleenex to wipe away the two channels of snot gathered above his lip.

"Yukky, Mommy," he'd say, twisting his pink mouth into a grimace.

"All clean," I said, sending him back into the classroom where juice boxes were arranged in a neat row beside plates of sliced apples and oranges. At first, he tried to cram the slices into his mouth, almost choking until I held his hand back, telling him to wait his turn.

Had I been too hard on him? Too intimidating? My voice too sharp?

At times like this, the pain came in waves. Real gut-wrenching pain. As if there was a hole in the world where Jack should've been. A deep, yawning emptiness at the center of my life. I'd see him in places I'd taken him to. The donut store where he always begged for the one with white icing and sprinkles, the play structure in the Burger King where I'd sit hugging a coffee and watch him play. The library at story time. The wading pool. The zoo. The swings at the park. I'd eradicated these places from my life since he'd gone. They were forbidden territory.

The memories welled up with such brute force, I couldn't even look when Shanti walked by and stopped at the bottom of the driveway. She waved and made a move towards my front door.

What was wrong with her wanting to drop by for tea? Why couldn't I just ask her in for a chat?

But I couldn't handle it, especially now that Nate was missing. The conversation would inevitably swing towards that topic and I was a terrible liar. Always was. Maybe it was something to do with having pale skin and red hair. We redheads were always the first to blush – a dead giveaway. So, I slipped back into the shadows. She hesitated, then turned away, while Rocky stood watching my empty window, thumb in his mouth, cute as a button in his red woolen hat and hockey scarf.

Angry at myself, I rushed into the kitchen and took out the half bottle of wine left from the previous day. The drinking was becoming a habit, but by that point I didn't give a damn. I'd lost my son, my husband had been lying to me since the first day I'd met him and I'd been marked for tragedy since my teen years.

I poured a glass and downed it, then sat and drank another one, loving the numbness that came with it. I knew then I should've moved away from this place and the cursed lake house opposite. Start a new life. Try to forget. But every time I started to look at listings in other areas, a panicky little voice started up inside me. *What if Jack was still alive? What if he came back to find me? If I wasn't here, he'd be lost all over again.* I had to stay here just in case, no matter how the grief gouged at my heart.

More dark thoughts were closing in on me when my phone pinged with a text message.

> Put tea on, chuck, and don't skimp on t' biscuits. There in five.

Stefan. The clouds retreated. Sucked away for another day. The unfamiliar sensation of laughter bubbled in my throat. It was our private joke.

Years ago, on Sunday mornings, we'd worked on the comic strip at his place. His grandma would settle down in front of the TV to watch two solid hours of *Coronation Street* on CBC, the recap of all the week's half-hour episodes. She barely understood what the characters were saying, but she loved all the intrigue and infighting.

"Why are these people always shouting and angry?" she'd say, eyes glued to the TV screen. "And then always *put tea on, chuck?*"

Stefan and I would kick off laughing. She never missed an episode. I had no doubt she'd kept up the habit in the seniors' home. They all probably had *Coronation Street* marathons every Sunday morning along with their tea and cookies. I reminded myself to ask about visiting her. That would surely cheer me up.

I roused myself from my lethargy and disposed of the empty wine bottle. It wouldn't do for Stefan to see me at my lowest point, reveling in self-pity and guzzling back wine in the early afternoon. After combing my pantry shelves, I came up with half a pack of ginger snaps and an unopened box of chocolate chip cookies. I quickly arranged some on a plate and poured the boiling water into my rarely used teapot. Two cups and saucers, and a sugar and milk jug completed the arrangement just in time for the sound of the doorbell.

Seeing Stefan still took me aback. He hadn't always had the broad, open smile that he greeted me with at the door. When I'd first met him, he tended to slouch around, his eyes trained on the floor. But as our friendship grew, so had his confidence, and now the fresh faced, self-assured man who strode breezily into my front hallway, was such a welcome sight. Honest, smiling, and totally lacking artifice, he was just what I needed.

He grinned when he saw the tea tray. "Just like old times. Except for the matrimonial cake."

I shrugged. "Sorry. Haven't baked that one in ages."

As a teen, Stefan had been fascinated with the name of that particular pastry, and he loved cinnamon and dates. Strangely, he also loved baking which was definitely at odds with his appearance. We'd often bake matrimonial cake together at his place. He'd be bent over a mixing bowl measuring butter sticks into flour, and with his burgundy crested hair, multiple piercings, and his *dude with the food* chef's apron, I'd imagine him as a quirky cooking show host.

"Guess I'll have to make do with the ginger snaps." He picked one up and wrinkled his nose.

"Think you'll survive?"

He nodded towards the cups. "Think so. You be mother, then."

We had such an easy rapport. It was like slipping back fourteen years to a simpler, safer time when I'd still felt the pressure of grief from Alex's death, but not the bone-crushing weight of losing a child. Now I longed for that carefree young woman who still had some shred of hope for the future. I turned away to pour the tea.

He settled down on the family room couch, and took out his notebook.

"I'll get right to it, Liv. About Nate's parents…"

I leaned against the counter, shaken. A tingly feeling settled on my skin. As if everything was about to dissolve into a shifting mirage.

"They don't live together. I followed Mrs. Barnett from her home in the north end of the city to a nursing home about ten minutes away. Made a couple of phone calls to the care home and found out Mr. Barnett's been there for years."

"But he can't be that old? Why would he be in a place like that?"

"The staff wouldn't share any medical details with me, but I suspect he either had some kind of stroke or accident or maybe early onset dementia."

I was still trying hard to accept the reality that Nate's parents actually existed when he'd lied about them for at least ten years.

"What was she like, Stefan? Nate's mother?"

"I couldn't get a close look at her, but I'd say she's in her early sixties. Tall, thin, gray hair. Nothing that stands out, really."

"And what about their house?"

"Small bungalow. Run-down. Siding and roof looked like they need repairs and it's not in a great neighborhood. Looks like they don't have a lot of money."

I slumped down onto the couch. "But why would Nate keep this from me? After all these years. Why would he lie to me?"

Stefan sighed and put down his cup. "I know it must be a shock to find this out now, but I have to ask if there's anything else that you're suspicious about. Any other lies you're aware of."

"I found out Nate's still gambling. The neighbor saw him at a casino in Niagara Falls just a few months ago. I thought he'd given it up. He promised me years back."

Stefan chewed his lip and gave me a pensive look. "Sorry to say, Liv, in my experience, once a gambler, always a gambler. It's an addiction that's next to impossible to beat."

"Sounds like you're an expert, Stefan."

"I'm on the vice squad. I deal with problem gamblers all the time."

I almost dropped my teacup, but quickly put it down on the coffee table, sloshing tea into the saucer. "Have you ever come across Nate in your investigations?"

"If I had, I couldn't even tell you, Liv," he said, sheepishly.

"Okay. I get it, but would you tell me if I was in any danger?"

He looked away from me, clearly uncomfortable at the question. "I hope it never gets to that, Liv, but I'm sure I'd find some way to keep you safe."

I sighed. "I suppose that's some comfort, then, but I do want to see Nate's mom, and I don't think that's a conflict of interest for you. I probably could have tracked her down myself. I have to talk to her. Can you take me there?" The idea scared me, but I felt compelled to follow any lead.

He shifted in his chair. "There's nothing to stop you, as a private citizen, from going to her house and telling her who you are. I can't approach her in an official capacity, but I can stay in the car and give you some moral support."

I leaned forward. "Tomorrow? Can we go tomorrow?"

"I'm off around five. I'll come and pick you up. That sound good?"

I nodded. "It'll give me time to rehearse. I'm not even sure what I'll say to her."

"Just be honest, Liv. That's all you can do." His phone buzzed. "Damn, there's no letup in this job."

While he stepped out into the hallway to take the call, I jumped up and poured a glass of water. A dull pounding had started up in my head. How was it possible that in all this time Nate's parents had never tried to contact him? Why had they cut themselves off from him so completely that they knew nothing about his life, his career and, worst of all, his child? Their grandchild? All those questions swirled around in my head, making me wonder what terrible things had happened between them to cause such a drastic rift.

Just then, Stefan popped his head around the door. "Sorry, Liv, I'm needed somewhere. Gotta make a quick exit *again*."

"When do you ever get longer than twenty minutes to yourself?" I felt the dreaded imminence of another lonely night.

He zipped up his parka. "They own me body and soul, it seems, but I like to be busy. I'm not great with down time."

"My door's always open," I said, my heart skipping a little. "Any time."

He stopped at the front door and smiled. "It's so great to see you again, Liv. I thought about you a whole lot since I left here all those years ago."

I pressed my lips tightly together and nodded. *What to say?* Everything seemed utterly pointless. "Tomorrow, then?"

He swung the door open. "I'll text you ahead of time… and… oh… I left the comic strips in your hallway."

"Can't wait to look at them," I said, as a frigid gust of wind blew in through the open door.

His car, a black SUV, was parked in the driveway. I stood watching as he pulled away, my mind turning over and over. I wanted to see Nate's parents, but hadn't a clue how to approach them. Or what to tell them. I could just imagine their reaction when I, a complete stranger, appeared on their doorstep and announced, *Hi, I'm married to your estranged son, Nate, but unfortunately, he's recently disappeared without a trace, five years after the same thing happened to the grandson you never met, and I have no idea how to find either of them.*

I pushed the door shut against the stiff wind that rustled around the trees and blew the snow into drifts. How on earth was I going to break this terrible news to someone I'd never met? Someone whose relationship to my husband had already been broken for years.

22

The garbage truck rolled by the window, stopping at the lake house where two giant containers stood, piled so full of junk the lids wouldn't close. The recycling bin lid was propped open by a stack of empty pizza boxes and a massive collection of beer, wine and liquor bottles that tumbled into the hold of the truck with such a clatter, the ground vibrated.

Despite the momentary distraction of watching Heidi set out for a walk with Toby in a small, red sled, my attention kept wandering to the phone. I'd check for missed messages, just in case I'd mistakenly slipped the phone onto silent mode. For once, the little boy looked relatively happy. He wasn't crying or whining. And she'd actually dressed him in suitable clothing for the weather – a bright red woolen cap and a navy snowsuit.

When they disappeared around the corner, I forced myself back to the sketch I was doing. It was a scene where the bullies are in the process of ambushing the protagonist, Parker, on the way to school. He's rescued by a quick-thinking little girl wielding a massive water gun. Try as I might, I couldn't get into summertime mode. Not when winter was raging like a beast outside.

Instead, I sat down with a fresh cup of coffee and the box of comic strips, imagining that when I opened it, I'd unleash the scents of my teens: stuffy school hallways, peach-flavored lip-gloss, musty textbooks. And with that the lost and broken dreams of my teens.

I hesitated. Did I want to revisit that time?

I decided I did, and edged the flaps up and open. The past came rushing back, spooling out like an old home movie. There on the first page was Alex Apollo, drawn from a photo of my brother. Alex Apollo, crowned with sunbeams, dressed in golden armor and riding a single, blazing horse across the sun, thunderbolts glinting from his shield as he tramples the snake-limbed giant. The next strip was one Stefan had drawn. I'd forgotten how good he was. First, he'd drawn a towering goddess with a wild mane of burnished red hair floating in a molten sky, rays of fire shooting from her head. Underneath was her bio: *Brigid, solar goddess, keeper of the fire held within each woman. Sacred and strong.*

A chuckle rose to my throat. We were so serious then, so intent on sticking rigidly to the mythology, and yet something about the picture unsettled me. I studied it more closely and wondered why I'd never noticed before, that it was my face on the goddess. Stefan had captured the seventeen-year-old me with my powder-white skin, my green eyes which I'd thought of as too small, my nose which I'd cursed for being too long, and my hair that I'd spent countless hours trying to tame. Stefan had seen the beauty in me and captured it in this incredible picture. *How could I have been so dumb?*

Holding that comic, a torrent of memories and scattered sensations tumbled into my head. I remembered myself at seventeen, eager for time to pass so I could see Stefan, the many *almost touches* that happened whenever we were together, my fascination with the tiny sun tattooed next to his eyebrow, his quirky sense of style.

The way I'd loved walking through the hallways with him because he had the guts to carry off the three silver rings in his ear, and the burgundy mohawk. He had an air of poise and assurance that prevented the jocks from teasing him. He was truly cool; a rarity among all the wannabes in high school.

I remembered then something I'd been thinking about ever since I ran into him again at that Halloween block party. Something about the night he left to go back to Hong Kong, when we were saying goodbye years ago.

We'd never kissed before, even though I'd wanted to. Looking back, I suppose we'd both had this unspoken understanding that it would alter our friendship too much. But that night I leaned against him and he tipped my chin up and kissed me full on the mouth. My heart flipped. I could have melted into him at that moment. His lips were so soft, the kiss tender, the scent of his skin so warm and clean. I clung to him as if I could never let go. I didn't want him to leave, but I was too shy to beg him to stay. Too timid to tell him exactly how I felt about him. But Stefan was so perceptive. He could almost read my thoughts.

"I have to go. My mom needs me. She's all alone there."

"I know. I understand," I said as he pulled himself away and got onto his bike. I remembered it was early summer and still light at ten in the evening.

"Bye," I called again, watching him until he disappeared around the corner.

The crickets were chirping loudly, but the racing of blood in my ears drowned them out. All I knew was that my soul was somehow bound irreversibly to this guy.

And now he was back. For a few seconds, I felt the faint stirrings of guilt when I realized how glad I was that Nate wasn't around. The idea of Stefan and Nate in the same room was inconceivable. Past and present in direct collision.

I turned back to the comic strip and imagined a tiny boy-hero amongst all the bold sunrays and glittering chariots. A small copper-haired boy with burnished wings. A fantastic trio of characters, guardians of the sacred fire that holds back the evil, slithering creatures of the darkness. Perfect. All I had to do was think of a name for the new little character.

My phone buzzed with an incoming message.

Pick you up in five. Be outside.

I sent back a thumbs up and placed the comics back into the box. My mind raced with the thrill of new ideas. Suddenly the prospect of seeing Stefan had tamped down my fear of confronting Nate's mystery parents.

23

Traffic was heavy for early afternoon, the road a messy wash of slush from the milder temperatures.

"Dammit, I forgot the window-washer fluid," said Stefan as a half-ton truck swished by, spraying the windshield with brown sludge. We'd just crossed the arched metal bridge that spanned the tangled network of rail yards and plunged into the north end of the city. Past rundown motels and beer vendors and the streets of shabby bungalows and soot-streaked apartment blocks. The occasional 7-Eleven store and tattoo parlor, pawnshops and payday loan places with their bright orange signage, the only shot of color in that bleak, treeless setting.

We'd been chatting about my ideas for the comic strip, so the ride passed quickly with no mention of Nate or any of my worries. But when we pulled up at a red light, Stefan turned to me.

"You sure you're okay with this?"

I nodded. "I have to see her. After all these years I want to know the truth about Nate."

"I talked to my buddy Raj at missing persons. He ran a check of hospitals all across the country and Nate's name hasn't shown up."

"So, we know he wasn't in an accident. Guess we can cross that possibility off. What next?"

The light turned green and he turned back to the road. "We can't do any license plate checks because you told me he didn't take his car, but if you give me his cell phone number, we could run a trace on that, maybe."

"I'll text it to you," I said, punching in the numbers and pressing *send*.

Stefan was wearing a gray ribbed wool hat pulled low over his forehead. I laughed. "Fourteen years ago, you wouldn't have been seen dead in a hat like that."

He smiled back. "Yeah, I'd have been too afraid it might crush my spikes."

His dark hair contrasted sharply with his pale skin, bold eyebrows, and the strong line of his jaw with its slight bluish trace of stubble. "What did your parents think of your punk hairdo – I mean, when you lived in Toronto?"

"They were cool with it, I think." He glanced sideways at me. "Mom was a bit of a bohemian type anyway. She was all for free expression. Didn't want to cramp my personal style. My dad not so much. He never knew what to make of me. That's why it was so important to spend those last months with him. We came to a greater understanding of each other. Learned to respect each other's choices."

"Why didn't you go with them when they first went back to Hong Kong? I don't think I ever asked you that. Guess I was so wrapped up in my own problems."

He sighed. "I was just a self-centered kid. I didn't realize how much it hurt my Mom when I told her I didn't want to go with them. But we'd traveled around so much, and I'd become used to all the wide, open spaces. I could breathe here – and still see the forests and lakes. Still drive around the perimeter of the city, park my car and watch thunderclouds rolling in from miles away across the big prairie sky."

"That's so poetic – and a beautiful tribute to the city."

"It's home," he said, smiling at me. "That's why I dug my heels in and said I wanted to stay and look after Gran who was living alone at the time. This city was the very first place my parents had settled when they emigrated, and she never moved since she landed here."

"She must've been so happy you chose to stay."

"Yup. She was over the moon. And I have to say, even though she could be strict, she was so much fun with all her stories of the old country, and she loved to spoil me. I ate probably better than any high school kid I know."

"I can vouch for that," I said, remembering the number of times I'd arrived there starving and tucked into a plate of fresh noodles or steamed dumplings.

My stomach grumbled as we turned off the main road and pulled into a narrow street of old bungalows and one and a half story houses, mostly in sad states of disrepair. The front porches were cluttered with old bikes and piles of boxes, broken windows patched with plastic sheeting, battered roofs with missing shingles.

I sank back against the headrest. "How is it possible I didn't know they existed, let alone lived like this?"

Stefan slowed the car down. "Be prepared, Liv. You might not like the story behind it all."

He pulled up outside a tiny bungalow with faded green wooden siding. The old, glassed-in porch was fogged with condensation, but I could still see the shape of a battered old sofa and the spidery outlines of plastic flowers in hanging baskets.

"This is it?"

He nodded. "The Barnett residence."

My heart fluttered in my throat. I reached inside my pocket. I'd brought a recent photo of Nate as well as the football picture from high school. "Guess I should just go and knock," I said, gripping the door handle.

He put up a hand. "Let's wait a minute. Yesterday, around this time, his mother left for the care home. Maybe we should drive around to the back lane and wait a few minutes. Just get a sense of who's in there and what's going on. I don't want to send you into a dangerous situation."

"Okay," I said, relieved. Showing up at the front door was a daunting prospect.

We crawled along past the houses, turned right at the end, and right again into a back lane even more chaotic than the front street. A *Beware of the Dog* sign adorned an ugly chicken-wire fence, backyards were cluttered with buckets and plastic tubs, and the occasional discarded toilet. Rusted bicycles sat atop piles of mangled old car parts and stacks of used tires. Ramshackle garden sheds were full to bursting with jumbled piles of planters, wooden stakes and beaten-up old watering cans.

In contrast, the Barnett backyard was bare, featureless but clean. An old navy Camry with blooms of rust on the fenders sat in the carport, sheltered by a corrugated metal roof.

"Must be tough for them to look out at the neighbors' yards," I said, feeling a surge of guilt when I compared it to where we lived. "They could have come over to see us. Nate should've helped them out."

"Seems there's a whole lot you don't know about him, Liv. I'm sorry this is happening to you."

The insistent prickle of tears made me turn away. "You mean happening to me *again*."

"You don't deserve this, Liv. Not you. After everything you've been through."

I focused my eyes on the back door of the house and sighed. "Guess trouble always has a way of finding me."

"It's time you had some happiness in your life."

I looked over at his warm, brown eyes. "I've had a lot of happiness. Can't say it's all been bad. And I decided two things today when I looked at those comic strips."

He smiled. "The graphic novel?"

"Yes. I already decided I'm going to create a new character inspired by Jack. And if and when Nate shows up again, I'm leaving him."

His eyebrows rose. "Whoa, that's drastic."

"It's over. Time for a new start. For both of us. We're not doing each other any favors staying together. Besides, I don't think I can ever trust him again."

He looked away and adjusted the fingers of his leather gloves. "It's your decision, Liv. You're still young. You have a whole life ahead of you. But don't get ahead of things. Just try to deal with everything one step at a time."

"I know. You're right. But I just can't stop my mind racing from one worry to the other. I keep going over and over everything until I can't sort out what to do." Just then, the back door of the house swung open. A tall woman with faded brown hair and a slightly stooped posture, stepped out. She wore a brown quilted parka and a red woolen hat.

"That's her?"

He nodded. I gave him one last look as I opened the car door. The woman was hurrying to the car. I had to stop her before she got in.

I picked through the ridges of snow and reached the fence just as she opened the back gate.

"Mrs. Barnett?"

She looked at me with faded blue eyes. Her brows knit. "I'm not interested in any religious pamphlets and my bills are all paid up."

"Mrs. Barnett. I'm Nate's wife."

I might as well have smacked her in the face. She stepped backwards, an expression of utter horror transforming her face. "You must be mistaken."

I stepped towards her. "We've been married eight years."

She stared at me with terror-filled eyes as she backed away.

"I didn't know anything about you and your husband. Nate never talked about you."

"I'm sorry. I don't have a son," she said, pulling herself up to her full height and glaring at me.

"But he's my husband. Your son, Nate Barnett. I'd have loved to get to know you. I still would."

I took the photos from my pocket and held them out to her.

She looked at them, her mouth twisted in disgust. "Is this some kind of sick joke?" she said, edging towards the car door. Her eyes were moist with tears.

I rummaged in my purse. "I can prove it. I have my marriage license." I took out the certificate, still in my purse from the bank visit. "See, it says Olivia – married to Nate Barnett."

She leaned forward and glanced at the paper as if it was some forbidden, top-secret document. Then she looked up at me, shaking her head. "I'm afraid you've made a big mistake, and I'm not sure who your husband is, but my son, Nate Barnett, is dead."

148

24

For a moment, I was dumbstruck.

"I don't understand. How?" I barely croaked the words out.

She squinted, then looked at me through narrowed eyes. "Look, I don't know who you are, or who this man is you say you've married, but my son, Nate, died in a car accident fifteen years ago. His father was driving. They were heading north on the perimeter, hit a patch of black ice and the car flew out of control. It crossed the median into oncoming traffic. My husband was the lucky one, if you can call it that. Living with a brain so damaged he can't function independently. The only blessing is, he can't remember what happened. My son Nate was another story. His injuries were so serious he was in a coma for five weeks. I sat by his bedside the whole time, barely sleeping in case I missed the moment he woke up. At the end of the fifth week, I held him like a baby and watched him fade away. Now I have to live with that truth for the rest of my life. I swear I only keep going because of my husband."

My face burned in the chilly air. "How is this even possible? I... I don't know what to say..."

She'd already started to climb into the car. "There must be some explanation, but I'm sorry I couldn't help you. You don't know how much I wish my son was still around to get married, so I hope you find the answers you're looking for. I have my own life now. I take things day by day."

"I'm so sorry for your loss," I muttered, my throat seizing up as I spoke. I completely understood her grief, but at the back of my mind a terrible question lurked. *Who exactly was I married to?*

She barely acknowledged my words as she got into the driver's seat and slammed the door.

I had a sudden thought and tapped on the window. Scowling, she rolled it down.

"Please, one more question, Mrs. Barnett. Did your son play football?"

She turned to me, tears pooling in her eyes. "He was about to transfer to a big high school in the south end of the city, because he wanted to try out for the football team. Our local junior high was too small to have its own team. He was a football fanatic like his dad. They followed all the games on TV like two old football buddies."

Her eyes shone with tears as she choked up, then began to close the window. I stepped aside to let her reverse into the lane. Then, with nothing left to lose, I remembered the photographs and pulled them from my pocket. "Wait, Mrs. Barnett. Do you know this man?" I showed her Nate's most recent photo.

She frowned and shook her head. "No. Can't say I do."

I switched to the old high school photo. "Then what about this guy?"

Tears were pooled at the rims of her eyes. She blinked them away. "You really won't give up, will you?"

"Please, Mrs. Barnett. It's so important to me."

She took the grainy picture and studied it, then looked up at me with wide eyes.

"Is this your husband?"

I nodded.

She leaned over and took a Kleenex to blot away the tears. "I know this boy. He does resemble my son, Nate."

My heart leapt.

"Who is he?"

She shook her head. "I don't know his name. But I remember him from the hospital when Nate was in a coma. Maybe he was a volunteer. I think he brought books around the wards on a trolley. For the patients to borrow."

"Which hospital?"

"Medical Sciences."

I looked again at the picture. "But why would he claim to be someone he isn't?"

"That, I can't tell you," she said, starting up the engine, "but right now I'm done. I can't talk about this anymore. I have to get to my husband."

"Do you want me to contact you if I find more information?" I said, as she revved the engine.

"You know where I am," she said, rolling up her window and taking off down the lane.

The bitter cold wind blew my hood back as I watched the car disappear around the corner. I looked over at Stefan who was beckoning me over to the car, his eyes expectant – questioning. My mind was a mass of confusion. *Should I tell him about Nate's stolen identity?* If I did, then the investigation might take a different turn. Maybe it would slow up the effort to find him. But then maybe I wanted to hold this new information to myself because I needed to be the one to face Nate and ask him why he'd lied to me all this time. Or did I still harbor some deep-seated loyalty to my husband that I was prepared to lie for him? Did I want to give him the benefit of the doubt? Hear *his* explanation for stealing someone's identity, before I gave him up to the police?

I couldn't come up with a clear line of reasoning, but instead acted on gut instinct. I wouldn't tell Stefan about this latest development. Not until I'd had a chance to think things through and maybe do my own investigation into Nate. At least it would be a way to hold onto some feeling of control in a situation where I'd had very little so far.

As I walked to the car, I decided what story I'd give Stefan. I'd tell him that Nate was estranged from his parents because he'd stolen from them and run them deep into debt, and his mother detested him so much she wanted to deny his very existence.

After I managed to get my version of the events out, Stefan looked pensive.

"There could be so many other reasons why she doesn't want to talk about him, Liv. Families are crazy, complicated organisms that sometimes don't make any sense at all."

I kept my eyes steady on the road as we picked our way through the dense traffic. I didn't want to look too directly at Stefan in case he could tell I was lying. "I know all that, but there was something about the way she reacted. Like she was terrified that I'd found her or something."

"Maybe we need to do a bit more digging about the family. I can check out a few things, but I have to be careful, Liv. It's not my case. I can't get too personally involved. You need to call Raj and fill him in. It might be relevant to the missing person's search."

I nodded. "Okay, I'll do that as soon as I get home, but I don't think there's any harm in me doing some checking around. See what I can find out about Nate."

"Be careful, Liv. I don't want you getting into any situations you might not be able to handle."

"You know me, Stefan. Once I've got something in my head, I don't let it go."

"That's what I'm worried about," he said, flexing his fingers on the steering wheel.

Stefan dropped me off with a promise he'd be in touch as soon as he got any leads on Nate. I tried to sound grateful, tried to summon up some enthusiasm, but I simply whispered a soft *thank you* and walked towards my house. I had the strangest feeling of detachment – disembodiment. That I was really sleepwalking and at any moment I'd wake up and Jack would be there, playing with his dump truck on the lawn, and Nate would be in the garage cleaning his car, and all the weirdness would simply slip away like a nightmare at sunrise.

But when I flicked open the frozen pin pad cover on the garage, my mind jolted back to cold reality. Nate's car sat there empty. A silent reminder. Why was I still kidding myself? My life was a mess. My marriage based on lies.

Who was Nate if he wasn't Nate Barnett? And why had he taken on a dead kid's identity?

25

I stood at the open garage door, paralyzed by confusion. My entire life had been marked by disruption: Alex's death, the loss of Jack, and now Nate's unexplained disappearance and endless lies. It was enough to drive a person towards complete disconnection from reality.

But I had to hold it all together. In case Jack was alive. In case he came looking for me.

I turned and looked towards the street. Stefan was still sitting there watching me through his open window. He waved and, in that moment, I realized I wasn't really alone. Stefan was there. He'd always had my back. I tried to smile and return the wave. Only then did he drive away.

Punching in the key code for the garage, I realized I'd only just begun to assemble the puzzle that was Nate's life. He'd deliberately hidden his past, pretending that he was all alone in the world with no family and no old, established friends. He'd taken on someone else's identity. *Why?*

And yet, at school it seemed like he'd been part of a tight group of football buddies. The picture of the football team told me that. Or was all that buddy-buddy stuff a charade, just like our marriage? I couldn't even recall running into any of his old friends when we'd gone out shopping. And when Jack was born, only a couple of our neighbors and colleagues from his work came to the baby shower. Admittedly I was no better off in the friend department. Jack's disappearance had turned me into a recluse. Easier to avoid the pain of constantly having to retell the tragic story. To endure the pity-filled eyes of well-meaning strangers as they struggled for something comforting to say.

Perhaps the fact that Nate and I were both loners had drawn us together.

Even after Alex's death, I'd pulled away from my friends. I'd become the kid with the dead brother. My best friends gave me furtive sideways looks. Like they couldn't be alone with me anymore because they had no idea what to say. How could you joke around with someone whose brother burned to death? I didn't have to be a mind reader to know they were picturing leaping flames, blood-curdling screams and burning flesh. So, I clammed up. Shut them all out. And gradually they drifted away from me. Like I was a walking disease.

Until Stefan came along, and I poured everything into my friendship with him. He was the only one who under-stood me.

The slow, whirring sound of the garage door moment-arily soothed my jangled nerves. Mrs. Barnett's revelations had terrified me and raised so many questions. If Nate had stolen their son's identity, how had he managed to keep the lie going? How had he carved out a decent high school career, then a successful life as an accountant and sales executive? When I first met him, he'd presented the picture of a well-educated, up-and-coming businessman. His colleagues liked him – spoke highly of him. So what had actually happened to his real parents? And how could I ever have known that the well-heeled, smooth-talking romantic was actually a liar and a fraud and a person capable of stealing someone else's identity and life?

A car door slammed behind me. My heart flipped for fear it was Nate, coming back with some lame explanation for his absence. How could I face him? Let alone live in the same house as this virtual stranger?

I turned, my heart thudding, and breathed a sigh of relief at my empty driveway, but across the street I noticed a white Mercedes had pulled up. Heidi's friend with the shaved head – the man who'd dropped Toby into the snow the other day – got out and was waving to someone. I slipped back into the garage and hid beside my car. Heidi turned the corner, pulling the little red sled.

It was empty.

Where was Toby?

The man held out his arms and she ran straight into them, her face lit up by a broad smile. I watched and waited for the little boy to appear, running after her, but no one came. I felt a sudden dryness in my throat, the familiar tickle of panic in the pit of my stomach. I'd felt it when I first noticed Jack wasn't with Nate.

Had she dropped him off somewhere? At a babysitter's house?

And yet it seemed strange she wouldn't have driven him there.

I was frozen to the spot, staring at them, when she turned towards me and gave me the finger, grinning as she held the gesture. My hand flew up to the pin pad and pressed the switch to shut the door.

I'd have to keep an eye out for Toby without her noticing. And if for some strange reason, he didn't show up, I'd call Rick again.

—

Later, after a good two hours on the magic lunch box project, I pulled out the comic strips again and took a good, hard look at them. I needed to create a shining little sidekick for Alex Apollo and Brigid? The name Rory kept turning around in my head. Then I remembered Stefan's very first piece of writing. About the rocket trails of fire burning from his heels as he flew across the sky.

It was perfect. *Rory Rocket Boy. That would be Jack with his fiery wings, jet-powered boots and star medallion.* Just like Rory, the lost puppy. Missing from the box in my closet.

Had Nate taken it?

I'd learned today he was capable of anything.

But was he capable of causing Jack's disappearance?

That niggling thought was like a piece of grit in a shoe. It kept digging at the edge of my consciousness until I pushed it away, only to feel it prickling again a few moments later.

He'd been a good, loving father. Hadn't he?

But what did I really know about him? Was it all an act?

How could I sit around here waiting for Stefan to call? I had to do something. I looked at Brigid – strong, decisive, a fiery force to be reckoned with. How long was I going to play the sad victim? How long would I flail around like an ineffectual kid when the truth was waiting out there? I had to make a move. Come up with a plan to piece together all these fragments of Nate's life. Find out who he really was, because that was the key to discovering what he'd actually been doing all this time he'd been lying to me.

26

THEN

If I was really honest with myself, I'd have to admit that after Nate and I married, I ignored a whole lot of hints and clues that something in our relationship was off. I'd turned my head away, telling myself I was being picky and difficult. Instead, I told myself I was lucky to meet an attractive, successful man like Nate, and continued to believe in the perfect illusion that was my new, growing family.

Looking back, a few odd incidents occurred right after we were married.

First, he didn't attend my dad's funeral.

In Toronto he'd been so supportive, cradling me while I cried my heart out. Helping me pack up boxes of books and art supplies. Taping and labeling them more perfectly than I could ever have done. Making arrangements to fly back home on the soonest possible flight. I remember him walking into my apartment waving a plane ticket. It had been pouring all morning and the shoulders of his navy coat were speckled with rain. Water droplets glistened on his dark hair. I kept thinking, *this kind, attentive, gorgeous man is my husband*, and I blinked as if the dream would fade away, but he was still there, smiling at me. He was so real. Flesh and blood.

"Pack your bags. The plane leaves in three hours."

Excited, I kissed him on the lips and grasped the ticket. "Where's yours?"

He looked away. A shadow fell across his face. The perfect moment suddenly soured. "I'm staying back, Liv. I thought you knew. I'm driving back once I've wrapped up everything and bringing your boxes with me. How else did you think we'd get all this back home?"

So I went to Dad's funeral alone. It was a somber, quiet event in a sunlit funeral chapel with a few of Dad's old coffee-time buddies there to see him off. Gran had passed away two years previously, and Mom had already retreated into herself now Dad wasn't there to look after her. During the eulogies, she gazed off into the distance as if her mind and body were disengaged, and when Nate finally arrived home a week after the funeral, he was the one who helped me get her into a long-term care home.

But he never came with me to visit her. He always had an excuse. Preparing for a conference or presentation, packing for a business trip, feeling unwell.

I never questioned him. Just gave him the benefit of the doubt, rationalizing that he had no parents and didn't want to forge any new parental links. Besides, my mother barely even recognized me, so what chance did Nate have? He constantly reassured me that I was the only family he needed, and told me that when our child came along, we'd start our own perfect family *with none of the fuckups that I endured as a kid*.

I only asked once about *the fuckups*.

His face darkened. "Leave the past where it belongs. In the past. The future is what's important."

After that, I never broached the topic again, until a couple of months after we'd returned from Toronto. We were at a football game. Nate's boss had given him free tickets, so he reckoned it might be a fun way to spend a Saturday afternoon.

It was a hot July day, the temperature soaring well into the 90s, and so humid the air seemed to drip moisture. I was already almost five months pregnant and definitely sporting a bulge underneath my light jersey dress, so I was totally unprepared for the blast of hot air that hit me when we stepped out of the air-conditioned car. It was like opening an oven door and stepping inside. The moment I moved a limb, rivulets of sweat trickled down the inside of my dress. Luckily, we'd brought bottles of iced water. I sucked greedily at mine, worrying I might drink it too fast and be left gulping hot air.

I needn't have worried. Once we got into the stands, it was way cooler under the canopy. A gusty breeze whipped around the crowd, providing a temporary respite from the stagnant heat. On the way in, Nate had bought hot dogs slathered with all the fixings and tall, iced cokes. Soon I was coasting. Loving the pre-game antics: the cheerleaders in blue and gold, the pounding rock music, the giant duck mascots careening around the field. But once the game got going, I hadn't reckoned with the weak bladder that comes with pregnancy. I tried to ignore the urge to go to the washroom, but by the second quarter I could barely think. I could've squatted right there on the spot and relieved myself. I tapped Nate's shoulder and told him I had to go, but he was so lost in the game, he didn't even turn to look at me.

"They've got another first down. Are you okay to go by yourself?"

I said I was fine, and not to worry, then began to edge my way past the other spectators in the row, trying hard to ignore their exasperated sighs when I blocked their view. Away from the row of seats, I began the tedious climb up towards the concessions at the top of the stairs. The heat ebbed and shimmered around me, and the sun dissolved my vision into buzzing pixels. Suddenly my legs buckled, and my ankles liquified as I stumbled to grasp the rail and make the next step ahead of me. In a second, strong hands grabbed my arm and someone stopped me from collapsing to the boards. I was aware of a hazy woman's face and the sound of her voice fading in and out.

"You need to get out of the sun. Let me help."

Another, stronger pair of arms grabbed at my other arm. "Help her up into the shade," said a man's voice. A familiar voice.

All I could focus on was the cool darkness up ahead of me. The cheers of the crowd echoed in my pounding head, and the brightly colored jerseys and streamers rippling and buzzed at the periphery of my vision, making my stomach roll. Next thing I knew, someone had placed me gently on a chair in the shade of a popcorn stand.

Two blurred figures stood in front of me. The familiar voice said, "Olivia? Liv is that really you?"

Then I heard a thundering of steps. Someone pushing the two people aside. Nate grasping my arms.

"Liv – what happened? Are you okay?"

I tried to nod but my head felt too big for my shoulders.

The other familiar voice spoke. "Nate? Nate Barnett? What the…?"

Nate pulled at my arm. "I'm taking you home, Liv. We shouldn't have come here."

"Nate, it's me, Max."

In my dizzy stupor I registered that this was Max Leonard. One of Alex's best buddies from the football team.

Nate lifted me upright, bracing his arm tightly around my waist. Then he simply guided me away from them saying, "Appreciate the help, man. But I have to get her home."

I protested weakly. "But, Nate, I feel dizzy, I…"

He didn't listen. Just propelled me towards the gate, his arm locked around my waist. As we stumbled along towards the exit, I remember hearing Max's voice protesting faintly in the distance, saying, "What's the hurry, man? Why don't you wait for the paramedics?"

But we were inside the elevator by then and Nate was completely silent, his mouth a tight, thin line, as if he was angry that he'd run into someone he knew from high school.

Later, I remember asking him why he didn't acknowledge Max.

"I was worried about you, Liv. I couldn't think straight. All I could think of was getting you home."

"But we didn't even thank Max for helping me."

That's when he dropped the cold cloth he'd been using to mop my forehead, and looked at me right in the eye, his brows knit into a frown. "I can't believe that you, of all people, should want to bring up anything to do with high school. I never want to talk about that messed up time. What did I tell you about the past? Leave it where it belongs."

And I did, consigning it to that growing garbage can of *crappy* experiences and memories that were banned from our everyday conversation. The rest of that day, he slammed around the house, making a terrible clatter wherever he went, which was totally uncharacteristic of him. He finally locked himself in his office, stayed there for two hours and re-emerged as his calm, charming self.

I never did find out what made him act so coldly towards someone who used to be a friend, according to his old football photographs.

And yet now, the more I thought about it, I realized Nate had always been on the outside of the group. A shadowy, elusive presence. Someone who was rarely around in the weeks before Alex's death. Though Stefan had claimed Nate was friends with Renny and Chad. The two guys who'd brought trouble into Alex's life. Or so it seemed. Because my brother became a different guy once they came into the picture.

There had to be bad blood there.

Was it the gambling? Did Alex owe money?

There had to be some good reason why Nate hadn't wanted to even talk to Max. Max had been in the basement the night my brother died. Did Nate know something about what happened? Something he couldn't tell me?

I was so jumpy I could barely get my lunch down. Afterwards, I thought about working, but immediately rejected the idea. I couldn't focus on anything while my mind was fixated on Nate – or the man who claimed to be Nate. The only way I could get some answers would be to go right back to the first thing I knew about him. That he'd worked as a volunteer at the hospital. Before he became someone else.

I gathered up my purse and coat. It was time to do a little research on the boy who actually stole Nate Barnett's identity.

27

NOW

The city's main hospital occupied several blocks, and with many research facilities attached, it resembled a small city. At fifteen, Mrs. Barnett's real son would have been in the children's section, so I circled the block several times before I could find a parking space. Parking spots were limited here, but the meter guys were like flies crawling on spoiled food. One minute late and they'd pounce with a ticket.

I decided to start with the main lobby of the hospital, a glitzy place with its own hotel, a Starbucks and a vast cafeteria as well as a pharmacy and gift shop. I reckoned the gift shop would be a good place to start since it was staffed by volunteers. If they'd been around a while, they might recognize Nate as the boy who brought the books around. Maybe they'd even remember his real name.

The gift shop was buzzing with people, browsing the flower arrangements and soft toys and candies. Trying to find some little knick-knack or keepsake to brighten up a sick person's day. Business was booming. Not surprising since it was winter and therefore flu season, which always inflated the patient numbers. I picked up a little book titled *Dreams of Andalusia*, attracted to its bright cover of blossom trees blooming around the Alhambra. Two women were manning the cash register, so I picked the older one with the silver bob and thrust the book towards her.

"My gran loves to read," I remarked as casually as I could.

She studied the cover and smiled. "Then she'll love this one. It's been a big seller. Something to do with the exotic locations."

"Yes, there's nothing like a good book to take you away from reality," I said, swiping my debit card. "Tell me, do they have a book lending service here for the patients?"

She handed me my book, wrapped in a paper bag. "Oh yes. It's not as popular as it used to be, but some patients still use it."

"Only I was looking to do some volunteer work, and I thought that might be a good place to start."

She laughed and handed me a receipt. "Then you'd have to fight Shirley for a job. She's looked after the book lending for years and there's barely enough demand to justify having her here."

"But it wouldn't hurt to chat with her, would it?" I said, regretting that I hadn't just gone to the front desk and asked for the person who delivered the books.

"You'll find her in the volunteer coordinator's office. Third floor."

I rode the elevator, cursing myself for wasting time and realizing I'd just have to get to the point with Shirley. No more fake offers about volunteering. I'd have to find some other tactic, though at that point I was flying by the seat of my pants.

The doors swished open onto a featureless corridor with drab cream walls. Totally dissimilar to the flashy lobby. A sign at the far end read *Volunteer Coordinator.*

The door opened onto a small reception area where a young woman sat scrolling through her phone.

"Can I help you?"

"I'm here to see Shirley. Er… I'm interested in donating some books."

She barely registered me and inclined her head towards a small office-cum-storage room in the corner. Behind some antique wooden trolleys loaded with dog-eared paperbacks, a small woman sat at a tiny desk, thumbing through a long list.

"Shirley?" I ventured.

She looked up, flashing a bright smile at me. Salt-and-pepper hair, pink cheeks and cornflower-blue eyes, Shirley in her lavender sweater was exactly the kind of person I would have chosen to sit by my bedside to read me a story.

"Yes. That's me. I've been a fixture here for almost thirty years. Everyone knows me here."

Her openness disarmed me for a moment and I floundered, trying to collect my thoughts. "I… I'm trying to track down an old friend of mine who used to work with you… maybe sixteen years ago."

She sighed. "This place was so busy then. Before all the internet and streaming and the e-books replaced the good old, honest-to-goodness feel of a real book in your hands. People are too lazy these days to crack open a book. They're all just glued to the TV. Bingeing on Netflix and all that."

"How right you are," I said, reaching into my pocket and pulling out the early photo of Nate. "Do you remember this guy?"

She squinted at the grainy photo for a moment, and that was all it took for the color to drain entirely from her pink cheeks. She looked up at me in shock. "You know this person? Are you a detective?"

"No… just an old acquaintance. I… I used to know him."

"Then if you know what's good for you, I suggest you stop looking."

"I don't understand."

"This boy… this little con artist charmed us all with his good looks and easy manner. Then he disappeared without a trace after stealing from every patient he loaned a book to."

I felt the nausea rise, sour in my throat. "Why didn't you involve the police?"

She shook her head. "I have a soft heart, Miss… Miss…"

"Barnett," I said.

"I knew about his background. He was from a bad home. I wanted to give him a chance. I didn't find out about the thefts until much later and then it was too late. Nobody knew where to find him."

"What exactly did you know about his background?"

"Father in prison. Drug addict mother. And somehow, he'd survived it all. He was well-spoken and beautifully groomed. A lovely looking boy. The nurses were all fond of him. And he played up to them. He was quite the gentleman. I have to give him credit for that. But I suppose he'd witnessed too much bad behavior from his parents from an early age. And it's so tough to undo all that harm once it's ingrained. Stealing and lying were the only ways he knew to survive."

"Do you remember his name?"

Holding up a finger, she swiveled around in her chair and opened the bottom drawer of a small filing cabinet.

I held my breath, waiting for her to reveal my husband's real name – his true identity. No more lies.

She rifled through the brown folders until she pulled out a thin file and flipped it open. "Ah... here we are. I'd almost forgotten. His name was Jack. Jack Sawyer."

28

My head was so scrambled on the drive home, I almost ran a red light, then narrowly escaped rear-ending a semi-truck.

I couldn't figure out what to make of Nate naming our son with his own, real name. The name that he'd buried at the age of fifteen when he somehow managed to steal a dead boy's identity, take his place at a popular new high school in the city's south end, but also slide right into a spot on one of the best high school football teams in the country.

It seemed unlikely he'd done it alone. Someone had to have given him a hand. Looked after the details. And if so, who? It seemed unlikely to be his parents. His mom was too far gone with the drugs, and his father was in jail — though it was possible he still had some pull. I thought of all those thriller movies where hardened career criminals were still able to wield their influence beyond the prison walls, depending on how powerful they'd been on the outside, who they'd pissed off and who was still loyal to them.

I was so eager to get into the house and start an internet search I forgot to open the garage door. Seconds before ploughing right through the gray metal door, I saw it coming and stood up in my seat, flooring the brake. The car juddered to a stop with a screeching jolt, millimeters away from disaster. *Get a grip on yourself*, I said, falling back against the headrest and trying to slow down the shallow breaths that had my heart pounding so hard my vision was blurred. Was I having a panic attack or something?

Finally, I managed to collect myself and pressed the remote door opener. The slow whirring noise calmed my racing heart. I eased the car into the garage, then slid out of the driver's side, holding onto the door frame for support. When I looked up, my heart caught in my throat again. Heidi was standing at the foot of my driveway watching me, her features knotted in an expression of disapproval and disbelief. Dressed in a fitted black parka and pale green woolen hat, she looked as if she'd just come back from a walk. My hair was stuck to my forehead with cold sweat from the shock. I pushed the sticky strands away from my face.

"You okay?" she asked. "Only I thought you were about to crash into your garage door."

I swallowed. *Of course, someone had to witness my stupid blunder.* And worse still, it had to be her. "Got a lot on my mind right now."

She was staring at Nate's car. "Good thing your husband didn't see. He'd be worried about you."

I glanced over at the car. "Oh… he's away on business."

She seemed to consider that fact for a while. "He's coming back soon?"

"I'm not sure. He didn't give an exact date."

She shrugged. "Too bad. Looks like you could use some help."

"I'm fine," I said, pulling my purse from the car. "I'm used to being alone."

"Not me," she said, pulling off the woolly hat and letting the blonde curls tumble onto her shoulders. She always seemed to look like she'd come from a photo shoot. "I like being around people. Love entertaining."

It occurred to me then, that Toby wasn't with her. I hadn't seen him since she'd taken him off in the little red sled.

"How's Toby? Haven't seen him around."

She looked away, almost furtively. "He's okay, I guess."

I moved towards her. "Where is he?"

She backed away, eyes narrowing. The friendly, casual manner replaced by bald suspicion "Oh, he's… he's…"

The shrill ring of a phone cut her off. She held up a finger and reached into her pocket. Pulled out her phone and started talking, her eyes flickering towards me. I stood watching, waiting for an answer. Not caring that I looked like the resident crazy lady as well as the local busybody.

Her face set in a dark look of vexation as she covered the phone. "Gotta go," she said, turning away and stomping towards her driveway, only turning to check and see if I was still watching. I stood there until she reached her garage door where she fumbled with the pin pad and waited for the door to open. Before she went in, she turned again, and with her left index finger, twirled a little circle by her temple.

Crazy bitch. I knew that's what she was thinking.

But at that point I was past caring.

Inside I waited for the coffee to brew, then checked my phone. No texts or messages. Nothing from Stefan or Raj, which confirmed that I was indeed doing the right thing, pushing on with my own investigation instead of driving myself crazy, sitting around the house agonizing – chewing my nails down to the quick and waiting for something to happen. I'd hand all of my findings over to

Raj in my own good time, once I'd pieced everything together.

My first search using the name Jack Sawyer revealed nothing except a general manager of a car dealership and a founding member of a bodybuilding association whose first name was actually Jacques. As I'd thought, Nate – I still couldn't bear to call him Jack – had somehow buried his identity, which wouldn't have been too difficult sixteen years ago. Social media hadn't been as widespread then as it was now, and phones hadn't yet become an essential part of our anatomy.

I tried another search – *Sawyer conviction*. A different story.

The screen displayed a host of hits related to drug trafficking, and the name Glenn Sawyer was mentioned on every one. I scrolled through, desperate to find a picture of someone who resembled an older version of Nate. By my rough calculations, at the time Nate changed his identity, his father could have been anywhere from thirty-five to fifty. Soon I came upon a mugshot of a slim tattooed man with a brush cut, a twisted half-smile on his face and the unmistakable piercing blue eyes I'd stared at across my dining table for the last eight years. But this man was smoothly shaven except for a thick goatee that sprouted from the tip of his chin. He also had a weird spider-web tattoo that crept across the left side of his temple and ended at the corner of his lips. His intense eyes seemed to bore into mine with a steely defiance I'd never seen in Nate.

This was one scary gangster you wouldn't want to run into alone in the daytime, let alone after dark. I felt a sudden flare of pity for Nate. No wonder he'd wanted to get away from this man who looked like he was bad to the bone.

More searches around his name revealed that Nate's dad, Glenn, was indeed a member of the Hell's Angels. In and out of jail for minor break-in and assault charges during the eighties, he'd finally graduated to the higher echelons of crime, forging connections with major criminal organizations in Montreal and Toronto. Eventually, he'd been imprisoned for twenty-five years on drug trafficking, money laundering and weapons charges. After serving seventeen years, he'd gotten out on good behavior, and on his release had relocated to British Columbia where he'd been killed in a drive-by shooting related to some kind of turf war in Vancouver. I checked the date and was shocked to see it happened just before the time I met Nate in Toronto.

There was some mention of a wife, Marion. But the only result from a search on her name was an obituary in a local paper showing she'd died around or just before the time Nate changed his identity. Cause of death wasn't stated, though there was a mention of a local rehab clinic, leading me to believe it might be a drug-related death. Considering the nature of the guy she'd married, I guessed a life spent high on meth or heroin was her only option for survival.

It seemed I'd finally stumbled on the one thing that Nate hadn't lied about; his parents were actually dead when he met me. The question was, had he changed his identity to escape the influence of his deadbeat parents? If so, I could hardly blame him for trying to cut all ties with an evil gangster dad and desperate junkie mom. Make a fresh start as someone else. Or had he somehow followed his father's lead and struck out onto his own criminal path with a little help from some old friends of the family? The only way to find out would be to talk to people who knew him around the time he entered high school, equipped with his brand spanking new identity.

I tried to put in a couple of hours' work, but my mind wasn't on it. I couldn't focus and ended up ruining the whole picture after I erased it so many times the paper was covered in gray smudges. I threw down my pencils, thinking maybe an evening walk would help me clear my head after all the revelations of the day. So, I set out into the chilly night. The sky had darkened already, and snow was falling in big, floaty flakes that settled on the tip of my nose and eyelashes.

By the time I hit the forest path, my brain had switched into logical mode. I'd started to put together the pieces of my husband's life from when Jack Sawyer became Nate Barnett. At the tender age of sixteen, I calculated. Now I had to continue to the next phase of high school. Since I didn't know anyone from Nate's high school, I had to focus on his connections with my school football team. Especially Max and Chad and the other guys in Nate's football photograph. They'd know more details about him at the time he entered high school, even though they were technically Alex's friends.

I wondered how many of them still lived in the area.

Max had been the star quarterback of the team. A typical prom king in waiting. After he graduated, I'd read somewhere he played college ball in Michigan, then a couple of pro seasons with the Detroit Lions. Too bad an ankle injury put him permanently out of action.

Max was a natural high school celebrity. Gold skin, green eyes and a surprisingly self-conscious smile that had the cheerleaders clustering around him everywhere he went.

He was one of Alex's best buddies. The trio of Max, Alex and Chad had been stars of the football team. When they walked through the halls of our school, the other students fell back in awe. I do remember though, that Max was like Alex: humble, friendly and with no trace of arrogance. Chad was another story.

As I walked across the bridge, past the snow-laden fir trees, I remembered the night of the deadly fire was only a few weeks before city finals. Apparently, they'd just left a grueling three-hour practice. According to gossip I picked up on afterwards, they were pretty buzzed up. There'd been a major showdown between Max and Coach Marshall, who was a real drill-sergeant when it came to football. He had this way of reducing big, tall guys to blubbering babies. Only Max wasn't having any of it this time and he'd walked out of practice. Coach Marshall had threatened to bench him unless he apologized. I'm not sure he ever did, because then the fire happened and everything afterwards was a blur.

I turned off the track onto the street that backed onto the forest. Max had lived on this street with his sister Darla. I kept on walking until I reached their place. A brick and stucco two-story surrounded by giant spruce trees, their branches drooping with heavy snow. Since there was no fence, I could see along the side of the house into the backyard, a huge lawn ringed with giant birch and linden trees. A stone fire pit sat at the center, surrounded by chairs.

The sight gave me quite a jolt – as if I were stepping back in time, one foot in the present and one in a past I'd badly wanted to leave behind me. But if this was the only way to get to the truth about Nate, I was prepared to remember everything, no matter how painful.

I stood in the shelter of a tall tree and found my way back to the last time I'd been in that backyard.

29

THEN

Darla had invited me over to her house one night maybe three months after the fire.

My family had been living with Gran, until the day Mom opened her eyes, crept out from her bed and said *it's time to leave*. That's when we moved back to a smaller bungalow on the edge of the park, close to our old house, because Mom said it reminded her of Alex. Every day he'd skateboarded through the park on his way to school, past the lake and fountain. I was so happy we came back to the area, and had missed the lake and the forest, and all its hidden trails.

After Alex's death our house was too quiet. Like when there's a power outage and everything dies. No electricity to jolt it back into action. I could never replace Alex or bring the same joy and happiness into our house. He was a natural. And me? I barely registered on their radar. I was the introvert, slipping around the place like a shadow.

I know they loved me. Dad ruffled my hair on the way to the kitchen and Mom always kissed me when she handed me my lunch bag in the morning, but the actions seemed detached – mechanical, with no substance behind them. Our family was like a deflated balloon. Collapsed in on itself and shriveled inside. We were afraid to reach out and comfort each other. At the time I guessed my parents never wanted to admit to me how much they craved Alex. How his absence had changed us forever.

We ate by ourselves. Mom at the kitchen table, her laptop open in front of her. She shopped online a lot for gadgets and kitchen tools. Useless, shiny things that arrived in padded envelopes every second day. Dad was always parked in front of the TV, watching hockey or football, while I was holed upstairs in my bedroom longing for some friendly conversation to break the monotony.

I went to Darla's because I couldn't bear the silence any more, and also because Stefan said he'd be there. He'd been in our class about three days, and was the only person who treated me like a human. Probably because he didn't know about Alex's death.

I stopped dead in my tracks as soon as I turned the corner into the back garden, my heart lurching at the sight of the leaping flames. Darla hadn't said anything about a bonfire. I thought we'd just be hanging out on her deck. But Stefan was already there, along with a couple of other kids from class. They took one look at me and kept on chatting as if I didn't exist. Stefan gazed into the fire, hypnotized, his face glowing red and orange in the firelight. He glanced up and smiled, then beckoned me over. I felt suddenly better.

Darla skipped down from her deck carrying a bag of marshmallows in one hand and graham crackers and chocolate in the other.

"Hey, Liv. These smores are gonna be awesome."

She put the bags down and handed me a roasting stick. "Glad you came."

I'd been acting like a mute since the accident, so that thing happened again when I wanted to speak but my body wouldn't let me. All I could do was nod and take the stick. Darla seemed relieved when I edged away and stood next to Stefan. She went right over and joined the other kids and soon they were laughing and talking up a storm. Stefan smiled, stared back into the fire and began talking in a soft voice.

"Did you know the Ancient Egyptians worshipped Ra, the god of fire, but the Koreans chose a goddess instead. Jowangshin, goddess of hearth fires. She actually helped the three death gods send the evil Samajangja to the underworld."

"How do you know all this stuff?"

He shrugged. "I studied it. I read anything to do with the gods and sun and fire. It's cool."

"Fire is cool?"

He glanced sideways at me. "Guess that's a contradiction. Or even an oxymoron. *Cool fire.*"

"You know how to make a smore?"

"I like mine without the chocolate," he said, spearing a marshmallow.

"Are you nuts? That's the best part," I said, building up a double-decker special.

We roasted in silence for a while, then ate our smores.

"You've got chocolate all around your mouth," he said, reaching into his pocket and handing me a tissue.

"Thanks. Sorry, I'm a slob when it comes to eating."

He laughed. "I built a Cyclops mask. Wanna come over and see it?"

I didn't tell him that was the weirdest, most random proposition anyone had ever made to me. "Maybe," I said, just as the deck door slid open, and Max emerged into the firelight. He didn't see me at first.

"Hey, save me some of that junk," he yelled, play-shoving his sister Darla so she dropped the bag of marshmallows on the grass. "Don't tell me that landed on Bennie's doo doo." Bennie was their black poodle.

"You're gross," said Darla, picking up the bag.

Max grabbed a stick. "Hey, Sasha," he said.

She grinned back. "Hey, Max." Everyone knew Sasha had a crush on Max. That was why she was so keen to hang out with Darla.

Max glanced at Stefan and nodded, but when he looked my way, his eyes widened. "Liv," he said in a choked kind of voice. "Didn't know you were coming. I mean, how are things?"

"Okay, I guess."

A long, tense silence followed. All eyes were on us. Then Max dropped the stick. "Sorry, guys. Just remembered. I gotta study for my finals."

He was gone in less than five seconds. I wasn't surprised. I should've known Max couldn't spend more than five seconds in my company. Not when he was probably holding onto guilty secrets about Alex's death.

"Weirdo," said Darla, turning back to the fire.

Sasha was so pissed her chin almost touched the ground. She was probably planning to impress him with the cute way she ate the toasted crust of her marshmallow without getting the gooey inside all over her mouth. She darted a killer look my way and leaned towards Ivy, another girl from our class, to whisper in her ear. Then they both looked my way, their faces set in a smug expression of disapproval. I was so mad I swear I could see the blood flowing through my eyeballs.

"If you've got something to say, why not just come out and say it?" I shouted. Everyone's stick froze in mid-air. All eyes were on me. "Well?"

"We weren't talking about you," said Ivy. "You're just acting paranoid."

I was on a roll. Couldn't stop. "You think I'm stupid? I know what you all think. Well, let me tell you all, my brother Alex was not into drugs. And he did not start the fire. And I'm gonna make it my business to find out who did."

I caught a glimpse of Stefan, his face a pale, horrified mask in the firelight. Then I shrugged my shoulders and threw my stick in the fire. "Well, that's my cue to leave. Thanks for the treats, Darla, and screw the rest of you."

Darla's eyes looked all watery behind her thick glasses. "Sorry, Liv," I heard her say as I stomped away around the side of the house and reached the darkened street, angry with myself for behaving like a petulant brat. But I just knew Max was hiding something, and I had no idea how to get at the truth. I couldn't exactly pin him down and demand he tell me exactly what happened that night in our basement.

I heard the sound of footsteps behind me, and wheeled around. Stefan was running to catch up. When he pulled up, he bent double and grasped his knees, gasping for air.

"Take it easy," I said.

"I gave up smoking a year ago. Guess my lungs still aren't a hundred percent."

"But you're only – what – sixteen?"

"Almost seventeen. Smoked since I was eleven."

"Glad you saw the light."

He looked up at me, his face slick with sweat. "What was that all about? That stuff by the bonfire?"

I kept walking. "That's my business."

"I missed the hot chocolate so I could come after you, so now it's my business."

"You can always go back and get some. I'm sure there's lots left."

He grabbed my shoulder and I stopped in my tracks. "I might just do that but only if you promise to hang out with me after school tomorrow. I'll show you my Cyclops mask and maybe some more sun god stuff."

I nodded my head. "You're pretty weird, but I like that. Now there's something you should know about, if we're going to hang out together."

He forgot about the hot chocolate and walked me all the way home.

30

NOW

My mind fast-forwarded fourteen years to my rapidly freezing toes. I had to keep walking otherwise I'd be in agony when I got home. I took a long look at Max's house and realized I was so tired of secrets. When they stay hidden, they fester like sores. I'd always known Max was hiding something, but I'd never had any idea how to get at the truth. Now I didn't give a damn. I wasn't that introverted, tongue-tied kid anymore and I wouldn't take no for an answer.

I crept around the side of the house. The lights from the family room spilled out onto the snow-covered lawn. I felt a tug in my heart at the sight of the blackened firepit filled with ashes. I'd stood there so many years ago, never imagining I'd experience another, even greater tragedy than the one I'd already suffered.

I pushed the thought of Jack from my head and thought instead of Max. I strode back around the side of the house and rang the front doorbell. The frosted glass door filled with light, then opened revealing a woman in her late fifties. Slim and stylish, she had Max's sea-green eyes and dark curls. She looked at me with a blank stare.

"Can I help you?"

"Mrs. Leonard?"

"Do I know you?"

"I… I'm an old school friend of Max's. Actually, he's also a friend of my husband. I was just passing by and I have a message for him."

She peered outside. "Did you walk here?"

I nodded. "I live in the area. Nearby."

Her brows knit. "Okay. He actually doesn't live here, but you're in luck. He's staying with us for a couple of days en route to Calgary. I'll get him."

Wings of panic fluttered in my chest as I waited, thinking I could turn around and hightail out of there and no one would be any the wiser. But just as my hand reached for the door handle, the floor creaked and a tall, muscular figure strode into the hallway. He stood under the light. Max, still the handsome football player, but now with a slight paunch underneath his black T-shirt and lines of hard living etched under his eyes. Sea-green eyes that narrowed at the sight of me. His full lips drooped at the corners.

"Liv?"

"Max."

"Why are you here?" he said, his head turning slightly as if to check no one was behind him.

"Well, I didn't come by to get an update on your football career."

One foot tapped nervously on the floor. He chewed at his thumbnail. "Nothing to say about that. As you probably know."

"I want information, Max."

He began to shake his head. "That's old history, Liv. I don't know anything. I told you before."

"I want info about Nate Barnett."

His eyes opened wide in an expression that looked like shock.

"Nate is my husband."

He stared at me, unblinking. "I can't believe you married the asshole that dragged you out of that football game when you could barely stand."

I nodded. "We were already married then, so why the look of disbelief?"

His shoulders sagged and his foot tapped faster. "Look, I'm not that kind of person, talking about people behind their back."

"It's okay, Max. You don't need to sugar-coat the truth. Nate's gone missing and I'm trying to figure some things out about him. When you knew him at school, did he ever talk about his family... his parents?"

He leaned back against the wall. "Okay... okay. Guess I owe you something after all these years. So now I'm gonna be out of town for good, I guess I can talk. We all knew Nate, but things were weird with him. He mostly kept to himself, but when we asked him about his family, he always said something bad happened and that's why he was living on his own. That guy had his own apartment and a car. *At seventeen.* Don't know how he got them, but he said they'd left him enough money to put himself through school."

"So you just assumed they were dead?"

Max chewed at his thumbnail as if he was really uncomfortable even talking about that time in his life. "Dead or he'd left them behind because they were deadbeats. No one really knew."

"Know where he was getting the money from?"

Max shook his head. "Sorry, Liv. But I still can't believe you'd end up with that guy."

"Why do you say that?"

"Everyone knew he was into bad stuff. Drugs. Gambling. We never had proof, but we always suspected. One time, just after my eighteenth birthday, I was out at Bar Q with Chad. We were sitting outside on the patio and Nate walks by in his football jersey with two other guys. One was this short weasel of a guy. So thin you'd swear he hadn't eaten for days, and all shaky like he was coming down from some kind of high. The other guy was some slick-looking dude who looked like he'd knife you if you glanced at him the wrong way. I only went to Nate's apartment once, but those guys were there. Maybe he lived with them. Who knows? But he'd make them leave when we got there. One thing I can tell you, Liv. They were the type of guys you just knew to steer clear away from."

"That's all you know about him?"

"That's it. After Alex… Alex's death, we didn't hang out together any more. Then I lost touch with everyone when I went to university in Michigan."

"Did you ever get the names of those two guys?"

Max narrowed his eyes at me. "Not sure. Maybe the dark-haired guy was Sonny or something. Hey… Liv… don't even think about finding those lowlifes. They're bad news. Don't get into that. Let the cops handle it."

I shook my head. "I know. I'm not crazy, Max."

"That's good." He sighed a long, deep sigh and put out a hand. Touched my arm. "I thought about you a lot, Liv. I always wanted to tell you that Alex was the best friend I ever had. I think about him all the time. I have so many regrets, Liv. The biggest is that I didn't stick around that night."

"You mean the night of the fire?" Now the blood was racing in my ears. "So, you didn't see what happened?"

He shook his head, his eyes trained on the floor. "Got a call from my girlfriend. Remember Tanya?"

I nodded. Tanya was the possessive type. Kept tabs on Max's every movement.

"I had to leave. Turns out she was pregnant. I promised I'd stand by her. But she ended up losing the baby."

His eyes filled with tears. It was hard to believe the heartthrob quarterback's life had been so complicated.

"I'm sorry, Max. Glad you leveled with me after all this time."

He started towards me. "The thing is, Liv, Nate was in your basement the night of the fire."

I felt shaky and reached out to the wall to brace myself. Nate had never talked about being in our basement that night.

"I never ever remember him being at our house."

"He was there. Trying to get some card game going, but Alex wasn't having it."

"And then?"

"Tanya called and I left. Chad and Nate were still there. Maybe a couple of other guys – Andy Kim and some other guy I can't remember came by as I left."

"Did you ever ask any of them what happened?"

"Like I said, nobody would talk about it afterwards."

"Is Andy still in the city?"

He shook his head. "Think he got into car sales. Left the city long ago. I don't know where he went."

"What about Chad?"

"I hear he's around. He has a band. They came back from British Columbia and did a few gigs around here. He also has a music store somewhere in the west end."

I felt a surge of hope. "Maybe I'm going to pay him a visit next," I said, turning to go. My heart was heavy. It gave me a sick feeling to know that Nate was in our basement the night of the fire. I was gradually getting the impression that bad things happened when Nate Barnett was around.

"Watch out, though. Chad is still an asshole."

"I'll deal with him," I said, opening the door. "But who knows? Maybe he's all grown up now like the rest of us."

"Maybe. Life has a strange way of knocking all the bullshit out of you."

I turned to him again, thankful he'd had nothing to do with Alex's death. Of all my brother's friends, I'd always liked Max the most. "Thanks, Max. Thanks for the help."

He held the door open. "Strange how you have all these dreams at high school. Big, bright hopes for your future. Then life comes and smacks you in the face just to remind you that reality sucks."

"I know what you mean. But I hope I can find a new reality soon."

A smile lit up his face. "Me too, Liv. Got a coaching offer with the Calgary Stampeders. It's a new beginning."

"Hope it works out."

"Look after yourself, Liv."

"I will," I said, stepping out into the starlit night and heading along the crescent.

According to Max, maybe Chad or Andy had the answer to what happened to Alex. Perhaps they knew more about the real Nate Barnett and whether he played a part in starting the fire that killed Alex and destroyed my family. Just like he'd ruined our marriage.

But that same, dark thought hovered at the back of my mind. Maybe, just maybe, if Nate was that crooked, was it possible he was somehow connected with our son Jack's disappearance? I shuddered at the terrible thought.

31

The Weather Channel issued a heavy snowfall warning the next day, and I prayed I wouldn't be forced to shovel the entire driveway just to get my car out. I stood at the bay window, watching the swirling snow. Heidi's driveway was deserted. No sign of life. No sign of Toby.

She hadn't surfaced since the previous night when I'd got back home from my walk and saw her standing inside her front doorway in full makeup and a figure-skimming blue dress, her hair cascading in carefully styled waves across her shoulders. A line of luxury cars had stretched along the drive, illuminated by the bright display of twinkling lights. She waited, shivering at the door until a glossy, black Lincoln pulled in behind a white Mercedes. Two guys and a woman got out, the men in dark suits and the woman in a fashionable camel coat. After many hugs and stooped air kisses, Heidi ushered them inside, but not before I caught sight of a glittering chandelier – heard the low buzz of people talking. It seemed a low voltage party. No loud music, no heightened voices, and strangely, no laughter.

I dug my nails into my palms. *Had she given up her boy in exchange for some fake party lifestyle? And what on earth was she doing in there that made such a cold-hearted decision worthwhile?*

Was she tired of being a mother? Maybe all she wanted was to party all night and sleep in all day.

And as if to justify my hunch, a pink Molly Maid car ploughed through the snowdrifts and pulled into the empty driveway. Four cleaners emerged, armed with buckets and cleaning supplies. Most likely ready to get the place in good shape for the next party, whenever that might be.

A large furniture delivery van arrived just after the cleaners. The delivery guys unloaded high-end chairs and a massive wooden bed frame – just the latest of a constant stream of deliveries that arrived on a daily basis since Heidi had moved in.

I took a good look at my own living room. The style could be summarized as *boring suburban. Inoffensive. Bland.* Beige leather couch and chair, light oak dining table and chairs upholstered in a drab gray stripe. Nate had taken charge of the décor. I didn't have time or the inclination. After Jack was gone, I could've sat on a wooden box and eaten from a TV table for all I cared about my surroundings.

Back then, I was numb. My sensations anaesthetized. I dragged myself through life as if I was lost in one of those dreams when you can't move your feet because they're stuck fast in some kind of sticky substance, and you can't cry out your pain because your voice is trapped deep inside you.

That thought brought me right back to Toby. I thought maybe I should call Rick again just to check if maybe he knew where the little boy was. I wandered into the kitchen and took his card from the fridge door where it was pinned under the Niagara Falls fridge magnet. First, I got a busy tone. Then the call went straight to voicemail and announced that his mailbox was full.

The *ping* of an incoming text distracted me. I'd try him again later.

It was Stefan.

That guy must have had a sixth sense about me.

> Hope you're okay. My buddy Raj – Officer Chandran from Missing Persons – will drop by this evening to talk to you about getting a judge's order to access Nate's cell phone records.

I texted back:

> Sounds good. Thx.

At least I might get some idea of Nate's movements, maybe even find out where he'd gone. I checked my phone. Ten o'clock. The waiting was unbearable. I wanted to move. Get things done and my mind was definitely not on the lunch box project. Besides, I'd sent Min pictures of the latest drawings and she'd been over the moon with them. For once, I was actually ahead of schedule.

By late afternoon, the snow had turned into a full-on blizzard. When I looked out from the window, I could barely make out shapes more than a few feet ahead. Just the blurred shapes of trees blown sideways by the wind. Great drifts of snow butted up against my garage door. Good luck digging myself out later, I thought, realizing I'd never get out to see Chad today. To make matters worse,

Officer Chandran had called to say he couldn't make it later because of the blizzard.

"If you send me an email confirmation of his phone number, I'll see if they'll accept scanned and signed documents. Keep an eye on your email and I'll get back to you as soon as I can."

I paced the house like a caged tiger, then made myself a cup of hot chocolate and sat down at the breakfast counter, opposite the three tall windows that looked out into the backyard. I could hear the wind whistling down the fireplace chimney in the family room, see the trees bending in the wind. Hopefully, there wouldn't be any broken trees crashing into roofs. It had happened before in blizzards and ice storms.

I searched Nate Barnett again. His old corporate profile came up first. With his groomed hair, snowy shirt collar, dark suit and smiling handsome face he looked every inch the perfect professional. Seeing him like that tugged at my heart. This was the Nate I'd married. The quiet, kind, considerate man. Or maybe I wanted so badly to believe in that person who really only existed on a corporate promo page.

A few other mentions were related to his recommendations for various pharmaceutical brands. Another showed him receiving a sales award. After that, nothing. I scrolled through many pages with no results. It was as if he didn't exist outside his job. Finally, I was about to give up when I came across a post from about fifteen years previous. It was a spotlight on the most promising young high school football players. Alex was up there along with Max. Someone had interviewed each one of them. My heart ached when I read Alex's responses, filled with anticipation and hope for his future. Further down I found Nate. Fresh-faced and smiling, he credited his father, Brian, for inspiring him to excel in football. Was that what he'd always wished for? A father who would sit in the stands and cheer him on at every game? Just like my dad had done with Alex.

Sixteen-year-old Nate with his lively expression and shining eyes bore little resemblance to the blank-eyed, quiet guy who'd left on a business trip a few weeks ago.

How had he, at sixteen, managed to steal a dead boy's identity and conceal the truth from everyone? He was either extremely desperate to make a fresh start, or utterly ruthless. A guy without a conscience.

I hoped to God it wasn't the latter.

Scanning the remaining players, I came across Chad, his jet-black hair slicked back from his pale oval face.

I sat back on the couch sipping a strong espresso. Chad was my next target. According to Max, Chad, Nate and Andy had been the last people to see Alex alive.

I closed my eyes and let my mind slip back to the last time I'd run into Chad. Fourteen years ago.

32

THEN

I'd gotten into the habit of leaving school at lunchtime to go to my favorite place in the nearby park.

The place I called the ice palace was actually a glass conservatory nestled among the trees, with a lily pond and fountain in front. Naked girl sculptures reclined on the edges of the pond. Molten hot in summer, they basked under the hot, prairie sun enjoying the steady sprinkle of water from a whole network of fountains. Their bare stone toes trailed in the cool water in summer and grazed the scum-line of the drained pond in winter.

I'd usually sit on the stone bench in the conservatory and wish I lived there. White sculptures in the glass cases smiled at me like they cared. Ceramic bears climbed a bronze log, an ivory bust of the Pope stared out onto the frozen tree line, and the pale winter sky was visible through the glass-domed roof. That room was so warm in winter, and cool in summer.

That particular day, I needed to settle my head. Think about my new friend, Stefan. Maybe even do some writing. I had my bicycle with me, so it was only a fifteen-minute ride to and from school. Through the gates, past the pavilion and round the duck pond. On the way there, I'd recognized a few other people from school breaking into the kids' adventure playground to goof around on the play structures. I didn't want them to see me, the loser loner, so I took the deserted forest trail towards the lily pond.

I had this half-finished sci-fi story about a brilliant scientist who discovers a dark secret about the Hadron Collider and then is kidnapped and imprisoned in a remote cave to keep her quiet. I read it to Alex a week before he died. I'd never shown my writing to anyone before. I remember feeling lightheaded, my hands clammy and my heart thumping. But he was blown away.

"I never knew you were this good," he said, his trademark wide grin lighting up his face. "You gotta finish this, Liv. Then you can get it into the school newspaper."

"You like it?" I said, feeling like the top of my head would whirl off with excitement.

"I love it. It's amazing how you mix science with action and you create a really cool world." He handed it back to me. "Promise me I'll be your manager when you become a best-selling author."

After the fire, I shoved it back into the drawer of my bedside table, but after I met Stefan, I felt that old urge creeping back again and I'd pulled out the old notebook.

I planned to do some free writing. Try to get back into that pretend world again. I'd left the scientist alone and scared in that cave, so I needed to somehow rescue her.

I was just pulling up to the glassed-in conservatory, when I heard raised voices. A girl burst from out of the tree cover, her face like thunder. Marnie something or other. I recognized her from math class. She bleached her hair white-blonde, missed every second class, and was always texting when the teacher put notes up.

"Asshole," she yelled to someone following her as she strode out towards the lily pond, zipping up her hoodie and shoving her hands into her pockets. A guy ran out into the open. Chad Hayes, my brother Alex's football buddy. He was pissed, his face flushed and angry under his black curtain of hair.

"Bitch. Teaser," he yelled, until he saw me watching, open-mouthed, notebook in hand. He dropped his arms and backed away.

Marnie stopped dead in her tracks and watched him retreat. Then she doubled over with laughter. "Always knew you were just a chicken, Hayes. 'Cos only cowards hit women." She turned my way so I could see the bruise on her cheek. "Your brother was too good to hang out with this loser, Liv. Too bad *he* didn't burn instead. He's a piece of crap. You should ask him what he knows about the fire in your basement. You might be shocked." Then she spat in his direction and headed off towards the children's playground. Chad threw me a look that could kill, then turned tail and ran the other way towards the forest trail, disappearing before I had a chance to reach him and ask what Marnie was talking about.

I never saw either of them again after that. Marnie dropped out of school and so did Chad. They even skipped their grad. After I met Nate, any conversation about high school was strictly off limits, and I hadn't heard any gossip or rumors about them from anyone.

Until yesterday.

Because, according to Max, Chad had emerged from seclusion, gone to British Columbia and made some kind of name for himself in indie music. I checked him out on Google. He'd released a couple of albums that made a moderate impact on the West Coast indie scene, then laid down some interesting YouTube videos in which he wandered up and down desolate, pebble-strewn beaches or walked across fields filled with chickens and sheep, or stepped out from the doorway of a rustic timber cabin. Most of them contained obvious symbolism such as white doves flying up into the sky or flies buzzing around a grisly carcass, or burned-out stumps of trees swarming with termites, and in all of them he wore the same rusty-looking jacket and cowboy hat.

He'd reinvented himself as a pro musician. Now he was back to conquer the prairie music scene and run his very own music store.

This I had to see.

As long as it stopped snowing so that I could dig my way out of my garage.

33

NOW

After a night spent tossing and turning, I woke to the sound of a shovel scraping my driveway. I threw the covers back, hurried to the window and pulled the curtains aside. Down below, under a bright blue sky was Stefan. Dressed in a red woolen hat and heavy parka, he shoveled like a madman, and was already halfway down the drive. I threw on my sweats and a heavy jacket, ran into the bathroom and splashed my face, then tore downstairs.

By the time I opened the garage door, he'd cleared everything almost to the street. I grabbed my shovel and went out to join him.

"You didn't have to do this," I yelled above the grating of his shovel.

He stopped for a moment and rested his hands on the handle. Two spots of red shone on his cheeks. He grinned. "No worries. This is better than a workout and cheaper than the gym."

"Thanks so much. I'm not sure how long it would've taken me to dig myself out from all this. Can I make you breakfast?"

"Got bacon?"

I shook my head. "I have eggs."

"Okay. Coffee, two cream and scrambled eggs on rye."

"You got it," I said, hanging the shovel back up and noticing a truck pull up behind him at the lake house. Two guys got out and unloaded snowblowers and shovels. Of course, Heidi would have the best service possible. She'd already lost one night of partying to the blizzard last night. Thoughts of Toby crossed my mind, but Rick hadn't called me back. I pushed the thought away, trying not to let panic overtake rational thinking. Toby wasn't Jack. *I'm sure he's fine, right?*

Soon the kitchen was fragrant with the scent of freshly made coffee and Stefan leaned against the breakfast counter wiping his hair and face with a towel. I stirred the scrambled eggs and waited for the toast to pop up. Sunlight streamed through the windows, and for the first time in ages I felt like this could be a normal, happy day. I hummed as I fixed the plates and put out fresh cut melon and strawberries.

Stefan threw the towel over his stool and picked up a knife and fork. "Looks great." I turned away before he saw the warm blush spread across my face.

"Did you say one sugar?" I said, pouring the coffee.

"You forgot," he said, chewing and talking at the same time. "I have a sweet tooth. Three, please."

I slid his cup along to him and watched as he finished off the eggs in record time, while I nibbled at a single piece of toast.

"Don't you ever make breakfast?"

He shook his head and wiped his mouth with a napkin. "Don't usually have time. Sometimes I grab a donut, maybe even a breakfast sandwich if I'm ahead of schedule."

"Same here," I said, picking at my eggs. "Often I can't be bothered to cook. But I have plenty of Pop Tarts in case of emergency."

He rested his elbows on the counter and checked his phone. "Zero nutritional value, but they taste so good."

"I've had a thing about them since I was a kid."

A slight frown line notched the skin between his eyebrows. "On a more serious note, Raj says he might have some info from the phone records by tomorrow morning. How are you holding out?"

I put down my cup and met his eyes. "Okay I guess, but it's been hard to keep my mind on work. I feel like I'm on pins and needles all the time."

"That's understandable. You guys have been married quite a while."

I thought I detected an edge to his tone when he spoke those words. Conversation froze. An awkward silence descended between us. Embarrassed, I slid down from the stool and made a show of clearing the dishes away. There was no way I could tell Stefan about Nate's stolen identity. Not until I'd had the chance to confront Nate about it. Face to face.

"I ran into Max Leonard," I said, turning away from him so he wouldn't spot the lie.

I heard the scrape of the stool legs as he got down and came towards me. He tapped me on the shoulder. "Liv, this is me, Stefan. Did you really run into him or did you go out and find him?"

I turned around to face him. "Okay. Maybe I did take a walk by his place. What's the harm in that?"

He placed his hands on my shoulders, his lips curving into a smile. "I guess you didn't knock on the door then?"

I felt a smile creeping in. "Well, maybe."

He shook his head. "Liv. You need to be careful."

"I have to know, Stefan. I need to find out about Nate and what he's been up to. And I'm discovering that I really didn't know too much about him at all."

He dropped his hands and turned to grab his hat. "I do remember something about you, Liv. You're a determined woman, and I know I can't do much to stop you once you've got an idea in your head. Just be careful, that's all I can tell you."

"There's something else, Stefan," I said, following him out into the hallway. "Max thinks Nate was into drugs or gambling to support himself in high school. Said he hung out with two guys. One short, really skinny guy with a sort of hunched-over posture, and a taller dark-haired guy named Sonny."

The abrupt way Stefan stopped dead in his tracks sent a tremor of fear through me. When he turned to look at me, his expression was deathly serious.

"You know them, Stefan? Tell me if you do."

He pulled his coat from the bannister. "I'll say it again, Liv, stop doing your own investigation. Stay clear and let Raj do the work. Just hang in there and we'll be sure to contact you as soon as we find something out."

I felt a rush of anger. "You mean like the police did with Jack's disappearance? Told me to sit back and wait like a good little woman. I listened to them and now I'm still here waiting, five years later, with no sign of my boy."

I couldn't stop myself. I doubled over, hands on my knees to steady myself as I tried to hold back the grief. I clapped a hand across my mouth. I couldn't break down now. Stefan wrapped his arms around me in a tight embrace. I rested my head against his chest, my whole body shaking as I bit back the tears.

"I'm sorry, Liv. Sorry for being such a smug, self-satisfied jerk. I can't imagine what you've been through. What you're still going through."

He held me there until I calmed down, then let me go gently before pulling on his coat. "I'll get Raj to come over and you can fill him in on all this new info. I'll tell him to keep this case top of his list."

"Sorry to fall apart on you, but the pain of losing your child never goes away."

"Don't ever hide anything from me, Liv. I want you to trust me completely. And you know I'll never judge you."

"That's a big comfort to me, Stefan."

He paused and thought for a moment. "I mean, I wish there was something more I could say or do to make it hurt a bit less, and I feel so powerless because there's nothing." He reached out his hand and cupped my chin. "But know I'm just around the corner if you ever need me."

I smiled. "It feels good that you're here."

He held my gaze for a while. "And you don't know how good it is to see you again."

"Hey – thanks for shoveling the driveway."

"You're welcome. Thanks for the breakfast."

"Just leave the invoice in the mailbox," I said as he stepped out into the daylight.

After I'd watched his car pull away, I checked my phone for the address of Chad's music store. Stefan was right about one thing. Once I had something in my head, I wasn't about to let anyone stop me. Not even Stefan. In fact, his urging me to stop had made me wonder what he was hiding. It seemed clear he recognized Sonny and his sidekick from my description. So I was even more determined to get to the bottom of this mystery. And now my driveway was clear, the first place I was headed was to see Chad and find out what he knew about my mysterious husband, Nate. Or should I say, Jack?

34

Later that afternoon, as I pulled out from my garage, I made a mental note to hire a snow clearing service. I couldn't rely on Stefan to help me out every time there was a heavy snowfall. He was a busy guy. And all this sudden urgency made me realize I had no time to waste if I wanted to find Nate on *my* terms. The thought of him simply appearing back home as if nothing was wrong, was almost terrifying. I had no idea how I'd face him without giving everything away.

I needed to find out as much as I could about him. Needed to know if I had to pack up and get out of the house because I might actually be in danger.

I eased my foot onto the gas and pushed through the heavy covering of snow. The side roads hadn't been plowed yet, but the temperature outside had risen to well above zero, turning the snow to slush, which made for slow going. And the roads were their usual mess after a heavy snowfall. There were smaller cars stuck in heavy drifts, and speedsters going way too fast for the road conditions, then spinning off into the ditch when they tried to brake.

"Doesn't matter what the conditions are," my dad had always said. "Slow and steady always wins the race." That had been in the good times. Before the fire, when Dad had been this reliable, sunny guy always there to cheer me on. To shake me out of my teenage angst. To pep me up when I was down on myself. Alex's accident had changed all that. Wiped away all his joy.

I was so lost in bitter reflection, I hadn't noticed my speed creeping upwards, swerving just in time to avoid a red SUV that had slowed down for a stoplight. The guy gave me the finger as I slid to a halt beside him, my brakes screeching in protest.

Crazy woman driver, he mouthed.

I turned away.

Pull yourself together, I told myself, slumping back against the headrest.

For the rest of the ride, I diverted myself by running over Officer Chandran's visit. He'd arrived promptly at noon. A trim man in his forties with a fatherly manner and the kind of easy humor that put me immediately at ease. After answering the requisite questions about when and where I'd last seen Nate, he questioned me about any other connections or people Nate may have contacted. I told him about everything – the gambling, the lies about his job, the unexplained business trips. Everything *except* Nate's stolen identity. Finally, he had me sign some forms. Explained he needed them to apply for a warrant to access Nate's cell phone records. There was no guarantee that would help, but he assured me it was the best chance of locating Nate, wherever he was hiding, and assured me he'd get back to me by the end of the week.

That went a long way to easing my mind just a little, though I was starting to get jumpy every time the doorbell rang, or there was a sudden noise outside. I wasn't sure what I'd do if Nate just arrived back home unannounced. It would be like letting a stranger into my house.

One I was unsure I could trust.

I crossed over the half-frozen river into the west end of the city. Chad's music store was located in a hipster area of town, a quaint, older neighborhood, its main road lined with artisan bakeries, organic produce stores, recycled clothing boutiques and tattoo parlors. I passed through streets of renovated late nineteenth and early twentieth century houses with clapboard siding, fancy cupolas and wide front verandas. It seemed like Chad had grown tired of middle-class suburbia and sought out a more *authentic* living experience. One more suited to a trendy, indie musician who needed to cultivate a certain cachet.

Finally, I pulled up to a small storefront, its sign written in bright psychedelic letters. *Archangel Music.*

Chad saw me coming.

One minute I was looking through the window at a guy with the unmistakable swath of jet-black hair hanging across his forehead and over one eye. He hadn't changed his hairstyle since high school.

Next minute, I was stepping into a cluttered music store, its walls festooned with a haphazard array of guitars, accessories and music posters. A skinny kid with cropped hair and an Alice Cooper T-shirt stood behind the counter stringing a guitar. He darted a quick look towards me, then went back to winding the keys tighter.

"Where's Chad?"

"Out," he mumbled.

"He was here. I just saw him through the window."

"Nah. Don't think so. He's on a delivery."

"When's he coming back?"

He shrugged his shoulders. "Couldn't say."

Okay, I thought. *You want to play it that way?*

"Well, thanks for all your help," I said, turning to leave. "It's been a real pleasure."

He barely flinched as I stepped towards the door, though his eyes flickered towards a curtain that covered an arched opening, probably the entrance to a back room. Right next to a stand displaying guitar picks and strings. I stopped. "On second thoughts, I need a new pick."

His eyes snapped upwards. "You do?"

"I play the blues. Snapped the last couple of picks playing a crazy riff."

"Huh?"

I sidled towards the display case, keeping my eyes on that archway, listening for telltale sounds. Within seconds I heard the drag of shoes on floorboards behind the curtain, and the slow whine of a blues guitar playing on a phone. The kid turned to hang the guitar on a hook and I made my move. Slipped through the drapes into a stuffy, windowless back room that smelled of musty old wood and marijuana. A lava lamp shed electric blue light on the walls and transformed the stark white face of Chad Hayes into something from a German vampire movie.

"What the f—" He moved behind a long workbench.

"Long time no see, Chad."

"What are you doing here, Liv? Looking for tickets to my next gig?"

"Just dropped by to ask how your music career's going. Didn't you see me through the window?"

"As a matter of fact, I didn't."

"Strange. I could have sworn you made a real quick exit to the back room. I'm wondering if it's part of your HR strategy to train your clerks to lie."

"Very funny. Jay thought I'd gone out on a delivery. He's a good kid."

"Doesn't look like you're too happy to see me."

He began to fill an open box with packages of guitar strings. "I tend to shy away from anything to do with high school. Too many bad associations. I've tried to erase it from my memory."

"So, I take it you don't attend high school reunions?"

He took a deep breath. "For me, high school was like a three-year prison sentence with no time off for good behavior."

"Even being on the football team?"

"That was the only good part."

"About the tickets. Maybe I'll take two. You remember Nate Barnett?"

He looked away and shrugged.

"He's my husband."

His head snapped back towards me. "You married Nate Barnett? You gotta be kidding?"

I moved closer. "I'm dead serious. Why? Something wrong with that?"

"He never told me he was married. In fact, I distinctly remember him saying he was single."

The light flickered, throwing quivering shadows on the wall. Time shifted as if the threads that tethered me to reality were fraying and I was about to float off into a bad dream.

Was I Nate's guilty secret?

"When? When did you last see him?"

"Oh – maybe three months ago. My band did a gig in the sports bar at the casino. He came up to me at the break. Said he liked my music. I told him to fuck off."

"Why? I thought you guys were all friends."

"*Were* is the operative word." I noticed he was wearing black eyeliner, which made his pallid face even creepier and added to his gothic look.

"So why would you talk to him like that?"

"Don't you know anything, Liv?"

"What am I supposed to know? I met him in Toronto. He was a salesman. Respectable. Successful."

"You hung around with the nerds. Always had your nose in a book. No wonder you don't know anything. You need street smarts in this world, Liv. Real life is fucked up. It's not a fantasy world. You gotta keep your eyes open and trust no one."

"Maybe it's only fucked up for some people."

He placed his hands flat on the workbench. "Look at me, Liv, and tell me your life has been all sweetness and joy since you married Nate."

I turned away, all my bravado ebbing away. "Parts of it have been a disaster."

"See. Told you. That guy's an operator. A liar. He has no conscience. Sorry to break your happy little family bubble. I was friends with him, but none of us really knew much about him or what he was up to."

"At least he doesn't beat women up."

Chad's face froze. "That day in the park. With Marnie. You saw us?"

"Her face was bruised."

"Yeah, and she spread the rumor around school that I'd caused those bruises. I couldn't ever go back to school again. They'd have expelled me."

"And you'd have deserved it."

"I never hit her. You gotta believe me, Liv. I'm not that kind of guy. Her dad did it. He was a bad drunk. After a few beers, he became a violent asshole. He'd start shouting and smacking her around. I felt sorry for her. I let her stay at my place a few times. Then I wanted to break up with her, and she threatened to finish me with everyone, so she accused me of hitting her."

"Why should I believe you?"

"Suit yourself. I know in my own heart what really happened and I'm at peace with it. And maybe she did me a favor. I hated school anyway. Always wanted to be a musician, and I can do it full-time now because I had a good run in BC and if the gigs dry up here, I have this store to keep me going. That's the one good thing my dad did for me before he passed away. He left me this store."

"You still didn't explain why you told Nate to fuck off."

He began to tape up the box, then stopped and looked me in the eye, as if daring me to listen. "You really want to know about Nate?"

"That's why I'm here," I said, leaning across the table and looking him straight in the eyes.

"Okay, Liv. You asked for it. This is what I know about your so-called respectable husband. At eighteen he was a compulsive gambler who funded his addiction by dealing drugs. A lot of guys at school owed him money from getting sucked into his card games. Then he'd force them to deal drugs as a way of paying him back. He'd give them some freebies and get them hooked, so he always had a hold on them. He loved to *own* people. Said it gave him a buzz. But we were small pickings compared to what he had going on outside of school."

"And what was that, exactly?"

He pushed the sealed box towards a stack of similar ones. "I might have been young and careless then, but I wasn't stupid. Everyone knew Nate was mixed up with the wrong people, and I wanted nothing to do with them. All I know is he hung out with some real gangster types."

"Was there someone called Sonny?"

He dropped the tape on the table with a loud clatter. "You know Sonny?"

"Just heard something about him and Nate."

"I'm gonna do you a big favor, Liv, because we go back all the way to high school, and I really respected your brother. If you ever run into that Sonny guy, turn right around and run the other way as fast as you can."

"Is that what you did the night Alex died, Chad? You left him there to die?"

He swept a box under his arm and stomped towards the back door. "I don't want to talk about it."

"Or maybe Nate was the one who did?"

He whirled around. "You'd better get out of here, Liv. I've come a long way since that night and I'm not going back. I told you all I know about your jerk of a husband."

"You and Nate were the last people to see Alex alive. You must know something."

"I swear I left before the fire, Liv. Marnie called me, crying. Said her dad was in one of his drunken rages again and she had nowhere to sleep. So I left. A couple of other guys were still there with Nate. Andy Kim and that other loser, Renny Beaumont." He pulled himself up so tall he seemed to tower over me. "Come to think of it, Liv, maybe you should just ask your lying husband about that night, because I've said all I'm going to say and now I'm asking you to leave."

I held tightly to the edge of the bench. "I'm not going until you level with me, Chad."

"Have a nice night, then," he said, steadying the box under his arm and opening the back door. "Because I have a delivery to make."

I shoved my card into his pocket. "Here's my contact info. Call me if you decide to come clean, Chad. You'll make better music because you'll finally be at peace with yourself."

"Fuck off, Olivia. You and your asshole husband."

He swept out and the door slammed shut, leaving me standing there like a fool. I hadn't learned anything of any value here, except that my husband was more dangerous than I'd ever thought possible.

35

I read a quote somewhere: *Grief is like living two lives. One is where you pretend everything is okay, and the other is where your heart screams in pain.*

When I left Chad's store, I felt like I was poised on the razor's edge between those two lives. I'd spent fourteen years thinking a whole lot about grief. And with all the new uncertainty about Nate, the pain was returning in waves. Now I'd lost my husband – or the man I thought was my husband – as well as my child. Eight years of marriage wiped out in the space of a few days. I'd been living in a false dream world, my mind occupied by the loss of my brother and son.

When I was a teen, thoughts of Alex would crowd into my head. I retreated into myself, until Stefan came around and talked me out of my depression. But after Jack was gone, memories of him would suddenly emerge and knock the wind out of me. Worse thing was, I never knew when or where that feeling might return.

It happened again after visiting Chad.

I didn't feel like heading back home, so I stopped by the art supply store, usually a happy place for me. The smell of paint, paper and turpentine always got my creative juices going. I loved discovering new paint colors with exotic names: *caput mortuum*, a dark violet-reddish brown, *tourmaline green, sfumato*, a fine, gray misty color like smoke. I'd say the names out loud, relishing the delectable sound of the words. But I needed brushes, and was sorting through a display case, picking ones with fine tips. Perfect for intricate details: the snaps on a parka, the *Star Wars* sticker on a lunch box, the texture of a blueberry muffin. The shine on Parker's bright auburn curls.

Then I saw the kid.

About seven years old, hair a cap of glorious red curls. His slight, narrow shoulders hunched under a navy parka, the hood lined with bright green silky material. He was sorting through piles of sketchbooks.

Jack would've been the same age as this boy. Would he have inherited my artistic streak? Or would he have been more like Nate? Good with numbers and patterns? With an eye for logic and symmetry?

A battle started raging in my head. *How could I hate everything about Nate? How could I reconcile the Nate I knew with the Nate that Chad and Max had described?* He'd been so patient and kind with me when we first met. And we'd had a wondrous child together. Maybe going back to gambling was his way of dealing with the grief of losing Jack. Heaven knows, we hadn't been much comfort to each other. Turning away, rather than towards one another. And yet, Chad said Nate had denied my existence. So how could I trust him? Unless Chad was lying.

Nate was an enigma. A puzzle. A contradiction. How could I reconcile what I'd heard about him and what I'd seen day after day? Year after year? Was it all a lie? What was real? What was forced by circumstance? And were all those bad things he'd been into at school, just part of a troubled teenage phase that he'd finally left behind? Maybe that was why he never wanted to talk about high school.

At that moment, the boy picked up a sketchbook, and I pictured myself coming to the store with Jack. Thought about what we'd have bought together. We'd spend time looking over all the paints and sketchbooks and brushes. I'd let him choose a paintbox and drawing tablet. We'd make plans to paint later.

But as soon as the boy turned his face, I knew it wasn't him. The line of the nose, the swell of his top lip, the clear brown eyes. All wrong.

Not Jack.

Hopes dashed once more.

I put the brushes back and ran out of the store, tears trickling down my face.

By the time I got home, I was a mess. Eyes red and swollen, jumping at the slightest noise when I pulled into the garage. Also, I'd been conscious of a car that seemed to be tailing me the moment I pulled into our street, which had made me drive faster than usual so I almost overshot my driveway. As I'd thought, the car had stopped in front of Heidi's house.

I climbed out from my car and saw the unmistakable long, lean snout of the Dodge Viper. Its front doors swung open and my heart flipped when I saw the men emerging from it. Two guys silhouetted against the bright white lights that decked the trees. One of them tall and dark-haired in a black overcoat, the other short and scrawny with stooped shoulders and a limp. *Could it be a coincidence?* Or was one of those guys Sonny? Nate's gangster buddy that I'd been hearing about from everyone. Were these the two men Nate had known since his teens? And why were they showing up here? Now? Right opposite my house – Nate's house. *Did they know he lived just yards away?*

My question was answered within seconds when they stopped and turned to look in my direction. The tall guy leaned towards the shorter one, listened to him whisper something, his eyes focused on Nate's empty car. I remained in the shelter of darkness until they shrugged and turned to walk towards Heidi's place. No wonder Rick had wanted his son out of there. Away from the drugs and the gambling that attracted lowlifes like Sonny and his friend. And where was Toby? I still hadn't seen any sign of him.

That thought was enough to send me flying inside. I double-locked all the doors and turned off all the lamps at the front of the house. Being so close to the lake house and the people inside it, made me feel even more uneasy about staying home alone. In semi-darkness I used the light from the fridge to pour myself a large glass of wine, then I sat in the family room in total darkness relieved only by the glow of my laptop screensaver. I took a long drink and leaned my head back against the sofa.

All the puzzle pieces were starting to fit together, but I still couldn't figure out what was real and what was simple coincidence. Had I imagined Nate stopping to watch Heidi when she arrived? Had she really looked at him as if she knew him? Why were his no-good ex-buddies hanging around here? Were they looking for him? And was that why he hadn't come back? Was he afraid to? Why? My mind was in complete turmoil. My thoughts racing ahead. I had to slow down. Had to concentrate on finding out the facts carefully and methodically as I had been doing up until now.

I closed my eyes and thought about what Chad had told me. He'd said two other guys were with Nate and Alex the night of the fire. Andy Kim and Renny Beaumont.

Maybe they could shed some light on what went on that night, because for some strange reason, I had this feeling that everything – every tragedy in my life – had somehow started with that one.

36

THEN

Back in eleventh grade, just after Alex's death, we had a new English teacher for the second half of the year. Our regular teacher, Mr. Koschuk, was away for an operation. Nobody knew what kind of procedure, but there was plenty of speculation; most of it related to his digestive system.

That particular day the new teacher arrived, it took twice as long to do the attendance because Kim, Jordan and Dom, the resident class clowns, decided it was a good idea to flick paper pellets back and forth until our sub clicked off the computer and swooped to the front of the class.

She'd written her name in bold letters across the whiteboard. *Miss Glow.* And she lived up to her name. Dangling earrings made of bright red feathers. Matching scarlet lipstick. Red and blue beaded pinafore dress over long-sleeved, floaty cream shirt. Blue tights. A life-sized doll, blazing with color. Totally unlike Mr. Koschuk with his rusty brown cord jacket and saggy-assed jeans.

"I'm so honored to be here," she said in a warm, singsong voice. "In my other life I'm a writer and a film maker. I'm dying to share some fun ways to get you all

219

writing. Because, after all, if you understand how literature is created, you'll have an easier time interpreting it."

I couldn't believe what I was hearing, and as she continued, I realized no teacher had ever talked with such understanding about the creative process. By the time she'd finished urging us to unlock our imagination and be bold and fearless when using language, I was ready to try out anything she suggested.

Later that day I decided to take out my writers' notebook and make some observations. I was usually a bit nervous when going into the park at dusk, but that evening I felt like I had extra high-def vision. Miss Glow had talked about looking at the world with a *writer's eyes and ears and senses* meaning you study every aspect of your surroundings. Textures, shades of color and sound, shapes, movement, background noise, scents, tastes, touch. She explained that most people just glance over the surface of everything without ever really seeing what they're looking at, because their minds are bogged down with mindless crap and trivialities. They don't really *look*, so they never actually *see* the truth of what's around them. I always remembered that lesson. I guess it helped me become a better artist.

So that evening, after her first class, I made my way through the park and tried to do exactly what she said. *Put on your pretend writer's glasses and really look beyond the superficial*.

It took me a few minutes, but soon it was like pulling a film away from my eyes. I began to truly see. The way a spider's web spanned the inside corner of the first step outside my front door; the yellow and gold leaves on the maple tree; a large hump on our front lawn alive with marching black ants; the slight, bald man that held his growling German Shepherd on a braided leather leash; the scent of wild sage by the lake; a sugar-pink front door on a house. It became easier the more I practiced.

By the time I reached the soccer field at the bottom of the hill, my mind was alive. I marveled at the red-gold sky splashed with violet clouds and the soft call of the loon on the lake.

I started the climb up the hill, feeling more relaxed than I had for months. A light breeze played across my face and the gentle trickling of the fountain in the middle of the lake lulled me into a deep sense of contentment. I was so into the whole writer thing I didn't notice the sweet skunk smell wafting down the hill until it was too late, and I stumbled upon three figures huddled around the covered seating area at the top of the hill, passing a fat cigarette around. I went to turn tail and run, but stepped on the gravel and made such a loud, crunching sound they all turned around. My heart did a downward swing when I realized it was Renny, Max and Andy. I shrank back against a nearby bush.

"You stalking us or something?" said Renny, standing up and walking towards me.

He was the smallest of the three guys, and was the kicker on the football team. He dug the toe of his runner into the gravel and glared at me, his eyes moist and sad looking. He and Alex were old video game buddies.

"Leave her alone, douche," Max said, grabbing Renny's arm.

Renny shook his arm free. "I wanna know why she keeps watching us. Like we've done something bad to her. She keeps staring at us every time we walk down the hallway at school."

I stood still, curling and uncurling my hands into fists. Digging my nails into my palm. I wanted to scream at them right there and then. Grab them by the throat and squeeze the truth out of them. Instead, I stood there like a wuss. Tongue-tied, silent, a coward. I didn't have the guts to demand the truth about what happened to my own brother. He would've done it for me. I know he would.

Max pulled at Renny's arm. "C'mon, asshole. Don't cause any more trouble."

I was tongue-tied. Mute. Couldn't summon up a word.

I set off down the hill, but when I was halfway down, I heard Renny yell after me, "Nobody could save your junkie brother. He deserved everything he got. He gambled with the wrong people and he lost."

It was like a bolt of lightning seared my scalp and my whole body was electrified. I whirled around and screamed for all the world to hear. "Lying creeps. Assholes. He was the best, the bravest brother a girl could wish for." Then I ran so fast I almost took a tumble at the bottom of the hill. I stumbled to a halt, my lungs heaving, and doubled over as if someone had punched me in the gut.

My knees gave way, and I fell to the ground, clawing at the grass, sobbing my heart out. Until a shadow slid across the moon and I knew someone was there, standing over me. I snuck a look at a white wrinkled face, with rubbery folds of flesh folding into a black cave of a mouth, jagged white fangs and one bulging bloodshot blue eye staring right at me. I fell back against the picnic bench, screaming like a kid, until a pale hand pulled down the mask. Stefan's face was a pale blob in the moonlight. His mouth moved but no sound came out. We looked at each other for a few long moments, then he offered a hand to pull me up.

"I wanted to surprise you with my Cyclops mask, but I scared you."

"No… it's okay."

"I heard shouting."

"It was nothing."

"Not nothing," he said, patting the picnic bench. "Tell me."

I sat beside him, my whole body aching inside and out. I couldn't hold it in anymore so I told him everything I hadn't yet properly explained. About my lovely, shining brother who burned away like a dying star and sucked the life from our family. About Mom and Dad who walked like shadows around the house, not talking, not touching, not living. About the empty hole in my heart that wouldn't heal, about the guys who ran out on my burning brother, let him die and now called him a junkie.

When I was done, he stayed silent. I cringed, waiting for the cheesy words of sympathy, the scared, empty sentiments, but Stefan was calm and quiet. Waiting until I was all talked out. Then he waited some more, stroking his chin and thinking. Finally, when I'd calmed down, he nodded his head and turned to me.

"Seems we've got two projects now."

"What do you mean?"

"Well, there's our comic strip and then the more important one where we find out who killed your brother."

He said it without blinking as if it was the most natural thing in the world.

"How will we do it?"

He tapped his forehead. "The way I see it, we both have more brainpower than all those goons put together.

We're gonna be spending a whole lot of time with each other so we'll come up with a plan."

"What kind of plan?"

"That's what you're gonna help me come up with. Where would *you* start?"

His eyes appeared dark and glittered with flecks of gold. Suddenly it came to me. "Everyone has secrets. You agree?"

He blinked and looked away. "True. You don't know much about me."

"I know you're a good writer and you like anything to do with fire and the sun, but there must be more."

He nodded. "Time for that much later. Keep going."

"Well, if we find out Max and Renny and Chad's dirty secrets, we'll probably find out who caused the fire."

He tapped the stud just above the flare of his nostril. "Brilliant. A little technology and some covert surveillance techniques and we'll dig out the dirt in no time."

"Then what? I mean if we find out, what will we do with the info?"

He took a deep breath, then exhaled. "I haven't thought about that yet. Let's just deal with it when we get there."

But I never knew if he found anything out. We became consumed with the comic strip, which made me so happy, the investigation just fell by the wayside.

Now, fourteen years later, I felt as if I'd picked up where we had left off that night at the bottom of the hill, though I was determined to find out if Stefan knew something else that he was holding back from me.

I remembered Renny's words.

He gambled with the wrong people and he lost.

Were Nate and his two gangster buddies the wrong people?

I had this strange feeling I was running out of time. As if I had to gather all the pieces together before it was too late. Before my husband came back and I wasn't ready for him.

Were Shuc and his two partiers hidden the wrong people.

I had this strange feeling I was running out of time. As if I had to gather all the pieces together before it was too late. Before my husband came back and I wasn't ready for him.

37

NOW

I never even made it up to bed. Mental exhaustion and worry finally wore me down and I passed out on the family room sofa. I woke up, half-covered with a quilt, just as the sun's orange light flooded the sky. My laptop was still open beside me, the battery leaked down to zero. Sighing, I pulled myself up and plugged it in. My joints ached, but I was hungry, gasping for a coffee and craving a shower. On the way upstairs I checked Heidi's place and felt an immediate rush of relief when I saw the Dodge Viper was gone. Only one car remained in the driveway.

By the time I was back downstairs, dressed and installed at the kitchen counter with a mug of coffee and a couple of Pop Tarts, the sun was up, blazing through the family room windows. I sipped the coffee, and started a search on Andy Kim. After a few false starts, I tracked the Andy Kim I knew down to a tech company in California that specialized in interactive video games, but the post was a few years old. Seems he'd found some success as a game designer and entrepreneur, but after that date there was nothing. No mention of Andy Kim anywhere on any social media platform. He'd vanished into thin air.

I took note of his last contact info and went on to search for Renny Beaumont.

It didn't take long to find him, or rather read the news articles about his murder.

Seems he'd been gunned down in the parking lot of a local burger restaurant. It had happened around nine years ago when I was still in Toronto. At the time, the police had no leads as to who was responsible, though they'd thought it was related to drugs and local gang activity.

A chill prickled my skin. *Now who'd been gambling with the wrong people?* He was only twenty-two years old when it happened. I closed the laptop lid wondering why neither Max nor Chad had mentioned Renny's murder. Come to think of it, Max hadn't even mentioned Renny's name. Worse still, Stefan hadn't thought to tell me about the shooting. He'd told me he was in the vice squad, so he was bound to know something about Renny's death. And now he knew I was married to Nate, why was he hiding information that might be relevant?

Suddenly I had an overwhelming urge to get out of the house and find some answers. I texted Stefan and invited him to meet me for lunch at a deli we used to frequent when we were at high school. A few minutes later he texted a time, said the place was okay, and mentioned he'd only have half an hour at the most. I texted back and said I'd have his order waiting for him when he arrived.

I had time before leaving to try to contact Andy. The contact info didn't give a specific extension, so when I called the general number, someone put me through to reception. A woman told me that Andy had left rather suddenly around nine years ago and they had no idea where he'd gone. He'd even forgotten to pick up his last paycheck and hadn't left a forwarding address. I thanked her and ended the call. *Andy had left nine years ago. Around the same time Renny was killed.* So, with Renny dead and

Andy vanished into oblivion, that only left Nate of all the people who'd been in the basement with Alex the night of the fire.

After a messy ride through slush and melting snow, and another try at calling Rick, I got his voicemail again. At some point I realized I'd have to pay him a visit just to put my mind at rest about Toby.

I got to the restaurant just in time to grab the last open table. Cohen's Deli was a small, stuffy place with an open kitchen counter and rough wooden benches. A perfect hangout in the dead of winter, it sold the best comfort food. Hearty soups, crispy falafel, and stacked corned beef sandwiches. When we were working on the comic strip, Stefan and I were regulars. We'd share a sandwich and a giant pickle, and we'd each have a steaming bowl of borscht with a blob of sour cream on top. Stefan always had money. Sent by his wealthy father to make up in some small way for their lack of contact.

I ordered our old favorites, then sat back to soak in the familiar atmosphere, cradling a huge mug of breakfast tea.

The place was packed with the lunch crowd, buzzing with noise – clinking cups, conversation, laughter, a welcome break from the deafening silence and lonely solitude of my house. Settling into the corner of the booth, I realized the décor hadn't changed much in fourteen years. The walls were still plastered with old black and white photos of the owner's family and ancestors from the old country, as well as a few signed celebrity pictures of visiting artists and actors who'd made a special journey to sample the famous corned beef and falafel.

I let the room's warm coziness wrap around me like an old blanket. And, like fourteen years before, I felt a thrill of anticipation at seeing Stefan. When he appeared in the

228

doorway in his black quilted jacket, my heart lifted. He pulled off his woolen hat, smoothed down the glossy tufts of his hair and looked around until he saw me. His face lit up with a smile and suddenly all those silly night fears were sucked away. I could have been any average woman, meeting her boyfriend for lunch. Not someone weakened by tragedy and stuck in a dysfunctional marriage with a mystery man.

Brushing those thoughts away, I beckoned him over. He squeezed by the crowded tables and plunked down in the booth opposite me, bringing the scent of fresh air and sandalwood with him.

"Hasn't changed a bit," he said, glancing around just as the waiter placed two bowls of borscht on the table.

I unfolded my napkin. "I was just thinking that."

"Food looks great," he said, lifting his spoon. "Just like the old times."

"I know. Makes me feel so old."

He stirred the sour cream into the deep maroon-colored broth. "Thirty-one hardly qualifies as old, Liv."

"Thirty-two next month."

His spoon hovered halfway to his mouth. "Of course. How could I forget? Remember your eighteenth?"

"We bought a whole ice cream cake at Dairy Queen and ate it between us while watching the director's cut of *Blade Runner*. Your gran kept coming and checking in on us because we had the surround sound turned up too high."

"It was pretty memorable, I have to say." He ladled the soup into his mouth. "Sorry. I gotta eat. I've been working since six this morning."

"I have more time on my hands, so I'll do the talking first."

He grinned. "Don't mind me if I slurp a bit too loudly."

"Already forgiven."

When I began to fill him in, starting with my visit to Chad, he dropped his spoon with a loud *clink*. "Liv, I told you not to keep digging around on your own."

I placed my hands flat on the table. "I can't exactly sit there alone in my house waiting for something to happen. Especially if I could be in danger."

"Danger? What danger?" He leaned in close, his voice lowered to a whisper.

I told him exactly what Chad had told me about Nate's early involvement with gambling and drugs and his association with the two guys, Sonny and the nameless short guy. Stefan sat back against the bench, watching me with a new level of intensity.

"You know about those guys, don't you, Stefan?"

He sighed and looked away, as if he was trying hard to think of something to say. "I can't reveal anything about our investigations, Liv. I'd lose my job."

I felt a flicker of anger in my throat. "Even if you know they're regular visitors at the lake house right opposite me? Not only that, but they've followed me a couple of times when I've been out walking. The other day when they pulled up at the lake house, they stopped and stared at my place for more than a few seconds, as if they were looking for someone. Maybe Nate."

He mopped at his lips. His left knee was knocking the underside of the table, a sure sign he was uncomfortable. "You think Nate's still involved with them?"

"Chad certainly hinted that," I said as the waiter brought over two massive pastrami sandwiches. "Can you pack mine up to go?" I'd suddenly lost my appetite.

I stared at Stefan, daring him to tell me something that might shed light on this puzzle that was slowly coming together.

He exhaled, his face set in grim concentration. "What do you want from me, Liv?"

"How about honesty?" I said, the ache of disappointment crowding my throat. I'd thought I could trust Stefan, of all people, to be totally honest with me. "I want to know if I'm in danger, or if you and your team have information about Nate that you're not telling me. I want to know if my husband was responsible for the death of my brother, and for the loss of my son. Dammit, Stefan, I want to know exactly who I'm married to – who I've been living with for the last eight years of my life."

My voice had escalated to the point that people at the other tables had stopped their chatting and were now looking over at me. I lowered my head and held my face in my cupped palms.

In a moment, I felt two warm hands cover mine. "I'd never let anyone hurt you, Liv. You have to trust me."

I pushed his hands away. "And how will you do that, Stefan, when you're away at work, and I'm sitting at home alone just a few feet away from a house that regularly entertains known gangsters? Where gambling and drugs, and heaven knows what else, motivated a father to try and take his young son from the place? And, incidentally, that little boy has gone missing. There's been no sign of him for the past week. What if he disappeared like Jack did? And besides all that, Nate could show up any time and I'd have no idea what to say to him. Hell, I don't even know who he really is anymore. Seems I'm the last person to know that my husband was a gambler, and possibly a drug dealer who hung out – or maybe still hangs around

– with known criminals. Hey, maybe he's the one who caused Renny Beaumont's death. Or perhaps you didn't know about that."

"Of course I did, Liv. That's old news and public knowledge. Beaumont was dealing drugs and he just happened to cut into someone else's territory."

"So Nate had nothing to do with it?"

"I was just finishing Police Academy training, Liv. I had no access to any of those case files at the time. I just heard a few rumors about Renny."

"I know Nate's still gambling, Stefan. Chad saw him at the casino three months ago. I found a bank slip in his pocket. The account balance was almost a million dollars. You telling me that's not suspicious?"

He chewed at his bottom lip before speaking. "Possibly. There might be many explanations. He could've picked up someone else's slip. Maybe it's related to work."

I shoved my soup plate away. The soup lapped over the side, spreading across the table. Stefan leaned forward and began to mop it with a napkin.

"Bullshit, Stefan. Tell me the truth. Is your team watching Nate? And is it just a coincidence that you're living on my street or are you staking out the lake house opposite me? I need some answers."

His eyes seemed to plead with me. "Liv, I can't talk about my job. Can't reveal anything. Our work relies on total confidentiality. If I break that, I'd not only jeopardize the entire operation, I'd also place a whole lot of people's lives in danger, and I'm not prepared to do that."

For a moment I wanted to bury my head against him until all the bad stuff just faded away, but my anger was so intense, I couldn't do it. I stood up, scraping my chair back across the floor.

"Then there's nothing left to say. Guess I'll have to find the answers myself."

I picked up the brown bag with my sandwich inside and edged my way out from the booth.

"Don't leave like this, Liv. Please. At least let me drop by and check on you."

I couldn't look at him. At those warm, brown eyes. "Suit yourself," I said, walking towards the door, my heart slamming against my ribs.

38

I hated myself for being so brutal with Stefan, and as I drove away from the deli, the logical part of my brain reasoned that I'd been unfair asking him to jeopardize his job and the safety of the people he worked with. And yet we'd always trusted each other, so why couldn't he just level with me? Especially when I might be in danger?

The early afternoon traffic was heavy, and my ability to concentrate on the road kept lapsing as I swerved to avoid parked cars that hadn't even registered on my radar. Thoughts swirled around in my head. All the accusations about Nate were mainly speculation. Nothing concrete. My only certainty – Nate was still gambling, and maybe in a big way. If so, then he needed help to kick the habit. What if the drug stuff was just something from his distant past? And maybe I'd imagined those two guys were Sonny and his gangster sidekick. After all, I did tend to let my imagination run wild.

Alex had always said I was the easiest person to play a spooky prank on. That's why, when I was eight, I'd made my mom take my new Elmo doll out of my room at night because I was sure it was watching me in the dark, and I'd swore I saw its eyes blink. Nine-year-old Alex had wasted no time pushing it around my open bedroom door to make it appear as if it was creeping back inside. I screamed the house down, probably traumatizing him in the process.

Was I overreacting now? Filling in the blanks with pure fiction dredged up from one of my comic strips?

Someone's horn sounded behind me and I realized the traffic light had turned green. I forced my focus back to the road ahead. Pulling up to the next traffic light, I rummaged in my purse and found Rick's business card. Maybe it was time to pay him a visit and finally see if he knew where Toby was, and maybe also ask a few questions about my new neighbor. His place was just ten minutes away, so I took a right turn and headed downtown.

Rick's bike shop was across the river in the French area of town. An area with a long history spanning from the early French settlers. The long, central boulevard was lined with trendy boutiques, intimate restaurants, French bakeries and quirky little bookstores that I could have lazed around in for the entire afternoon, had I not had a pile of pressing questions weighing on my mind.

Rick's place was at the far end of the boulevard towards the more industrial section. Housed in a featureless brick strip mall, next to an Autoglass store, the yellow sign read *Rick's Custom Bikes: We Specialize in Parts and Services for All Harley-Davidsons.*

I pulled into the parking lot and sat for a moment looking at the front window display. A long, lean Harley painted inky black with cobalt blue accents, occupied the entire window. I wasn't a big fan of motorbikes, but I could imagine a bike fanatic just salivating over this beast of a machine with its gleaming chrome rims and polished black leather seat. There were no other parked cars there, so I headed straight for the front door and opened it into a long, low-ceilinged room that smelled of car oil, paint and the burning stink of a welding gun. Shelves of bike parts lined one wall, a stand filled with bike-fanatic magazines stood against the other, and a gleaming array of custom bike parts took up the central island. A display of fancy license plates provided a backdrop to Rick who stood at a glass counter sorting through a pile of receipts. He did a double take when he saw me.

"Hey, Olivia. Did you get lost or something? Or maybe you're interested in a bike?" He grinned, revealing even, white teeth.

I shook my head. "I'd rather ride a horse any day than get onto a bike."

"Don't know what you're missing. The wind in your hair. The open road. There's nothing like it," he said, stacking the receipts and stapling them together.

"I'll get a convertible. Same experience."

"So what can I do for you?"

I averted my gaze, afraid to meet his eyes. "Okay, I guess I'll get right to the point. Toby's gone. I haven't seen him around for a few days now. Heidi took him out for a walk in his sled and came back without him. I'm worried, Rick, and…"

I was on a roll. When I glanced at him again, he was smiling, his hand raised, palm facing me.

"You know about this?"

He nodded. "I met Heidi in the school parking lot. Rosa, my girlfriend, came with me. Heidi called her a slut and asked if she was going to try and play mother. I said she'd do a damn sight better than Heidi ever has. Then I told her if she didn't hand Toby over right then and there, I'd call the cops to come and pay her a random visit to see how an innocent toddler is living in a place with cocaine lying around in candy dishes just waiting for

236

a vulnerable kid to taste it. I also reminded her that her so-called friends would soon drop her if the cops came nosing around her party house. So, she had no choice. She handed him over to me and Rosa."

"And how is he?"

His eyes gleamed. "As it happens, he's great. Tearing up a storm at nursery school and eating through my pantry as if he never ate a square meal in his life. Which he probably didn't, living with his mother. Knowing Heidi, he'd be lucky to score a cold piece of pizza or some leftover French fries."

"Makes me feel good to hear he's doing well," I said, my courage faltering a little and wondering *Why was I really here?*

"You okay, Olivia?" he said. "Something bothering you?"

I nodded. "I know you hinted that bad stuff is going on at Heidi's place, but I need you to be more specific. What exactly is going on there? If I'm living just a few yards away, I think I have a right to know."

He sighed and ducked down to open a drawer where he stowed the bunch of receipts. When he straightened up again, the easy smile was gone. "It won't help you in any way to know what's happening in that house, Olivia. In fact, it may work against you, and I sure as hell don't want to jeopardize my son's safety by talking about Heidi and her crowd. Just take my word for it and stay clear away from there and nobody will bother you."

I ground my toe into the concrete floor to channel my irritation. "Stands to reason, Heidi has to be into something big to afford that place."

He laughed, though his eyes were unsmiling. "You think she owns that monstrosity?"

237

"I… I assumed she did."

"Are you kidding? The same guy has owned the house for the last ten years."

My blood froze. "But there was a *For Sale* sign up there."

"That was just for show. The guy who owns it wants to make people think he has nothing to do with the place. He likes to stay under the radar. That's why he left it empty for a long time. Got some bad publicity a few years back when a kid went missing from—"

I couldn't stop myself from flinching – felt the corner of my lip twitch, and my face twist into a grimace. He saw it all, and his eyes fixed on me, wide with disbelief. "Was that your…?"

I nodded, biting my lip to stem the tears. Always the tears. When would I ever stop crying?

"I'm so sorry, Olivia. I had no idea. God… I can't imagine losing Toby."

"Is Heidi a friend of the owner?" I asked, trying not to break down on the spot. Trying to extract a coherent thought from the swarm of possibilities buzzing around in my head.

He nodded. "She rented the house from him. They go back a long way."

"And are they in the same line of work?" I asked in a voice that sounded disconnected from me. I dreaded his answer.

"I told you, Olivia. I feel sorry for your loss and everything, but that's all I can tell you. I've said enough already. But if I was you, I'd think about selling your place and getting the hell out of that street. You have no idea who or what has just moved in across from you."

"I'm not stupid, Rick. I see all those fancy import cars there almost every night. They're not dropping over for a glass of wine and a book chat."

He twirled the end of his beard and sighed. "That's Heidi all over. Loves the party life. Always drawn to the hotshots and big spenders. I should have realized earlier on in our marriage how shallow and materialistic she was. She could never settle for the quiet life. We'd be doing something together with Toby – like going to the zoo – and she was already thinking about what we could do next, or where we could go for drinks that night. She never lived in the moment. Something better was always just on the horizon and she couldn't stop herself from running towards it, grasping everything she could get her hands on."

"Sounds a lot like my husband. He always wanted more, and wanted it faster. I'd talk to him and he'd be somewhere else. Like he was planning his next big move. It got to be so lonely."

Rick's eyes softened when he looked at me. "Oh, I know that feeling, Olivia. I was so lucky to meet Rosa. She's a dancer, and she's really in tune with herself and especially with Toby. He loves her already. I hope you can move on and find someone like that. Find some happiness."

I sighed. "Actually, I just met up with an old friend. We were kind of soulmates at high school."

He grinned. "There you go. Sometimes old and dear friends become something deeper and more meaningful to us. You'll see."

"I hope so." I remembered the picture of Nate in my purse. "Oh – just on the off chance – do you or Heidi know this man?"

Rick squinted as I passed him the photograph, then suddenly dropped it and shoved it across the counter towards me. "Who is this guy?"

The fear in his voice sent a tremor through my body. "He... he's my husband."

Suddenly his entire body stiffened. The easy, friendly manner wiped away. He glanced beyond me at the parking lot, his eyes darting left then right. "You need to leave. Now." His voice was controlled, but the edge of a threat sharpened it.

"You know him?"

"I told you to leave. Don't ever come back here."

I backed away, dumbfounded. How could seeing my husband have had this effect on him? I reached behind my back and opened the door. At that moment he killed the lights and when I was finally outside, he rushed over, locked the door and pulled the shutters down, his face a white blob in the darkness.

I'm not sure how I staggered out to my car without stopping to press my hands against my ears and scream. Nate knew Heidi. Rick was afraid of Nate. It was obvious. Everything bad in my life was somehow connected to Nate and that cursed lake house. Heidi knew Jude, the guy who'd owned the house when Jack went missing. Jude was probably into the same illicit line of work that Heidi was. Maybe she was even running his business for him.

Nate had said Jude was a friend from work when he convinced me to go to that damned party. Was Nate involved in their business too? I remembered the feeling I had the first day Heidi moved in – that she'd looked at Nate as if she knew him. I thought I'd imagined it all, but it seemed a strange coincidence that Nate had left and not come back, the moment Heidi and her entourage showed up on our street. Was he running from them?

I was just trying to grasp the significance of that question and get my key into the starter when my phone pinged with a text. I slammed the door shut and opened the screen. It glowed blue in the darkness, illuminating a message from Stefan.

> Raj accessed phone records. They show Nate is in the city now.

I missed a breath and clapped my hand across my mouth. Another text followed.

> If you're worried, come to my house tonight.

Sweat beaded my brow despite the freezing air. I jumped when the bright lights of a car swished by in a blue-white blur. *I should go home. Face Nate if he's there*, but the thought of being alone with him at the house sent a tremor of fear through me. *It would be so easy and comfortable to stay at Stefan's.*

I started the car, suddenly conscious of the falling temperature and my breath fogging the windshield, and was just about to drive away when another text came in. *Probably Stefan*, I thought as I put on the brakes.

But when I glanced down, my vision blurred and my heart slammed into my throat. It was Nate. The text was brief. To the point.

> Hey Liv. Where are you?

I stared at that one-line message. It was almost threatening in its simplicity. Maybe Nate or Jack – whatever his name – was back at the house waiting for me. Swallowing loudly, I typed.

> Out grocery shopping. Where are you?

I waited. My eyes focused on the glowing digital numbers of the dashboard clock.

Silence for a few long seconds, then the short message flashed up.

> Still out of town.

Liar. The word echoed in my head. *Liar.* But I couldn't let on I was suspicious. I typed.

> Why haven't you called?

The three little dots pulsed for an eternity. He was thinking. What to say? What new lie to spin?

> Something important came up. I'll get back to you.

When? I typed madly.

I waited. Nothing. I tried his new cell number. No answer. It went straight to an out-of-service message. What was he up to? Was he trying to find out if I was at the house? Suddenly the fear was replaced by frustration, even anger. At that moment I decided I would not sit at home like a helpless victim. I had to do something. He was in the city somewhere and I needed to find him.

But on my terms.

I thought about the place Chad had seen him most recently. The casino. It was only ten minutes away and had a hotel attached to it. Maybe I could catch him at his own game.

243

39

It was clear no expense had been spared in designing the main entry hall of the casino. A sweeping, red-carpeted staircase and glittering monster chandelier that wouldn't have looked out of place on the *Titanic*, graced the neon-lit lobby.

To my right and left, a chorus of ringing, *pinging, whirring* issued from row upon row of slot machines. That strange cacophony echoed through the maze of endless halls. Lights flashed, jingles played, and illuminated wheels spun, adding to the frenzy of excitement when the clink of electronic coins cascading across a screen followed the occasional *whoop* of someone winning a jackpot.

I stood watching the circus, imagining how easy it would be to get hooked on the possibility that you could *hit it big* at any moment. That twenty bucks might net you twenty thousand. Blind instinct drove these people to sit at the machines pumping in ten and twenty-dollar bills, like lab animals in a conditioning experiment.

Muted lighting ensured that the players could get maximum impact from the flashing lights and colors. And everyone was too glued to their screens to give a damn about one woman skulking around in the background scoping the place out. I'd tied my hair back and jammed a baseball cap on. That and my dark zip-up jacket and an old pair of glasses were enough of a disguise to blend in with the background.

I wove around the rows of machines, half expecting to see Nate throwing in money as fast as he was losing it, but my instincts told me he'd probably graduated long ago to the gaming tables. Roulette, blackjack or poker were probably more his style. Those games were set up on a platform at the far end of the gaming hall, while the more high-stakes card games could be accessed through a small, curtained doorway in the far corner.

I edged towards the roulette tables, scanning them to see if I could spot Nate's familiar dark, groomed hair. He wasn't there. At least not at the roulette tables. But my gaze soon settled on a tall, blonde woman sitting with a bald-headed guy in a leather jacket. Heidi and her boyfriend. I slid behind a nearby pillar and watched as the croupier raked in the losing chips. Heidi was quick to throw more chips onto red, laughing as the bald guy nuzzled at her neck. She sipped a tall, colorless drink stuffed with greenery and watched as the wheel began to spin again.

A collective sigh went up when it landed on black. Heidi stood up, cursing under her breath, and scooped a still-sizeable pile of chips into a black and gold embroidered bag. Bald guy took her arm, and they made their way around the tables, stopping to whisper in the ear of at least one player from each table. Those exchanges were followed by a cursory nod and sometimes the quick exchange of a business card. I was intrigued and wondered if this was how she recruited people for her parties?

I followed them to the cashier's counter and hovered behind a coffee machine, watching as the girl behind the Plexiglas screen dumped the chips and counted them.

Heidi tapped the toe of her crocodile skin boots on the tiled floor and inspected her manicured nails, until the girl came back with a cashier's check, which Heidi slipped into her designer bag. She headed towards the entrance where her boyfriend retrieved her coat from the coat check.

I decided to keep following them for two reasons: I wanted to know more about what they were up to, and thought maybe they'd lead me to Nate.

I hung back and followed them into the parking lot. Outside, the stink of cigarettes lingered in the air from the ragged clusters of gamblers taking a smoke break by the exit doors. Almost gagging, I wrapped my scarf over my mouth and nose and stood behind a large fake palm tree to watch as Heidi and her friend lit up cigarettes and waited.

Over the next few minutes at least four different people – a young, clean-cut guy, two middle-aged women, and a burly biker type – approached them, slid an envelope into their hands, then slunk off into the shadows. Heidi had some kind of racket going on here. People working for her inside the casino. Was she running some kind of loan racket and collecting high interest or laundering dirty money?

After a few minutes of no-shows, the two of them made their way to Heidi's SUV, parked only three rows away from my car. I waited until they were hidden among the cars and ran over to mine. Once they pulled out and headed towards the exit, I made sure I was right behind them.

I gripped the steering wheel, my heart racing as we sped through darkened streets in the direction of downtown. When they took a sharp left turn onto a pothole-damaged backroad running parallel to the railway tracks, my hands began to sweat. We'd entered a sketchy, rundown area. I checked my dash. I was low on gas. Cursing myself for not checking earlier, I prayed I had enough to get me safely out of the place should I need to make a quick getaway. I was so caught up with worry I almost overshot them when they slowed down and turned off into a parking lot near a strip of old warehouses.

I carried on past the turnoff for a few yards, finally slowing down to do a U-turn into a deserted strip mall nearby.

I decided to wait for a while, then drive by the warehouses to see what was happening. I couldn't waste any time, considering how low my gas tank was. Killing my headlights, I let the darkness swallow me up. My mouth tasted like sandpaper. Not surprising since I hadn't eaten or drunk anything for hours. My eyelids felt heavy, so I let myself sink back into the seat for just a moment, but my head jerked suddenly forward as my phone blared out into the silence. I snapped back to reality and hit the Bluetooth. An unfamiliar number came up on my screen. Was Nate keeping tabs on me?

I clicked *accept* and waited for his voice, but instead a muffled sobbing or coughing sound came across.

I muted my voice. "Who is this?"

More choking noises and the clink of glass against glass. A slurred voice answered. "Hey, Livvee... it'shh Chad."

"Are you okay? You sound... er..."

A hiccup first, then, "Drunk, pissed, loaded? Guilty. All of the above."

"What's wrong, Chad?"

"I... I've been thinking about you a lot. Ever since you showed up at my store. Can't get you out of my damn stupid head. Then I found the business card you gave me, and it was like an omen. I had to get back to you."

"You sure you're okay?"

He answered with a gulping, sobbing sound. "Your brother, Alex… he was the best friend a guy could have. An angel. You know that, don't you, Livvy?"

The old sadness welled up, pressing like a weight against my eyelids. "I know that, Chad. I loved him so much. We all did."

He let out a plaintive cry, as if he was in pain. "That's why I have to come clean with you and to hell with my own miserable life."

"Are you in danger, Chad?"

"Just shut up and listen, Liv. I have to get this out because I can't look myself in the eye until I do."

I waited, barely breathing, in case I missed what he was going to say. From the corner of my eye, I noticed another car approaching from the opposite direction. I watched as it turned and entered the same parking lot Heidi had parked in.

Chad's voice continued, dry and raspy with emotion. "Guess I just have to get right to it. Here goes… there's a good reason Andy Kim left the country just after Renny Beaumont was shot." A long pause. My stomach rolled. "Your… your husband Nate arranged the hit, and Andy knew it."

Prickly fingers of dread clutched at my throat. "What are you saying? I don't… I…"

"I didn't know about it at the time, but once Andy got somewhere safe, he called me from some payphone in the middle of God knows where. Told me to be real careful. Said that Nate was into something scary big – some drug thing – and they'd ordered him to tie up any *loose ends* as

248

they called it, otherwise he'd be in big trouble. Too bad Renny was a loose end."

My mind darted from one thought to another. "You mean Renny knew what happened in the basement with Alex?"

Chad seemed to be sobering up, the longer he talked. "Nate couldn't risk anyone opening that whole thing up again. He wanted to stay under the radar. A respectable, hard-working guy with a squeaky-clean past."

I tried to swallow, but my mouth was completely dry. "Happily married. With a wife and kid. Living in the suburbs?"

"You got it, Liv."

Suddenly I had the feeling that everything real and solid was slipping away from me. Like I couldn't grasp onto anything tangible. "Guess I was a loose end. That's why he married me."

The choking sobs started again as Chad tried to talk. "We should have warned you. I told Max. But you were away. In Toronto. We had no idea he'd go and look for you there."

Look for me? He searched for me. Tracked me down. Married me and kept me right where he wanted me, so I'd never suspect him. I wanted to vomit. I pushed the door open and heaved. Dry-retching, then spitting out sour-tasting bile, because I had nothing inside me to throw up. I heard Chad's voice.

"You okay, Liv?"

I croaked something to let him know I was still there. He started to talk again.

"Andy never told me what happened that night. Guess he was too scared to explain it all, so I don't actually know if Nate caused the fire. I just know he was there when it started and then he disappeared, leaving Renny and Andy to face the cops."

I swung back into the car and wiped my sleeve across my mouth.

"How can I ever find out what happened, Chad?"

There was a long silence then, "Whatever you do, don't ask your husband. Andy's the only other person that knows the truth and he's disappeared. He called from a payphone. I have no way to get back to him."

"I have to know, Chad."

Chad's voice ratcheted up a few notches. "Liv... Liv. Forget about finding out. You need to get away from Nate! But don't let on why. That's why he came to see me three months ago at the casino. It was no accident. He was with those two guys again – made sure he introduced them to me. Sonny and the little guy – Mel. He just wanted to see if I'd talked to Andy. Make sure I was being a good boy and keeping my mouth shut. So now I've told you, I don't know what's gonna happen to me, but you know what? I don't care anymore."

The red, blinking gas light snapped on. I had to make a move. Had to get back home. Had to figure out what to do about my so-called husband.

"I gotta go, Chad. And thanks... thanks for this."

"You gonna be okay, Liv? You want me to come over?"

"No... no. I'll be in touch."

"But, Liv... I'm worried for—"

Click. I disconnected. My battery was getting low.

I felt disoriented, confused as I edged the car along towards the turnoff into the warehouse parking lot. Any doubts I had about Nate – any sympathy for him – had been wiped away by Chad's words. This new version of Nate was chilling.

My husband was a man who'd stop at nothing to cover his tracks. How could I even contemplate going home? Suddenly, I'd lost interest in Heidi and her gambling operation. But as I got closer to the warehouse, a door opened and light spilled out onto the concrete. Silhouetted in the glare were two familiar figures, one stooped with a jerky gait, the other tall and skinny: Sonny and his sidekick, Mel, their familiar Dodge Viper clearly visible in the parking lot.

I pulled in behind a dumpster, big enough to hide me, but not so large that I couldn't see inside the building. The door was open, revealing a brightly lit storehouse with small tables scattered around the room. At least three were occupied by people hunched over hands of cards. I remembered watching a movie starring Jessica Chastain, about an illegal gaming operation. The secret high-stakes games that happened in hotel rooms, abandoned storehouses, private homes, and all run by a woman who recruited her clients by word of mouth.

Sonny and his friend, Mel, moved into the shadows at the side of the building as two other men emerged dragging Heidi's bald-headed friend with them. One of the men slammed the door shut with his foot as the bald guy struggled to shake them off. They kneed him in the back, propelling him towards Sonny who lunged forward and punched him hard in the stomach.

The bald guy doubled over, retching and coughing, then straightened up only to take another fist square on his jaw that sent him reeling backwards. Sonny cursed as he rubbed his knuckles. He nodded and the two men dragged bald guy back. Sonny then reached into the guy's pocket and extracted a sheaf of white envelopes. *The checks from the casino?* He handed the envelopes back to

Mel, then took out a long, sharp object from the back pocket of his jeans. With a lightning-swift movement, he lunged towards the bald guy and shoved the knife into his gut. The guy grabbed his stomach and lurched forward, gasping as he slumped in a heap to the ground. Sonny kicked him to the side.

I plastered my hand in front of my mouth to stifle a scream, but just then the door swung open again and Heidi flew out, hair streaming behind her like a blonde scarf, her face contorted with fury. She shuddered to a halt, almost slipping in the pool of blood that oozed from her friend who lay there moaning. Instantly she covered her face with her hands and began screaming. Mel shoved Sonny out of the way and lurched towards her, but another man emerged from a dark doorway behind Sonny, and grabbed the back of Mel's jacket before he reached the blonde.

My blood went cold when I saw his face.

It was Nate. Nate, tall, suave and imposing in his navy overcoat. In one swift move, he reached out and grasped her face, his thumb and finger pressing into her cheeks. She froze instantly and went silent.

Who was he, that he had this effect on her? I gasped for air. Breathed short, sharp breaths as if a fist was pressing on my chest. The slow, calculated deliberation of that movement seemed more violent than the stabbing.

I kept saying to myself: *This man is my husband. This man is my husband.*

He held her that way for at least thirty seconds, speaking directly into her face as if he were spitting out the words, then shoved her away. She stumbled against the brick wall and stayed there, her head bent, as Nate and his two cronies walked away towards the Dodge Viper. I felt the sudden urge to back up and drive as fast as I could in the opposite direction before they pulled out of the parking lot and spotted me behind the dumpster.

But did I have time?

I followed their progress towards the Viper. Sonny and Mel got in, while Nate flicked a key fob, and the lights to the shiny black Mercedes next to them flashed on. He turned again, bending his head to talk to the two men through their open window. Now was my chance to get away. I'd seen enough to know that my husband was mixed up in illegal gambling and maybe something even worse. That he had known gangsters working for him. That he was capable of calculated violence. That he used other people to carry out that violence and retribution. What more did I need to know? Only that I had to get away from him. Quickly.

I shifted the car into reverse and slowly backed away from the dumpster, my sweaty hand slipping on the wheel. But somehow, I miscalculated and smashed into a pile of metal drums, making a loud crash. Nate's head snapped upwards. I struggled to gather myself together and shifted the car into drive. Only one thought pounded into my head.

He can't know it's me.

And he'd definitely recognize my car if he saw it. I had to get away without crossing the opening to the parking lot. I slammed the car into reverse again, crashing into the oil drums one more time, then swerved the car in the other direction, bumping over the kerb in the process. Then I gunned the car into the safety of darkness, praying I had enough gas to get me to the nearest station.

My whole body was numb. I knew now, Nate was capable of anything.

But one question kept racing across my mind. Was he also capable of harming his only child?

40

Once I reached Main Street, I eased my foot off the gas, checking in the rearview mirror to see if anyone had followed me. I had to conserve what little fuel I had to get home. *Home?* I had no home now. Everything was turned upside down. My marriage. My life. I couldn't think straight. How could I make any plans while Nate was still lurking around, living this other terrifying life?

Only one certainty became clear in the swirling confusion of my mind: I had to tell Stefan about all this. Couldn't hide it anymore. There was no doubt now that Nate was involved in some serious criminal activity and I probably didn't even know the full extent of it. At the back of my mind was the realization that I'd finally have to move away from the lake and the park. Give up the dream that Jack would somehow still come back home. Unless I discovered that Nate knew something about his disappearance.

When I considered that possibility, a sharp current of anger coursed through me. I'd seen a dark, menacing side of Nate, but I still had the courage to look him in the eye and ask him if he was responsible. Nothing would stand between me and the truth about my son. Not even fear for my own safety. I didn't care about all the other lies and the changed identity. All that mattered to me was knowing what happened to my boy.

A blinking light alerted me to my dashboard – the gas light. I was going to run out of fuel sooner than I thought. I passed the art gallery, a long, gray cube of a building. The street was deserted and not the kind of place I'd want to be stranded alone. I pushed on across the bridge, praying I'd reach The Village, a gentrified area that had seen better days. My heart fell as I passed a shuttered gas station – the only one in The Village, so I pulled into a Safeway parking lot just as the engine sputtered to a stop. I'd have to call a cab and come back the next day with a canister of gas.

I checked Stefan's number first, but it went straight to voicemail. Either he was still working or fast asleep. Not surprising. After what I'd seen tonight, the vice squad was probably working overtime. I had no other choice but to go back home and hope Nate didn't show up.

The nearby Starbucks was just about to close, so I squeezed in just in time to order a large coffee. It would keep me up but I didn't give a damn. It was probably better that I was on alert in case anyone tried to enter my house. Cradling the coffee, I called a cab and waited by the door, letting the hot liquid slip down my throat.

Despite the shot of caffeine, I almost fell asleep in the back of the taxi. It was such a relief to have someone drive me, my whole body almost shut down. But far too soon the car pulled up in my driveway and I reluctantly climbed out and paid the driver. For a moment, I considered asking him to wait while I checked the garage to see if Nate's car was still there, but the crackling sound of his radio messaging him to get to the airport put an end to that idea. He reversed quickly out of the driveway leaving me alone in almost total darkness.

The lone streetlamp at the corner spilled pale light onto the street. Heidi's house was dark. I wondered if she'd called an ambulance. If so, she'd have a whole lot of explaining to do when they saw her injured boyfriend. But I reckoned she'd have time to come up with a good story on the ambulance ride to the hospital. One that didn't implicate Nate and his cronies.

My heart leapt as the garage door swished upwards. Nate's car was still there. I could breathe. He hadn't been here. But why would he want to drive a dull Toyota Camry when he had a fancy Mercedes at his disposal, a car that was much more suited to his extravagant tastes?

I let myself into the house and immediately took a kitchen chair and wedged it under the back doorknob. If someone tried to get in, they'd make a whole lot of noise, which would give me plenty of time to make a swift exit from the front door. I stood back and wiped my forehead with my sleeve. Fear was making me jumpy and feverish. I told myself I had to stay calm until I could get in touch with Stefan and tell him everything.

Rather than sleep upstairs in my bedroom, I curled up on the sofa with a couple of pieces of toast – the only thing I could stomach – and a glass of milk. I put on some mindless romance movie. Something feel-good and escapist, set on a sprawling ranch with misty mountains on the horizon. I wrapped myself in a blue and white crocheted blanket my mother had made in her crafting days, and soon my eyelids were drooping. I lay my head against the cushion and let my exhausted body drift off into sleep.

I dreamed I was out walking, but the moment I hit the lake shore, the wolves appeared.

Silent gray shadows flitting between bare trees. Drawn by the scent of human fear, they padded like phantoms over the snow, gathering ahead, their blood-scented breath crystalizing in the air. Waiting like frozen ghosts until I was separate.

Apart.

Alone.

Then they pounced with a rush. Tearing along the narrow track, their claws gripping the icy crust.

I froze. My limbs paralyzed by cold and fear.

No escape route in sight. Only the half-frozen lake. Nate was standing on the other side, watching me. He cupped his hands around his mouth and shouted something, but I couldn't make out the words.

Stumbling down the bank, I slid onto gritty ice, aware suddenly of a gurgling noise under the fragile surface. Too late to sidestep the blooms of black water.

I fell forward into the darkness of the rippling pines.

The water held me in its frigid embrace, flooding my lungs to bursting point, but as my body quieted, I saw a face. A child's face. A small, translucent pearl. Hair curling like tendrils of weed. Wriggling and writhing in the shifting currents. I reached out to touch it and the illusion shattered into a million pixelated fragments.

–

I struggled to open my eyes. The dream was still tugging at me, pulling me back into the hazy world that exists between dreams and reality. Red bars of light streaked the sky. Dawn. I was lying on the family room couch. A scraping sound came from somewhere in the kitchen. The sound of drawers opening. I pulled myself up, my head still groggy with sleep, rubbed my eyes and saw someone rummaging through the kitchen drawer.

Nate.

I stuffed the blanket in my mouth to stop the scream in the same moment his head jerked around to look at me.

"Where are my car keys?"

That was it. No apology, no explanation, no expression of concern. Just one blunt question. After all the worry and craziness I'd gone through. Something wild sparked off in my head. I sprang off the couch and lunged towards him, pounding at his chest with my fists, screaming.

"Who the hell are you? You liar, cheat, asshole!"

He grabbed me hard by the shoulders, digging his fingers into my flesh. "Shut it," he said, through gritted teeth. "I'm Nate. Your husband."

Outrage and fury swelled into my throat. "No, you're not. You're a liar. A criminal. Always have been. *Jack Sawyer.*"

He dropped his hands. The anger was wiped from his eyes, replaced by a look of utter disbelief. "I'm not that person anymore."

"Then who are you? Some kind of *Godfather?* A gang boss? What exactly have you been up to? Why did you marry me? Just to keep me quiet about my brother, Alex?"

I must have struck a chord. He grabbed me again. Pulled me towards him, so close I could smell the light scent of his cologne, see the navy flecks in the pale blue of his eyes. He'd silenced Heidi only a few hours before – how might he try to silence me? "I married you because I loved you. I still do."

How could I believe him? No matter what he said. Even now, he was probably still lying just to keep me quiet. "And Alex?" I almost spat the words at him.

The *ping* of a text was almost deafening. He let me go, pulled out his phone and turned away to study the message. Tears welled from my eyes. My heart was torn apart. Nate, my husband was standing right in front of me, and yet everything about him was wrong – all a terrible lie. I reached for my phone. This had to end. Now. I'd call Stefan and tell him Nate was here.

I was just about to tap out a text when Nate whirled around and grabbed my phone from my hands, throwing it down onto the floor.

"What the fuck are you doing?"

"What I should've done a long time ago."

"You're gonna turn me, your husband, in?"

I nodded. "Then I'm going to divorce you."

"Liv, just listen—"

I scoffed. "To what? More lies?"

Something dark flickered across his face and I took a step back. Had I gone too far? He thought for a moment, chewing the inside of his lip and glancing from me to the back door. "Liv, I'm going to ask you for something. The last favor I'll ever ask of you. And afterwards, when this is all over, I'll tell you the truth. All of it."

"What do you want?" My heart swelled and crowded into my throat. I remembered him marveling at Jack's perfect little fingernails. *Like tiny seashells*, he'd said.

"Don't call anyone yet. Let me find my keys and leave. Then you can do whatever you want. But you have to decide quickly. I need to get away from here. Now."

I grasped his arm, feeling the slight twitch of his muscle, warm under the fabric of his coat. "On one condition. That you swear on our son's life that you didn't harm him."

Nate's mouth drooped at the corners. He looked at me as if I'd shoved a knife in his heart. "How can you even ask that?"

I felt a stab of regret but stifled it. Hot tears pooled in my eyes as I tugged at the front of his sweater. "I mean it. *Swear.*"

When he looked at me again, I thought I could see a glimpse of honest sorrow and pain in his expression. But how could I tell if it was real? Was my husband really just a brilliant actor?

"I swear," he whispered.

I dropped my hands, bent my head. "Your keys are hanging on the wall next to the fridge. Take them and get out of here before I change my mind."

He watched me as he ran to the fridge and took them. As he passed me on the way out, he turned. "I'm sorry, Liv. Believe me."

I kept my eyes on the floor. "Get out and don't come back unless you're ready to tell me the truth and turn yourself in."

He nodded, pausing at the doorway. "One last thing."

"Nate, you've got to be kidding me. I—"

"Just give me a bit of time, please. I know as soon as I leave here, you're probably going to call the cops, but think about it first. Please?"

He could sense the rebellion in my silence, because the pleading expression quickly vanished from his face. "Better listen to me, Liv, because you'll soon find out I'm not the kind of guy you want to cross."

I turned away, dumbstruck by his brazen threat, and silenced by a new sense of fear. I'd never seen this side of Nate. Ever. I backed away from him.

"Get out," I whispered.

He paused for a split second as if he was going to say something, then turned and slipped out into the garage. I slammed the door shut and listened for the roar of the car engine, then collapsed onto the couch and cried.

41

I must have drifted off again, because I woke to the sound of car tires on gravel. Springing up, I ran to the front window. The sun was barely up, but the reddish glare in the air was not from the sunrise. It was from the swirling lights of the two police cars and two armored vans parked at the foot of Heidi's driveway.

I hurried then, to the back door, saw the chair lying on the floor and swung the door open.

Nate's car was gone.

And I still hadn't called Stefan.

Racing back to the living room window, I watched as a line of cops in flak jackets stooped low, guns pointed, crept in a tight line across Heidi's lawn. They stopped and held their position just before reaching the paving stones that bordered the front of the house. Two other officers extracted a ladder from the back of one of the SUVs, while another two stationed themselves at either corner of the driveway watching to turn any onlookers away.

A man emerged from the first SUV, dressed in a stiff bulletproof vest. I blinked in disbelief. It was Stefan, looking as if he'd stepped right out of a scene from one of those cop procedurals. Drawing back from the window, I watched events unfold. Stefan spoke to the guys standing sentry at the corners of the driveway, then adjusted his peaked cap and walked slowly towards a large truck and past Nate's black Mercedes. I clung to the window, face hot with guilt. I'd betrayed Stefan. Now he'd know I'd let Nate get away. Unless I kept on lying and said he'd taken his Camry without my knowledge.

I felt nauseous again. Why hadn't Stefan told me there was going to be a raid? He'd left me so vulnerable, at the center of a dangerous situation. He must have known that Nate was involved. Especially with Sonny and Mel around. And Nate had known the raid was about to happen. That's what the text was about. That's why he'd been in such a hurry to get away.

By now Stefan had reached the front door of the lake house, and despite my anger at him for keeping me in the dark, I found myself silently praying that he'd be safe. I clutched the blinds so tightly I snapped the opening mechanism.

First, he checked in both directions to see that he was covered, then rang the doorbell. No answer. He waited a few moments then knocked on the door. No response. Then he waited again. Nothing. He banged at the door with his clenched fist. I could hear him calling something. Once he'd established that no one was coming to answer, he backed away from the doorstep, then turned and made his way down the driveway. The men with the ladder moved in, followed by the armed guys. Soon, they'd put up the ladder to the second-story bedroom window and one of the officers climbed up, followed by several armed officers. By now, backup had arrived in the form of more patrol cars. They pulled to a standstill, lights flashing.

My phone rang and I froze. Without taking my eyes from the scene outside, I held my breath and reached for my phone on the coffee table. It was Vera from next door. I exhaled. Ignored the ringing. There was no way

I wanted to get into a long discussion about the dramatic scene unfolding on our quiet street.

The first officer had reached the top of the ladder and leaned back towards the next guy who handed him a metal club. He used it to smash the bedroom window. The glass shattered and, with gloved hands, he pushed away the sharp edges from the frame. As soon as it was cleared, the two other armed guys followed him up the ladder and they all climbed inside. I waited, barely daring to breathe, expecting the sudden crack of gunshots. None came.

It seemed like an age before Stefan, talking into a head-piece, strode up the driveway with two backup guys and the front door swung open to reveal Heidi, head bowed, hands cuffed behind her back, accompanied by one of the officers who led her out towards the waiting squad cars. Another man followed close behind, cuffed as well. His face contorted in fury as he cursed at Stefan, spitting on the ground as he walked by. I waited, taking shallow breaths, for Nate to emerge, but instead Stefan beckoned the other cops towards the house, and they swarmed inside as Heidi and her friend were placed in separate squad cars.

Over the next half-hour, various officers emerged with large plastic bags filled with bulky objects and others bulging with bags of white powder. So, Rick had been right about the cocaine lying around there. The house had been a hotbed of gambling and drugs. But what was Nate's part in all this?

I sat back on the living room couch, a helpless spectator to the drama unfolding on my own street. I couldn't have written a more suspenseful story myself. This was the stuff of sensational cop shows and movies. Not the content of my own, average life. I closed my eyes and wondered when and if Stefan was actually ever going to come over and tell me what was going on. Would he come clean and let me know he'd actually been investigating Nate all this time he'd been pretending to help me? And did he suspect I knew anything at all about Nate's other life?

The pictures hanging on the opposite wall shifted and swam in front of my eyes. They depicted scenes from our trip to the Napa Valley wineries a month before we were married. I was powerless, trapped in a situation I couldn't control. If I ran, it might look suspicious – as if I'd known exactly what Nate was up to. And I couldn't stay, because I was still afraid of staying alone in my house. So I almost jumped out of my seat when my phone pinged again with an incoming text. With trembling hands, I picked up the phone and looked at the screen at a text from Nate.

> Are the cops still there?

My hands began to shake as I considered what to say. How to respond? Lie or tell the truth? I typed:

> No.

I waited, tiny fingers of fear crawling up my back, my neck damp with cold sweat.

> Liar.

I let out a sharp scream. He had to be in touch with someone, and that someone was close by, watching the raid as it happened.

It was then I realized the significance of what I'd just done. Nate was testing me out to see if I was loyal to him. And I'd lied, and failed the test miserably.

42

I rested my head in my hands and stared at the floor. All I wanted was a simple, uncomplicated life. Nothing exotic. I wanted to make plans, go out for drinks with friends, book a sun vacation or just sit in the park and read. I hadn't enjoyed anything close to a normal life for years and I was tired. So tired. I'd forgotten what it was like to be free from grief and worry. Free from the fear that played in the back of my mind every time the doorbell rang.

I had to tell Stefan everything I knew. Maybe he'd have time to talk now the operation looked to be drawing to a close. Patrol cars were leaving, taking Heidi and her friend away, and leaving only a few officers to finish searching the house. Stefan had been at the center of the action, directing everyone's movements, but finally he stopped and ran a hand through his hair. He turned towards my house, and with a quick look in both directions, crossed the street and made his way up my driveway. I was there waiting before he got to the front door. Dark shadows framed his eyes and his expression was grimmer than I'd ever seen it.

"Come in?"

"Sure." He took off his cap. "Got a glass of water?"

I ran to the kitchen and poured one and handed it to him. He gulped it down in one massive swallow.

"Another?"

He shook his head. "Better not."

"Want to tell me what's going on?"

"Let's go in there." He pointed towards the living room. "I have to keep an eye on the house."

I moved towards the sofa while he stood framed in the bay window. "You'd better sit down, Liv."

Feeling suddenly disoriented, I lowered myself onto the sofa.

"So… we've been watching your neighbor, er…"

"Heidi?"

"Yes, we've been watching Heidi's house since she moved in. We'd been scoping out her last place for almost a year, then she just up and left. We finally traced her here and for the last two weeks we've done drive-by and walk-by checks, parked a surveillance van on the street every day, even tapped her phone to confirm she was still up to the same tricks."

"What kind of tricks, Stefan?"

He sighed, turned his cap around in his hands and looked at me with sad eyes. "Officially, I shouldn't be telling you this, but I will because of the other information I'm about to share with you after." He took a deep breath and leaned his shoulder against the window frame. He was making me feel so fidgety, I wished to hell he'd sit down. "So, Heidi and her cronies run illegal gambling parties. Invitation only, big stakes games. She recruits the high-roller guys looking for no-limits play. For these guys, the bigger the risk, the greater the thrill. With just a few well-placed phone calls and some carefully orches-trated word-of-mouth, she organizes a big high-thrills, maximum-stakes game. Heidi hosts, provides the lavish setting, gourmet refreshments and complete assurance of anonymity. Everyone's happy. Especially the people she's laundering dirty money for."

"Laundering money? Which people?"

"I can't disclose exactly who they are. They're local but affiliated with larger criminal organizations situated on the West Coast and in Eastern Canada."

"I saw her at the casino, Stefan."

He frowned. I'd rarely seen Stefan look annoyed. "When? When were you at the casino?"

"I got a message from Nate. He lied and said he was still in Toronto. So I went looking for him. I saw Heidi instead. I followed her to some warehouse near the railway yards. They had a game going in one of the old, converted buildings. Then I saw Nate. He had two guys with him. They beat up and stabbed Heidi's friend, a bald-headed guy I thought was her boyfriend. He was over at her house all the time. I couldn't tell if he was dead."

Stefan's face was frozen in shock. "You saw all this and you didn't tell me?"

"I tried to afterwards, but the call just went to voice-mail."

"Did they see you?"

It all came back to me. The warehouse, the men, Nate giving orders. The sight of the man's head snapping backwards as Sonny's fist hit him square in the chin, the hard thrust of the knife into his gut.

I shook my head. "No, I don't think so. I don't know how I got away. They might have heard me. I floored the gas, drove to The Village, ran out of gas and called a cab. When I got here, I locked and barricaded the doors and woke up to a scene right out of a crime drama."

"Has Nate been here?"

I swallowed, then took a deep breath and nodded, deciding to keep things deliberately vague. This was the last favor I'd do for Nate. "His car was gone from the garage this morning. And just a few minutes ago he messaged me. Here – check this out." I handed my phone to him.

He glanced over the texts and immediately switched on his walkie-talkie.

"What's he driving, Liv?"

I gave him the details.

A scratchy voice came over the other end, and Stefan recited instructions in a steady, businesslike voice. "Send units out to find suspect of interest, Nate Barnett. Driving a black Camry." He took the license plate number from me and repeated it over the phone. "Bring in for questioning. Treat suspect as armed and dangerous. Approach with extreme caution."

He shoved the phone into its holder and stood for a moment, thinking and stroking his chin as if working out what to do next.

"I can't stay here, Stefan. I'm not going to sit around wondering when Nate is going to show up. I don't even know who he is anymore."

He chewed at the inside of his lip, then exhaled. "I don't need to tell you, Liv, that Nate is into some big-time criminal activity. But you already know that, don't you?"

"I swear I had no idea how deep he was into it until last night. I knew he was hiding things from me and lying, but it's like I've been asleep for five years and now I'm just waking up from a nightmare to find out my husband has not only been living a double life, but he's also mixed up in some massive illegal gambling racket."

He shifted from one foot to the other. "It may be more than just gambling, Liv. We suspect some large-scale shifting of cocaine and other drugs are involved, but we don't know how widespread the entire operation is. Right now, we're coordinating with units from BC and Ontario. Possibly even going international."

I flopped back against the sofa. "But why did he stay with me? Why live this quiet suburban life in this average neighborhood when he's spending the majority of his time rubbing shoulders with rich and powerful criminals?"

"Hate to say it, Liv, but you and this place. This street – this house – are a perfect cover for him. Nobody would suspect what he's been up to. I mean *allegedly* been up to. And that's probably what his bosses want. Staying under the radar, acting as the perfect family man with the respectable career – hell, nobody would suspect him."

"But we didn't turn out to be the perfect family. Not when Jack disappeared."

Stefan sighed and turned to look outside again. "Maybe he didn't bargain for that to happen. I hate to say it, Liv, but he wouldn't want the added police attention a missing child brings, if he was mixed up with organized crime."

I picked at my fingernail, my mind spinning. "But I keep thinking, Stefan, that maybe he was involved in some way with Jack's disappearance. I hate the idea of that, but I have to consider it, now I know the full extent of his lies."

He shook his head and sat on the arm of the sofa. "It seems unlikely, but all I can say is, if we find him, we can certainly question him about that. No promises that he'll open up, given his track record."

"You do know, Stefan, that Nate Barnett isn't his real name?"

He stood up again quickly. "Do you know something we don't? If so, you'd better tell me now, Liv."

I hung my head, afraid to meet his eyes. "I didn't want to say anything. I had to make sure about it on my own before I told you. I first got wind of it the day we went to see his mother." And then I told him everything I'd found out about the real Jack Sawyer and the way he'd simply stolen a dying boy's identity and forged a new life for himself away from his gangster father and junkie mother.

Stefan's flushed face was drained of color. "This information changes *everything*, Liv. Everything. You should have told me earlier."

Embarrassed, I hung my head. "I had to make sure, Stefan. Remember, he's my husband. I've lived with him for eight years."

"Still, I thought we weren't keeping secrets from each other."

"You haven't exactly shared everything with me either."

"Then we're even now."

"Guess so. But I just can't believe how Nate got away with changing his identity. And none of us suspected. We just accepted him as Nate, the guy who lived on his own. I keep thinking that maybe he was trying to get away from his father. Escape his past."

"There are way too many questions and not enough answers, Liv. All I know is, right now we have to get you somewhere safe. It's too dangerous for you here. Do you have any relatives – friends you can stay with?"

I looked away, ashamed. "You're going to think I'm a major loser, Stefan, but there's no one I can turn to. I shut myself away when Jack disappeared. Lost the urge to socialize."

"I'd never judge you, Liv. I don't know how you survived the loss of your son. But now I'm gonna talk to my supervising inspector. We'll get you into a hotel."

"There's more, Stefan. I haven't told you everything."

He exhaled, his face creased with worry. "What else are you going to surprise me with?"

"Chad called me. According to him, Nate was one of the last people in the basement with Alex the night of the fire. I keep thinking he had something to do with Alex's death and that's why he married me… to keep a close eye on me."

Stefan covered his mouth with his hand. His toe tapped frantically on the floor.

"You know something, Stefan. Spit it out if you do."

He looked up at me with damp eyes. "I always meant to tell you, Liv, but I couldn't. You loved Alex so much. Had him on a pedestal."

I grasped Stefan's arms and tugged on his jacket. "Tell me, for God's sake. I'm not a child anymore."

"When I did a little investigating all those years ago, I discovered that Alex had gotten into the basement gambling tournaments in a big way. He lost so much money, he had to borrow from Nate. He owed Nate over a thousand bucks – a whole lot for a high school kid at that time. So, Nate had a hold over Alex. But that's all I know. I never heard anything about Alex dealing drugs."

I felt an instant stab of regret. "So that's why he changed overnight. He was holding all that worry inside. He couldn't tell Dad about it."

"Once we find Nate, we'll question him all about Alex – but only after all this other stuff is sorted out. Fair enough?" he said, holding me gently by the shoulders.

"Okay. I'll pack some things," I said, getting up. I noticed my easel and the unfinished pictures of Parker. "Better take my work, too."

"I'll wait down here for you and don't skimp on the packing. You may be away for some time."

43

From my hotel room twenty stories up, I looked out at the downtown office towers, bustling city streets and the broad sweep of the half-frozen river in the distance. I was safe, but it was a hollow kind of comfort. I'd been torn away from everything familiar – the lake, the trees, the wildlife that formed such a major part of my everyday routine. But worse than that, coming here had broken the link between me and my lost son.

I turned to survey the room. A plain, ultra-modern rectangle, with one slate-gray feature wall, abstract gray and white flower paintings and stark white, freshly laundered bedding. But I'd slept well for the first time in ages, sinking into the plush mattress and falling asleep in the middle of a movie. The extra sleep made my head a little wooly, but a hot shower followed by a strong cup of coffee and a packet of chocolate chip cookies from the mini fridge sharpened me up. My bulging suitcase lay on the bed and I'd already set up my easel with the latest drawings on it.

Parker gazed out at me; the drawing showed him hiding his lunch box in the hollowed-out trunk of a gnarled ash tree, right by a lake that looked just like the one I'd left behind. A broad ray of sunlight trickled through the branches, turning his tousled red hair to gold. Preserved in all his innocent perfection, his sea-blue eyes stared balefully out from the page. *Protect me*, he seemed to say. *Protect me from the bullies and the people who want to hurt me.* I gulped back a sob and flung my sweatshirt over the image. I couldn't even think about drawing. Especially when I'd created a character who was the model of Jack.

Stefan had left me here with the promise that he'd drop in later to give me an update on new developments. In other words, let me know if they'd found Nate.

Just thinking of Nate was enough to chill me right through. When I thought about his betrayal, I wondered if the entire marriage had been just an act on his part. And yet, he'd told me the previous night he still loved me.

How could I believe him after all the lies? I searched my memory for something real and honest about our relationship, then I remembered the day Jack was born. When the nurse had handed Nate the small bundle wrapped in a blue hospital blanket, he'd cradled the tiny body against his chest and gazed at our child with such wonder, his eyes shining with tears. I'd never seen such a look of genuine emotion on his face – ever. That moment was so real, so sincere, as if he couldn't fathom the miracle of the gift he'd been given. I had to believe that was at least one perfect moment of truth in our marriage.

I threw my suitcase onto the floor and slumped onto the bed. Flicked through news channels, cooking shows, home renovation contests, afternoon soaps. Nothing held my interest. How could I stay here for hours without exercise? Without the trees and the sky and the lake? I wasn't tired or hungry, but I was so restless. The only thing that excited me was the thought of a long, cool drink. I grabbed my phone and threw on my denim jacket, remembering to take the key card from the side table on my way out the door.

The hallway was empty. Not surprising since the business types who usually stayed here were probably all in afternoon meetings. I reckoned I'd have a couple of drinks – just enough to relax me – and maybe get some supper before going back to the room and settling in for the night. I pressed the elevator button and counted the ascending floor numbers. When it stopped and the doors swished open, I took a quick look to establish it was empty, then hopped inside and let the doors close.

The bar looked like an extension of the lobby; a square space with lipstick red basket chairs arranged around black lacquer tables and all dominated by a massive abstract wall painting comprised of blurred, multicolored squares. I sat in the corner, partially hidden by a tall rubber plant, but with a clear view of the main entrance.

Five minutes later, I was nursing a large gin and tonic, enjoying the smooth liquor as it slipped down my throat. But I was so jumpy, I drank it too quickly. The waiter, an awkward looking guy who couldn't have been older than twenty-one, raised his eyebrows when I held out my glass for another.

"Tough day," I said, smiling and taking another sweating glass from him.

He nodded and scurried away. Probably thought I was hitting on him. I chuckled to myself, imagining him texting his buddies and telling them some drunken older woman was giving him the eye. Starting on the next drink, I fixed my attention onto the TV screen in the corner where some big bake-off show was happening with teams competing to make the best cake for the grand opening of a dance academy.

I was feeling pretty mellow when I first heard a whisper in my ear. The booze had made me so sluggish it took a while to register that someone was standing behind me. But not standing. Hovering. I placed the glass on the table and turned around to see Sonny, the tall guy from the Dodge Viper. My first instinct was to scream, jump up and tear over to the reception desk, but as quickly as I thought of it, a large hand clamped across my mouth. I glanced around the room, hoping the waiter might come back and check on me, but the lobby was deserted.

"Cooperate and nobody will get hurt," the quiet voice said as I felt something dig into my back. "Now walk out slowly and calmly and stay right beside me as if we're the best of friends."

I struggled to breathe, my head light and dizzy as I made my way around the chair and came face to face with Sonny. Up close, he looked older than I'd thought. Two deep grooves ran from the side of his nose down to the corners of his lips. The rest of his face was pulled tight and smooth as if he'd had cosmetic work done. His manicured eyebrows gave him the appearance of a mannequin from a shop window, and his hair had the dull, inky look that only comes out of a bottle. His eyes were flat and expressionless. Devoid of any trace of emotion. I felt the stirrings of panic inside my chest.

He placed an arm around my shoulders and steered me through the lobby then out the front door where a black SUV was waiting. Opening the back door, he shoved me into the rear seat. I heard a sharp click as the locks snapped down and, suddenly, we were off, speeding through the busy afternoon streets.

A Plexiglas shield separated me from the front of the car, but I could see Sonny's sidekick, Mel, was driving. He could barely reach the steering wheel and strained to see the road ahead. I felt my phone in my pocket. If only

I could tap out a message without them hearing me, I could alert Stefan, but as I went to pull it from my pocket Sonny's head whipped around and the shield slid open.

"Don't even think about it," he said, sitting up and twisting his arm through the space. "Hand it over or you get a bullet in the foot and that might put an end to all that walking you do through the forest near your place."

"You've been watching me?"

He laughed. "We've known about you for a long time thanks to our buddy, Nate."

"Where is he? Where's my husband?"

He laughed again. A kind of tuneless, dry laugh. "D'you hear her, Mel? She still wants to know where that piece of crap is." He turned to me again. "I'm surprised you're still interested, considering the lies he must've told you."

"Like he's not really Nate Barnett?"

"Yeah – we heard you'd been doing some snooping around. You like the name, Nate, or d'you prefer Jack? We kind of thought Nate had a better ring to it when we helped him all those years ago. He had to lose the surname that his rat of a father, Glenn, gave him. Had to undo a whole lot of bad parenting. Gotta tell you, Olivia, we – that is Mel and me—we *made* your husband. Took a pimply, sniveling shoplifter from his trashy home and made him into a polished, educated businessman. Did everything for him including paying for that damned university degree. A regular *My Two Dads*, the two of us. Eh, Mel?"

"Right, Sonny," said Mel, his baritone voice surprisingly deep for such a short man.

Chad and Max had been right. Sonny and Mel had been around Nate right from the start. Grooming him and guiding him into the world of crime. It was like a bad remake of *The Great Gatsby*.

"So, what's his loyal wife doing in a fancy downtown hotel instead of waiting with open arms to welcome him back?" asked Mel.

"He didn't come back. I don't know where he is."

"It's too bad you're lying," growled Mel. "We were kind of hoping you'd help us find him since you saw him only last night."

"You mean at the warehouse? By the railway tracks?"

Sonny wheeled around again. "How do you know about the warehouse? You in on that too?"

"No... no... I went to look for Nate at the casino."

"Gotta give you credit. That's a good place to start. That guy doesn't feel alive unless he's holding a hand of cards," Sonny chuckled. "And the sound of the roulette wheel gives him a better high than a line of coke."

"Always got him in deep shit," said Mel. "It's a serious addiction. Worse than drugs, they say."

"Clouded his judgement," said Sonny. "Made him forget who his friends were."

Mel nodded. "Too right, bud. So how did you know about the warehouse, Olivia?"

I was so confused by what they were saying – couldn't make out whether Nate was with these guys or had turned against them. "I saw Heidi at the casino and followed her there."

"Hey, we got a real honest-to-God amateur sleuth here, Mel! Maybe we ought to be hiring her instead of her ungrateful rat of a husband. What d'you think?"

"She's got guts," growled Mel. "I'll say that for her. She had to have, sticking with that loser for so long."

We'd left the city and were heading up the main road towards the turnoff for my place.

"You know they're going to check on me at the hotel. When they find I'm not there they'll come looking for me."

"The cops have had us on their radar for years and they've still got nothing on us. They're after your husband and that greedy bitch, Heidi. Nate thought he could have his own operation on the side, keep all the profits and not show his gratitude to the folks who set him up. But then Heidi got greedy and tried to cut him out. That's when Mel and me found out about their little side operation. But last night she squealed on Nate to save her boyfriend who just got to hospital in the nick of time. Too bad Nate made the big mistake of forgetting who's running things in this town. Especially when he knows how far our connections go."

We'd already turned into the treelined streets a few blocks from my house. I leaned forward, pleading. "Why can't you let me go? I don't have anything to do with this gambling. I don't want any of the money. I just want a quiet life."

Sonny turned around again. "You seem like a real nice lady, and it's too bad you got mixed up with a no-good scumbag. But the problem is, you married him and that makes you part of it. But now we need your help to bring him right here to us so we can deal with him."

We pulled into my street. "What makes you think I want to help you?"

Mel glanced at me in the rearview mirror. "When we tell you the truth about your husband and what he's done to you and your family, you're going to be begging us to help find him."

44

I felt a cold sense of dread when we pulled into the driveway of the lake house. The place was deserted. After all yesterday's action, no signs of police activity were visible. And I'd seen nothing on last night's TV news about the raid.

"Where are the cops?" I said, looking at the front door. There was no yellow police tape. No officers guarding the house. The only evidence of yesterday's raid was the boarded-up bedroom window on the second story.

Mel killed the engine. "They're probably keeping things under wraps. They think they can wait around and catch the big fish now. They're like bugs, just wanted to nip at us first. Get us all riled up so we panic and play right into their hands."

"But they're dead wrong," said Sonny, getting out and opening the passenger door for me. "They have no clue what or who they're dealing with."

Sonny took my arm and pulled me out. I looked over at my house, at the empty driveway. I prayed that maybe Vera would open her garage door and see me, or that Shanti might walk by, spot me with these two strange guys, and suspect something was up. But as usual, the street was deserted, and I cursed myself that I'd chosen such a secluded place to live.

"Don't keep looking. There's nobody gonna help you," said Sonny, as he walked me towards the front door. "We've scoped this place out long enough to know what goes on here and when people are usually around. The place is dead this time of day."

Mel shoved me forward. They were right. It was a quiet street. People kept to themselves. And that's what I'd loved about the area. My legs felt sluggish and heavy. My stomach churned as I dragged my feet past Nate's Mercedes, still parked in the driveway.

"Is Nate here?"

"Hell, no," said Sonny, opening the car door and checking inside. "But it's mighty kind of him to leave the keys for us. I'll take this one when we leave, Mel."

Mel nodded at me. "Guess Nate paid you a visit the other night and took his old junker Camry."

The lie was quick on my tongue. "I didn't hear him. I'd barricaded the doors. He couldn't get in."

"He was probably in a big hurry to get away, considering what he'd just done," said Sonny, shoving me towards the front door.

What had he done? I still couldn't figure it out, but whatever it was, they were mad as hell about it.

Mel sorted through a bunch of keys. "Real kind of Heidi to give us the run of the place. Guess she's getting used to a way smaller living space right now."

He pushed the front door open and I stepped inside the lake house. The place I'd watched from the outside for so many years, hating everything it represented. But now the feeling of dread so overwhelmed me, I thought I'd pass out.

Sonny's fingers dug into my arm as he yanked me upright. I looked around at a grand tiled entrance hall with a sweeping staircase on the left. French doors on the right opened onto an elegant dining room dominated by crystal chandeliers and a long dining table that looked as if it had been carved from a single tree trunk. A vast hallway stretched ahead, at the end a massive room made larger by the floor-to-ceiling windows that looked out onto the lake and the terrace and the trees. The frozen lake gleamed in the cold light of the sun.

We walked into a spacious, open family room. A gleaming gourmet kitchen was visible to one side. At the other, there was an ornamental stone fireplace that reached to the ceiling. Cream leather chairs, fur rugs and teak coffee tables were dotted around, but the stunning beauty of the place was marred by food-encrusted plates, brimming ashtrays and the rancid stink of cigarette smoke. I thought I heard the buzzing of a phone. Sonny touched his pocket. He had my phone in there. I cursed myself that I'd turned the ringer off. I wondered if it was Stefan or Nate trying to contact me.

Sonny stood, surveying the mess. "No wonder Jude was pissed off with Heidi. She's a damned slob."

"Beautiful place and she couldn't take care of it," said Mel. "Talk about ungrateful. Some people don't know how lucky they are."

Sonny shoved me onto a chair. "That's one thing you could say about Nate. He was really grateful for everything. *At first.*"

"Too bad it went to his head," said Mel, opening the fridge that looked to be filled with bottles. "Nobody eats anything around here. Just pickles and booze. Not even a piece of fruit or a vegetable."

"No wonder Heidi's old man took the kid away," said Sonny.

Mel took a bottle of water and shut the fridge door. "Yeah. The brat got in Heidi's way, so she probably wasn't too upset about it."

"Unnatural, I call it," said Sonny. "A mother not wanting her son. Sounds a lot like Nate's old lady. She'd have sold the poor kid for a few dollars to buy a shot of heroin."

Mel unscrewed the cap and took a slug of water. He was balding, with stringy hair and a thin moustache. "Little tyke had to fend for himself when his dad was put away."

Sonny stood over me. "But we know what that feels like. Let's put it this way – me and Mel have never felt the urge to celebrate Mothers' Day for reasons I don't wanna get into now. But that's why we helped young Jack make a life for himself. He was eager. Ready to sign up for anything we asked him to do. And we spotted the potential right away. He was a real charmer – a budding con artist. So we got him a new identity, an education, polished him up so we could prepare him for what was up ahead for him. Big opportunities if he played his cards right."

"Problem was, he got too fond of playing the cards," said Mel, perching on the edge of a couch. "We should have known it would cause big trouble right from the start."

I was shivering from cold or maybe fear. I'd seen what these two guys were capable of, but they seemed to want to talk. I wondered if I could keep them going long enough for Stefan to discover I was gone and come here to find me.

"What do you want from me? I don't know anything."

"Big surprise, O-livia. We know you don't." Sonny took my phone from his pocket. "But you're gonna help us find your husband. He has something we need really, really bad."

"But I don't know where he is. He went missing weeks ago and I didn't know anything about all this stuff he's mixed up in. I thought he was working in pharmaceutical sales."

Sonny shook his head and looked over at Mel. "Did you hear that, Mel? He sure scammed this poor, innocent woman. Even married her to tie up his loose ends."

"What do you mean *loose ends*? What are you talking about?"

"I feel sorry for you," said Mel. "I really do. You seem like a nice sort of lady. Too bad your brother got mixed up with a no-good delinquent kid like Nate."

I shot up in the chair, my eyes prickling with tears. "What's this got to do with my brother?" I screamed.

Sonny shoved me back down. "Cool it and we'll tell you. Then you'll really want to help us. Christ, you'll be begging to come along with us so you can put a bullet in your husband's head."

I sat back in the chair, tears streaming down my cheeks, my chest heaving.

He continued, a slight grin twisting his mouth. "Bet you always wondered what went on in your basement the night your brother, Alex, died?"

I felt a rush of anger. "Don't even say his name. He wasn't into drugs, and he didn't cause the fire."

"Did you hear me say anything about drugs, Mel?"

"I didn't, Sonny."

"I'll excuse the rude interruption and continue then if you'll just shut the fuck up."

I slumped back, panting for breath.

Sonny looked out at the lake and started talking again. "As a matter of fact, you're right. Your saint of a brother wasn't into drugs, but he was heavy into gambling. He owed Nate big money." This, I already knew. "That's why Nate went over to your house that day. To collect it." This, I didn't, so it felt like the wind had been knocked out of me.

Sonny continued. "He got real mad and said he'd ask your dad if Alex couldn't come up with it. Then his other buddies showed up. The weird musician guy, Chad, and some little junkie rat called Renny and two other football players, but they didn't stay long apparently. Your squeaky-clean brother didn't know Renny had asked Nate to bring some of the good stuff along that night. When he pulled out the pipes and the junk and all, your brother went ballistic and threatened to call the cops.

"At the time, Nate had a short fuse. He wasn't the calm Mr. GQ man you know today. We taught him all about control a lot later. Nate called us for help, but while he was waiting, he got real mad when your bro actually tried to dial 911. Before we got there, he'd already beaten your brother up, and threatened to burn him with a barbecue lighter. Problem was, he held the lighter too close. The flame shot out way further than he'd bargained and set your brother's clothes on fire. Your brother's friends tried to get to him to put it out, but he panicked and fell against a pile of craft supplies and Christmas decorations. The whole thing caught fire. When we walked in the place was an inferno. We ripped Nate out of there and told the other two if they breathed a word of it, we'd strap them to a chair, beat them to a pulp and then go get their parents and do the same. Then we all escaped out the back door. Your folks were upstairs in bed. Guess the whole thing went up with your brother still down there, and your parents got downstairs too late."

I bent over, sobs tearing through me. I couldn't get the picture out of my head. My brother, burning to death, while the others ran out and left him to die.

"Now you've gone and upset her," said Mel. "Gotta say though. He did feel bad about it afterwards. Poor guy had nobody to tell him how to behave until we came along. His asshole father used to use his wife like a damn ashtray. No wonder she got hooked on junk."

"Guess that's why he married you. Maybe he wanted to make up for it," said Sonny.

"Bastard," I yelled, feeling the words rip through my throat. "He's a liar and a murderer."

"My theory is, he wanted to keep you close. Make sure that little incident never caused him any trouble in the future."

"If I knew where he was, I'd drive you to him right now," I said, gritting my teeth to stop myself from screaming again.

I heard the *ping* of a message on my phone.

"Wonder if that's him," said Sonny, taking my phone out from his pocket and glancing at the screen. "Well, look at this. It's your friend the cop wondering where you are."

I felt a shot of hope rise in me. "He's gonna be here soon if he doesn't find me at the hotel."

Sonny put the phone back in his pocket. "That's good. We want him to come here. We've got plans for him. He's causing us way too much trouble. But it might take him a bit too long to figure it out, so you're going to call him and tell him to get his ass over here now."

"Why would I do that?"

Now both of them were standing over me. A slow smile spread across Mel's face. "You'll do it because we have the answer to a question you've been asking for five years."

I couldn't form the words. I opened my mouth, but nothing came out.

"Yes, Mrs. Barnett. We know all about what happened to your son."

45

I lunged at Mel with a force I didn't know I possessed and grabbed him by the throat, knocking him back against the kitchen table. But before I could make another move, an arm clamped around my neck, pressing against my throat and choking the breath from me. All I could see was blackness. Pinpoints of light exploding in front of my eyes. I was going to die right there. I'd never find out what happened to Jack. I tried to pull his arm away. Tried to beg.

"Okay... okay." I raised my hands. Sonny threw me hard against the wall. My head slammed against a picture frame, knocking it to the floor, shattering the glass.

"I get really mad when someone tries to hurt my buddy," he growled. "Now take this fucking phone and call your friend the cop. Tell him to meet you here in twenty minutes because you've found out something really important, then we'll think about telling you what you want to know."

He handed me the phone. It showed three missed calls from Stefan and a text from Nate. "Nate just texted me. I thought you wanted *him*."

"That's the next call. Just do as you're told," said Sonny, cracking his knuckles and glowering at me.

I dialed Stefan's number and put the phone on speaker. He picked up immediately. "Liv? Are you okay?"

"Yes, yes… I'm good."

"You weren't in your hotel room. I was worried."

Sonny loomed over me. "I… I… forgot something at home. I just wanted to pop back and get it."

"It's not safe, Liv. I told you. I'll come and pick you up, then we'll go get your car."

Sonny mouthed *here* silently.

"Oh, could you meet me outside the lake house? Nate's car is here and I found something important in it that might tell us where he is."

Stefan's voice took on an anxious tone. "Don't go over there, Liv. Stay away."

Sonny made a gesture to cut the call. "See you there, Stefan."

He yanked the phone from me. Mel, meanwhile, was pouring a glass of water, a livid expression on his face.

"Now your husband," said Sonny. "Text him and tell him we've got you and we'll kill you if he doesn't tell us where he is."

"What if he doesn't care? If he's as bad as you say he is, it won't make a difference."

"Do it," yelled Mel, turning towards me, "or you get this in the gut." He walked towards me brandishing a long knife.

I shrank back against the wall, as if I could press myself into it. Sonny handed me the phone and I typed the text out, sent it, then waited, a loud, rushing sound flooding my ears. My heart leapt when the phone pinged.

Heidecker's Barn, Jct. Highway 2 and 223.

Then another message.

I shook my head. "No. I don't want to. Please."

But Sonny dialed the number. "You're gonna scream so he knows you're in trouble."

I heard the ringing, felt my heart slam against my ribs, felt the nausea rising in my throat. Nate answered. "Liv?"

I started to scream. "Bastard. Murderer."

"Looks like she doesn't want to talk to you, bud," said Sonny.

"Don't hurt her," I heard him say. I felt sick at the familiar sound of his voice, but then I remembered what they'd told me about Alex.

"Told you we wouldn't, if you cooperate with us. You got what we're looking for?"

"I've got it here with me. Just let her go."

"Unlike you, we keep our promises. But if you don't hand over what we want, you know what happens. I have something lined up in case. A backup plan. Understand?"

"I got it."

Then he shouted something that blew my mind. "Liv... I'm sorry. Rory. Rory."

Sonny shut the call down. "We gotta move, Mel. Now."

Mel had a sick, twisted look on his face. "I think I want to kill her first for what she just did to me."

"Time for that later. I gotta get the stuff from the van. You watch her."

Sonny shoved me back into the chair and tied my hands behind me with a tea towel, while Mel pulled out a gun and stood in front of me, smiling as Sonny headed out the door.

293

"Just because I'm small doesn't mean you can push me around. That's why I'm going to give you a long time to think about the fact that you're going to die."

The room seemed to spin around me. Tears pressed against my eyes, but I couldn't cry. My body was a hollow shell.

"Go ahead. I have nothing to live for anyway," I croaked.

He shook his head. "But you want to know – before you go – about your kid. Don't you?"

I strained forward, twisting my hands. Wishing I could have strangled the life out of this guy. "Tell me," I said, my voice hoarse with crying.

Sonny came back inside holding two red gasoline containers. He handed one to Mel. "Too bad it has to go up like this, but we can't let the authorities take everything. Jude says he'd rather torch the place. He's got some crooked guy at the insurance company might put a claim through. And if that doesn't work, the lot alone is worth big bucks. Some fool will buy it and build something new here."

They strode around splashing gasoline over the couches and tables. Mel passed by me and I screamed as he splashed the colorless liquid over my arms.

He grinned. "Oops, I slipped."

"You said you'd let me go."

"I don't remember that," said Mel, throwing the empty container down. They were going to set fire to the place and leave me here. I would die like Alex had. I'd never know what happened to Jack. Never see Stefan again.

"I know you're going to kill me, but tell me what happened to my son… please," I said, struggling with the

294

tea towel and realizing I could see the way to the driveway outside. Sonny had left the front door ajar.

Sonny stopped for a moment. "Maybe we should tell her. What do you say, Mel?"

Mel nodded. "Sure… she'll die suffering more when she knows it was her rat of a husband that did it."

"He wouldn't hurt his son," I screeched. "He's not that kind of monster."

"Sorry, Mrs. Barnett, but our good friend Jude said when you guys came to a party here, he remembered you going off for a drink and leaving your kid with Nate. Then he saw your husband lead your son to the gate that goes into the forest, at the side of this exact house. When he came back, your son wasn't with him. Of course, Nate denied it completely. Too bad we don't know what happened to your kid, all alone in a place with coyotes wandering around or maybe weirdos passing by and a big, deep lake only a few steps away."

At that moment, it felt like an explosion went off in my head. As if a bolt of lightning had charged right through me, I ripped the loose towel away from my hands and leapt to my feet, hurling the kitchen chair at them. It glanced off Sonny's shoulder, knocking him backwards, giving me enough time to run towards the open front door, fly over to Nate's car and get in. The keys were in the ignition. My hands shook so badly I could barely turn the key. The stench of gasoline was everywhere. My breath tore out in rasps when I finally started the car up just as they ran out into the driveway. They'd never leave me alone. I knew I couldn't shake them off. But then a crazy idea shot into my head.

I backed the car up, put it in drive and headed right towards them. I could see their eyes, white-edged with disbelief as they jumped aside. It was then that I floored the gas pedal, crashing straight through the open side gate towards the lawn and the boat dock and the frozen lake. With seconds to go, I threw the side door open and flung myself out among the bulrushes, smashing my shoulder against a jagged chunk of ice. I heard the car crash onto the half-frozen lake.

Crawling through the bulrushes, my arm screaming with pain, I pulled myself into the shelter of the shrubs that bordered the park. Sonny and Mel ran down the back lawn and watched as the car's nose turned downwards into the cold, black water. Then they turned and made their way back to the house, stopping suddenly at the sound of a car pulling into the driveway.

All I could do now was sit back in my cradle of bulrushes and stare at the broken gate that separated the lake house from the forest. To watch the car go down.

To find myself in the exact place where Nate had left our son Jack five years ago.

46

The lake house was burning.

I had to get back there.

Right away.

Before there was nothing left but a pile of burnt rubble and the person I truly loved was buried underneath it all.

Mel and Sonny had already left, which was exactly what I wanted. I needed them to think I was dead. That my body had sunk down into the frigid water along with Nate's car.

But I could swear I'd seen Stefan standing in the window of the burning house.

I started running, the same thought spooling through my head. Over and over, *He thinks I'm still in there. He's gone in to rescue me.*

I tore up the garden and past the side of the house. Mel and Sonny's truck was gone, but Stefan's SUV was still parked in the driveway, the driver's side door hanging wide open.

The front door of the house was shut, and the heavy concrete planter shoved against it, so it would be next to impossible to open the door from inside. Sonny and Mel must have hidden at the side of the house and watched Stefan arrive, then shut him in once he went inside to rescue me from the fire.

They'd thrown gasoline everywhere, so there was no time to waste. I had to get inside before everything went up in a massive blaze. I start to shove at the planter, but I couldn't budge it. Then I began to scream for help, at the top of my voice.

My screams were suddenly drowned by the rush of flames rocketing into the air like cascading fireworks, dispersing into a heavy pall of black smoke.

Almost immediately, front doors opened all along the street.

Vera's garage door slid upwards and she appeared, tearing towards me, her coat flying behind her.

"I called 911," she yelled.

Then Shanti's front door slammed open, and Dev was sprinting down the street towards me. Sam from next door rushed out holding a shovel. In a matter of minutes neighbors from all down the street, including some I'd never met, were gathered in the driveway.

"Is anyone else inside?" shouted Dev.

"My friend's in there," I screamed above the noise. "Help me get to him."

Dev and Sam and a guy I'd never met, grabbed the edges of the concrete planter, and together we shoved it away from the door in an effort to open it. But the door was locked.

They lured him in there and locked the door on him. My heart lurched. I couldn't lose Stefan now.

My throat felt so dry I could hardly force the words out. "My friend's a cop – he's in there. They locked him inside. I saw him in the family room window."

Sam ran back to his garage and returned with a ladder. "If we can climb up to look inside, maybe we'll see him."

We ran to the back of the house. The family room was filled with smoke.

"We can't break the window," said Dev. "It'll make the fire worse."

I felt like someone's hand was clamped across my throat as Sam propped the ladder against the wall and began to climb upwards. Dev and I steadied the base.

"I hear the sirens," said Vera, rushing round to join us. "They're almost here."

But all I could picture was Stefan fighting back flames, just like Alex did that night so long ago. Or maybe he'd passed out in the noxious clouds of smoke.

"Can you see him?" I screamed to Sam as the sound of sirens filled the street.

"I'm not sure. Maybe I see a foot sticking out from behind a wall."

"Let me look," I yelled, and was about to climb up too when Dev grabbed my arm.

"Leave it to the pros, Olivia. They're here."

The sound of squealing brakes was quickly followed by the heavy crunch of boots on the gravel.

Two firefighters appeared. "Anyone in there?" yelled one.

"I think someone's lying on the floor down here," Sam shouted back.

Within seconds the crew cleared us all away from the area and banished us to the end of the driveway where two massive fire trucks were parked, their lights flashing. We all moved further back onto my driveway as an ambulance arrived, followed by the police. Only then I realized I was a mess – bruised, filthy, terrified. Vera put an arm around me and cradled me against her shoulder.

"They'll get him out," she whispered. "It'll be all right."

I leaned sideways against her stout, warm body, and next thing I knew everything went fuzzy and my legs gave out from under me.

-

I struggled to open my eyes – to get a sense of my surroundings. I was at the end of my driveway, propped against the back of an ambulance in a beach chair. Red and blue lights whirled around my head and the air was thick with the stink of smoke and damp, burned things. I looked up and a pain shot through my skull. Shanti was standing over me holding a mug of tea.

"Wh— what happened? How…?"

"You fainted, Liv. With shock. The fire. The car in the lake. Drink this."

"Stefan," I screamed, trying to jump to my feet but everything went black and I slumped back down into the chair.

"Stay still, Liv. You need to rest." She handed me the tea.

"Did they get him out?" I said, cradling the warm cup.

"You mean the cop?"

I nodded.

"I saw a stretcher taken into the other ambulance."

"Was he alive? Or was his face covered?"

"Sorry, Liv. I didn't see. But I think they got the fire under control."

I grabbed her arm. "Can you try and find out? Please?"

"I'll see what I can do. But promise me you won't move from here."

"Okay. I promise. Just go see. I have to know he's all right."

She took off in the direction of the other ambulance, and I waited, fingers crossing and uncrossing. He had to be okay. Suddenly that was all that mattered.

Because if he didn't make it, I couldn't handle losing him again.

47

I lay, propped against a mountain of pillows in the emergency room bed, my left hip stiff and bruised. The entire right side of my leg and arm was bandaged all the way down. I figured I must have bashed and scraped myself really badly when I rolled out of the car as it plunged towards the lake. Thinking about that crazy stunt from the safety of a hospital bed, it seemed inconceivable that I actually went through with it. It was like something from an action movie – or a comic strip. Like the one Stefan and I created.

Then a memory slammed into my head. Stefan had been carried out of the lake house on a stretcher, but I still didn't know if he'd made it out alive. The ambulance had taken me away before I could find Shanti. Then as soon as I reached the hospital, the doctors checked me out and a nurse dressed my wounds. After that, two officers came and took a statement asking me to recall everything I remembered from the moment Sonny and Mel brought me to the lake house. They already knew about Nate's involvement. Stefan must have told them before he came rushing to help me out. But I gave them the location that Nate had sent to Sonny and Mel, so they left in a hurry, telling me to stick around the city, because they weren't done with the inquiry.

I'd fallen asleep then, trying not to think about Nate and what was happening out on that country road. Since I'd found out he was responsible for Alex's death *and* Jack's disappearance, I hated him with such a passion that if he'd come into the room and stood in front of me, I'd have torn him apart with my bare hands. Instead, I prayed that Sonny and Mel reached him, found whatever they were looking for and delivered some kind of gang justice to him. Preferably something slow and excruciatingly painful.

The rush of anguish made my head woozy again. I thought maybe I had a concussion, so even though I felt the need to sleep, I tried to fight it. But I was so tired, I started drifting off. Then the sound of a familiar voice nudged me out of my drowsy state. I opened my eyes. Shanti was standing by the side of the bed. Something about her bright eyes and wide smile made me glad to be alive. She clutched a large bunch of yellow daisies and a bag of Maltesers.

"Hey, stranger. I got munchies and good news for you."

I sat up. Hope flared like a light inside me.

She plunked the candies on the bed. "The cop. He's okay."

"They got him out? He's not injured?"

She shook her head. "Seems he crawled across the floor to the back passageway of the house. He managed to shut that door so the fire couldn't spread there. He got out almost unharmed, except for a bit of smoke inhalation. Guess they train those guys on what to do in those situations."

"I can't believe it. That's the best news I've heard in ages," I said, ripping the bag of chocolates open and holding the bag out to her. "Want some?"

She grinned and grabbed a handful. "Don't mind if I do."

We were over halfway through the bag of Maltesers when Stefan walked in and my heart skipped a couple of beats. Shanti looked from me to him, a bewildered expression on her face.

Stefan looked pretty good for someone who'd escaped from a major fire. One side of his face was covered in deep scratches. His hands were both bandaged, but there were no visible burns. "Olivia and I are old friends from high school," he said, pulling a chair up to the side of the bed.

"We go way back," I added.

She exhaled deeply. "Oh… I was wondering what the connection was."

"Thanks for looking after Olivia," he said. "You guys are all great neighbors. I heard how everyone worked together to get me out. Can't thank you enough."

"We look after each other. That's what neighbors do," she said, smiling.

I was grinning like a kid on her birthday. I'd almost lost Stefan again, and now he was sitting right next to me, solid and real. He smiled back.

"Okay," said Shanti. "It looks like you two have important things to talk about, so I'll go and see if I can find a vase for the flowers."

We watched her leave. Once the door shut, Stefan's smile disappeared as he took my hand. My heart dropped.

"I'm afraid I have bad news for you, Liv. It's about Nate."

I leaned back against the pillow and gritted my teeth to stop the tears squeezing from my eyes. "I don't want to talk about that monster. I'm done with him."

"Wait, Liv. You haven't heard me out. Raj just came to see me. They found Nate."

I sat up, the anger rushing to my throat. "Good. I hope they've locked him up and thrown away the key."

He pressed my hand and spoke in a softer voice. "He's dead, Liv."

My mind whirled in confusion. "What do you mean? How?"

"They found him in his car. Out on the road by the barn where he'd told Sonny and Mel to meet him."

I swallowed. Tried to force the words out. "How did he die?"

Stefan looked away. "It was bad, Liv. Sonny and Mel killed him."

"I don't care, Stefan. They told me he killed my brother and did something to our son. I hate him. And now I'll never know what happened to Jack, because Nate died without telling me. I wanted to stand face to face with him and *make* him admit to what he'd done."

Stefan squeezed my hand again. "How do you know those guys were telling the truth, Liv? Maybe they were the ones responsible."

"We'll ask them. You can make a deal with them or something. Aren't you guys always doing deals?"

"Not with dead people. Sonny and Mel are dead too."

"How?" I gasped.

"Looks like they strangled Nate in his car with a piano wire and cut his tongue out."

The brutality of the image hit me like a blow to the skull. I squeezed my eyes shut.

"Sonny and Mel were monsters, Liv. They belonged to a major organized crime syndicate. But it looks to us like Nate rigged the barn with explosives, so as soon as they crossed the threshold, the whole place went up. Blew into a million pieces with them inside it."

Seeds of doubt began to sprout in my mind. "Nate set them up?"

"We're not sure about everything yet, but we believe Nate was trying to set something up on his own. Get out from the main organization. He had something they really needed and was using it for leverage. Apparently, he'd orchestrated their entire financial structure – set up a bunch of offshore accounts and phony shell companies. They wanted all the details – all the passwords and account numbers. He said he'd give it to them if they let him go. He'd told them he had it all at the barn and was waiting for them. But if they didn't give him a free pass to safety, he threatened to give all the information and more to FINTRAC, that's the national Financial Intelligence agency. He'd make a deal that would put them all away for life."

"I don't get it." I shook my head. Closed my eyes. It was all too much to take in.

"We'll spend the next few weeks finding out more details and filling in the blanks, answering the questions. Trying to find what they were looking for."

"Can I go home?"

"They won't let me drive yet, but I'll get someone to take you as soon as the doc gives the okay."

I remembered my car, back in the Safeway parking lot and asked if someone could fetch it to my place. Stefan went off to make the call and I lay there staring at the ceiling, feeling nothing but numbness. I thought I'd feel relieved to learn that Nate was dead. That he'd died a violent, painful death. But I didn't feel that way at all.

One thought still chipped away at my brain, and wouldn't let me rest. Now I'd never find out what happened to Jack and I'd have to live with that unanswered question for the rest of my life.

48

Two weeks later, I was back home sitting in an easy chair by the bay window, staring at the burned-out remnants of the lake house. It was a perfect metaphor for my life. A hollowed-out shell haunted by ruined memories. A grotesque reminder of what could have been. My easel stood on the other side of the window, on it a blank canvas. I hadn't touched it since before the fire. Min called me the day I got home from the hospital and told me not to worry.

"Take a month off, Liv. Check in with me then and let me know how you're feeling. We understand."

A month off? I needed a new life. A fresh start. A chance to put everything behind me. But how?

The neighbors were really kind and helpful when I came back from the hospital. Vera and Shanti kept bringing food. Left to my own devices, I probably wouldn't have eaten much if they hadn't dropped by with casseroles and soup and pies. But it took a while to get my appetite back. At first I was afraid to look in my fridge at all the food there, so I made a lot of tea. Pots of it. I also did a whole lot of sitting and thinking about nothing, because if I allowed it, my mind went to places I didn't want it to go. I craved sleep, sometimes crawling out of bed between eleven and noon.

I was just considering whether I should drag myself out for a walk when Stefan's car pulled into the driveway. I hadn't seen or heard from him since that day at the hospital, and was hoping he'd pay me a visit.

He looked rested and healthy. Clean-cut in his padded jacket and a crisp white shirt over his jeans. Self-conscious, I ran a hand over my tangled hair – tried to straighten my rumpled T-shirt.

"Hey, Liv. You look…"

"Like crap."

"No… like you're on the mend."

"I wish," I said, turning and heading towards the kitchen. "Tea?"

"Sure. Whatever you're making."

I boiled the kettle as he settled onto the stool by the breakfast bar. I liked seeing him sitting in my kitchen. His smile was a welcome relief in all the chaos of the past few weeks.

"Lemon-ginger okay?" I said, pushing a steaming cup towards him. "So, what's new?"

"We're learning more about Nate – or Jack. You want to hear?"

I shrugged. "Guess so. It won't make any difference to me though."

"From what we've been able to pull together, it seems Nate got mixed up with Mel and Sonny when he was fifteen. They'd worked a few scams with his father and owed him a favor. They'd heard he was a really bright kid, and good looking too, so they saw an opportunity. They had no problem pulling him out of his mom's place. She was too far gone with her junkie lifestyle to put up any kind of protest. They helped him steal a shiny, new identity and set him up with his own place. They got him into a good school and in return, he started dealing drugs for them and ran his own little dealership around all the local high schools. Once he graduated high school and went on to university, he did some small-scale work for the organization. Mostly casino-based laundering of their dirty drug money. Then when he graduated university and got a respectable job as a cover, they had him set up all the big-time laundering – the offshore shell accounts and the phony businesses and real estate companies. Even got him to set up an illegal online gambling site, which was a major success. Basically, he became indispensable to them. And even if he wanted to get out, he couldn't."

"So why did they kill him?"

"He struck out on his own. The big guys in Montreal and Vancouver didn't know anything about the Heidi operation. Nate hadn't cleared it with them. We think he was trying to pile up enough money to strike out on his own or maybe get out completely. They were worried he was going to make a run with all the financial information. Too bad he didn't realize they'd never leave him alone, no matter where he ran. And too bad that Heidi and her boyfriend got greedy too and started stealing from Nate."

I sighed. It was a sad story, but I couldn't feel any sympathy for him. Not after everything he'd done to the people I most loved. I folded my arms around my body. I was chilled to the bone, and wondered when I last checked the heat setting.

"You're shivering, Liv. Can I get you a sweater or something?"

I looked up at him. At the familiar face I knew so well.

"Just hug me, Stefan. Please."

And he did. Wrapped me in his arms and rested his chin on the top of my head. I felt the warmth of his breath on my hair.

"I always remember your hair smelled like strawberries."

I pulled back, smiling up at him. "Must have been someone else. I used peach-scented shampoo."

"I didn't smell anyone else's hair but yours. Promise."

"Liar. Weirdo."

"Not anymore. I'm a boring working professional."

I touched the corner of his brow where he'd tried to hide the sun tattoo under concealer. "Never boring. Still the sun guy." I pulled his face down and kissed him full on the lips.

"This is unprofessional conduct, Liv," he whispered.

"So? I'm very unprofessional."

"In that case, so am I," he said, taking my face in his hands, just like he did thirteen years ago, when we said goodbye. He kissed me again, and my insides melted. This time the kiss wasn't bittersweet. This time he was staying around.

The light citrusy scent of his cologne was so familiar. "How is it that you always smelled so good? Even when we were in high school."

"Guess I got into the habit at an early age. I think scents can create the most powerful memories."

"Like the night you left to go to Hong Kong? I always remember the scent of you. And it was the only time we kissed. Until now."

"I remember it clearly too," he said, stroking my hair. "I never forgot that moment, Liv."

I traced a finger around the curve of his lips. "Then maybe it's time we do something about that. Create some new memories."

"I'm down for that," he said, tipping my chin upwards.

We looked at each other for a long moment with a look of complete and total understanding. "It's always been you, Liv."

My heart turned as I held his dear, familiar face in my hands. "You and me, Stefan. I always knew that."

We kissed again and my whole world filled with the most intense kind of happiness.

"I have something for you," he said, holding my hands. "When the guys were done searching Nate's car, they found this hidden under the cargo cover beside the spare tire. I knew you'd want it."

He held out a bedraggled puppy with a silver heart dangling from the band around its neck. "Rory. It's Rory. Jack's favorite toy. I couldn't find him."

I clasped the animal to me. The stringy fur smelled of car oil and grease. I held it out and studied the wide, startled eyes and the tiny ears. The furry brown and white face.

"Any idea why Nate would have it?"

"None," I said, a current of anger buzzing in my chest, overwhelming my newfound happiness. "It's like everything related to Nate. A mystery. Another question I'll never know the answer to. *Damn him.*" I flung the toy across the kitchen. As it bounced off the opposite wall, a wave of guilt engulfed me. I covered my mouth, disgusted with myself. "Why did I do that?"

Stefan lunged downwards and retrieved the little puppy. As he lifted him, the heavy head tilted over and fell off. Something dropped out from the hollow head.

Stefan put the puppy down and studied the small square package in his palm. He unwrapped the paper and studied the black flash drive hidden inside.

"Maybe this is what they were looking for. This could have all the business and financial information we need to bring the whole organization down."

He looked so pleased; I tried to be happy for him. "That'll be good for you, to get this breakthrough."

"You bet. This would be the biggest bust I've ever had."

"You deserve it, Stefan. You're a good, hardworking cop and a loyal friend. You stuck by me through everything."

He glanced at the piece of paper. "Looks like there's an address written on here. I wouldn't be surprised if Nate's hidden even more inside information somewhere. Guess he wanted to make sure the whole organization would go down. I'll have to go right away and check this out. You sure you'll be okay?"

I nodded. "Shanti's coming to keep me company for a while before she has to pick up Rocky from school."

He handed me the broken puppy. "Maybe you want to do a little first aid here."

I clutched the toy to me. "It'll be a painless operation. I promise."

Then he smiled, and leaned in to hug me. "I promise, when you're ready, I'll take you somewhere beautiful for dinner. Just the two of us."

"No phone?"

He shook his head. "No phone. No work talk."

Then he headed out the door, already dialing a number.

49

A week later I'd managed to start drawing again. I still hadn't finished Parker's lunch box story, but I found some small comfort working on the superhero graphic kid's novel. Two pages of drawings were complete and I was so happy with them. It had been quite a journey of discovery, developing Alex Apollo and his sidekick, Rory Rocket Boy. Min absolutely loved the idea. We'd even talked over some ideas on how to market it, although I didn't really care how many copies I sold. For me, it was a great way to honor the memory of two people I loved so much. The only way.

I was so lost in crafting the latest drawings, I almost missed the phone ringing. It was Stefan.

"Liv. Do you still have the puppy?" he blurted without any intro.

"Yes. I fixed it. It's right here in the living room. Why?"

"We… we need to do some tests on it."

"Did you find something at that address?"

"We did. A whole lot of useful information. We think Nate must have planted the flash drive and the address in the puppy's head the day he died."

I felt a dull ache in my heart. After everything that had happened, Nate was still the man I'd been married to for eight years. I had loved him once – had even had a wonderful child with him. So even if our relationship had

314

been broken for most of that time, and even though he'd lied, I'd gotten past the gut feeling of wishing harm on him. "So he knew they were going to kill him?"

"It sure looks like that. But can you bring it to the station? Now?"

"Okay. I'll be there as soon as I can." I ended the call wondering what else I was about to discover about this whole twisted situation.

—

Twenty minutes later I pulled up into the parking lot of the station, a modern glass and concrete structure with a sloping roof. Stefan was waiting for me at the door, a broad smile almost splitting his face.

"Looks like you're happy about something. Did you get a promotion?"

"Not exactly. Just come in," he said, taking my arm and steering me inside the bright, airy lobby, then down a narrow hallway.

"You're hiding something. It's obvious. No wonder you never got involved in poker games at high school."

"That's me. An open book."

"So where did that address take you?"

He stopped and placed a hand on my shoulders. "It took us two days to find the place. Way up north near Flin Flon. Off the highway just outside the town."

"What on earth would Nate be hiding up there?"

"I need you to talk to someone, Liv. In here."

He directed me into a small office where three chairs were arranged in a circle. An older woman sat in one. Tall, with graying hair, brown parka and a smooth, kind face, she tapped an empty paper coffee cup on the table.

Stefan motioned me to sit down. I lowered myself slowly, wondering what the hell was going on and why the buzz of the overhead strip lighting sounded so loud.

"Olivia, this is Kate Bannister, Nate's aunt. His mother's sister."

The buzzing became louder. "I didn't think he had any family."

She smiled. "He didn't really. I tried to see him when I was in the city, but his mom, my bad baby sister, had wasted her life on that no-good gangster she married and he wouldn't let her have visitors."

I looked from this stranger to Stefan. "I don't get it. What's going on?"

She continued. "I've wanted to meet you for such a long time, Olivia. Nate always spoke so highly of you when he came to see me."

"You've seen him? Recently? How? When?"

"Tell her, Kate," urged Stefan.

Now I felt a racing, rushing sensation in my gut. I wasn't ready for any more revelations or surprises about Nate, but the woman leaned forward and spoke so gently I stayed quiet.

"Nate had his faults. How can you blame him with a criminal for a father and a junkie for a mother? But he was always good to me. Said I was like a mom to him. And that's why I agreed to help him when he asked me. I'd moved up north, but he called me. Said he needed me to come down to the city and do something for him." She faltered. Tears pooled in her eyes. She stopped and covered her mouth. "I hope you can forgive me, Olivia, but it was for the best. Nate said he'd got mixed up in something that was too big to control and he'd been trying to get out. The guys at the top had just sent him an ultimatum. Keep

316

working for them or they'd do something to his family. Threatened his kid. Said they'd make him disappear. Sell him to the highest bidder."

Tears pressed at the back of my eyelids. "What did they do to him? What did they do to my boy?" I sobbed, my whole body shaking.

She shook her head. "No, no... it's not like that. Nate gave me directions to a bridge near a lake. Told me where to wait. Said he'd bring Jack there and I was to take him back up north right away, hide him and keep him safe until he could get out from the organization. I did it. I didn't know what else to do."

The room swam around me. It wasn't possible. After all these years... after waiting, and hoping, and fearing the worst, it would be cruel to give me this hope and take it away. But it felt like she was telling the truth. I jumped to my feet, barely able to contain the rush of emotions.

"Where is he? Where's Jack? Let me see him!"

Stefan steadied me, holding onto my shoulders. "You can see him, Liv. But you have to calm down. He's been away for a long time. He might not know you."

I slumped back in the chair, my insides rolling with doubt, disbelief, but most of all, excitement.

Minutes later, the door opened and a beautiful seven-year-old boy stood there, his hair a cap of auburn curls, his eyes hazel, flecked with green. My heart flew to my throat. *My boy.* Taller, his face thinner and more angular than I remembered. He fixed a serious, pensive look on me.

I took Rory from my bag and held him out. "Remember this little guy, Jack?"

He nodded and chewed his lip. "Yeah. It's a kid's toy. I played with it when I was a kid. I'm grown up now."

"You are. You've grown into a wonderful, handsome young man. Your friend, Rocky, will be so surprised."

He grinned. "Rocky. I remember him. We played at the sand table."

I ached to hold him, but I didn't want to scare him off or crowd him. "Yes, that was at moms and twos. But that's a long time ago. I expect you're in grade two now."

"Yup. I'm good at drawing too. Are you really my mom? Aunt Katie says you are."

"I am. And I've missed you so much. We have a whole lot of catching up to do now."

"Is this you?" He held out a photo of me with him at the zoo. He was nestled in my arms outside the bear enclosure.

I tried to fight back the tears. "It is. Where did you get that?"

"Dad gave it to me and he said never to forget you because you're such a great mom."

I swallowed, realising that Nate – or Jack – hadn't lied about everything. Despite his capacity for cruelty and deception, he'd apparently had some real feelings for his family, too. "Then I guess you could say he was a great dad."

I held out my arms to my son and he stepped forward. A little timidly at first, but soon I was holding him in my arms, knowing he was really here with me. He was solid and real, because I felt the warmth and weight of his body against mine and my heart was so full it felt like it would burst from my chest.

A Message from M. M. DeLuca

Thank you so much for reading *The Perfect Family Man*. I hope you enjoyed reading it as much as I enjoyed writing it!

If you'd like to keep up to date with any of my new releases, please sign-up for my newsletter. Your email will never be shared, and I'll only contact you when I have news about a new release. Sign up by visiting the website below!

www.marjoriedeluca.com/thrillers

If you have the time to leave me a short, honest review on Amazon, Goodreads, or wherever you purchased the book, I'd very much appreciate it. I love hearing what you think, and your reviews help me reach new readers – which allows me to bring you more books! If you know of friends or family that would enjoy the book, I'd love your help there, too.

You can also connect with me via Facebook, Goodreads, Instagram and Twitter. I always love to hear from readers.

Instagram: mmdelucaauthor
Facebook: marjorie.deluca.3
Twitter: @DeLucaMarjorie

Goodreads: www.goodreads.com/author/show/20984340.
M_M_DeLuca

Thank you again, so very much, for your support of my books. It means the world to me!

M. M. DeLuca

Book Club Questions

1. How do you think losing Jack has impacted Olivia's life? How has it changed her day-to-day activities and interactions, her hopes and dreams? Her relationship with her husband?

2. Olivia is clearly unhappy in her marriage to Nate. Why do you think she stays?

3. Why do you think Olivia feels such a strong bond with Stefan?

4. Is Nate the novel's villain?

5. Olivia has always lived near the lake and the urban forest. Why is she so tied to the area?

6. How would you describe Olivia's relationship with her brother, Alex, and how did his death impact her family and her life?

7. Why is Olivia so concerned with Toby? How do her feelings develop from first seeing him to later in the book? Do you feel she's justified in reporting Heidi's behavior? How would you deal with a similar situation?

8. Why do you feel Olivia finally takes it into her own hands to investigate Nate's disappearance instead of reporting all her findings to Stefan and the other officers? Do you feel she's justified in doing so?

9. Olivia is a very solitary person even though she's living in a suburban neighborhood. What do you feel her neighbors could have done to support her? How do we as a society tend to treat lonely, solitary or grieving people?

10. How would you describe Olivia's feelings towards Nate by the later part of the book?

11. The novel touches on the issue of compulsive gambling and its impact on a person's life. Can gambling be a harmless form of entertainment? Have you come across people with gambling problems? How has it impacted their lives? What can be done to help them?

Acknowledgments

Many thanks go to the incredible publishing team at Canelo, most notably my editor, Leodora Darlington, whose optimism and unflagging support for this book inspired me to produce the best work possible. Also, a big thanks to the other team members who helped make this an incredibly smooth and exciting journey: cover designer, Lisa Horton; copyeditor, Jane Eastgate; proofreader, Claire Rushbrook; sales, Francesca Riccardi and Claudine Sagoe; marketing, Nicola Piggott; publicity, Elinor Fewster, production, Konrad Kirkham.

A big thanks to Brent Lusty, retired City of Winnipeg police officer and Manager of the Manitoba Gaming Control Commission (retired) for his help and advice.

Thanks to my local group of readers whose interest in my work spurs me to keep on going: my sister, Janet, friend, Kay, friends Laura H and Olivia, also the ladies of my book club: Janice, Pam, Laure, Tracy, Kerry, Deb M and Deb D. Hope we'll be able to have real meetings, soon, Fingers crossed!

To my amazing and successful kids, Mike and Laura. Your support and interest keep me going. To my husband, Fausto, thanks for all your support!

Thanks also to my Zoom family in the UK: brothers Trevor and Janet, Ken and his wife, Linda. Alison and Kev, June and Graham. Your interest and unwavering support have spurred me to keep on writing and our weekly Zoom calls have been a lifeline during lockdowns.

To my ex-home in Lindenwoods, opposite the beautiful lake houses and close to the loveliest urban forest and walkways. I miss those daily walks by the lake and the ornamental lamps in wintertime that remind me of Narnia and Mr. Tumnus!

Finally, a huge thank-you to all the readers and wonderful reviewers out there. It's your love of reading and your amazing commitment to the written word that keeps me striving to produce the best work I can. I couldn't have done this without you!